T0147132

A mind is a terrible thing to destroy . . .

Kathy has been hired to assess the threat of patient Henry Banks, an inmate at the Connecticut-Newlyn Hospital for the Criminally Insane, the same hospital where her brother is housed. Her employers believe that Henry has the ability to open doors to other dimensions with his mind—making him one of the most dangerous men in modern history. Because unbeknownst to Kathy, her clients are affiliated with certain government organizations that investigate people like Henry—and the potential to weaponize such abilities.

What Kathy comes to understand in interviewing Henry, and in her unavoidable run-ins with her brother, is that Henry can indeed use his mind to create "Tulpas"—worlds, people, and creatures so vivid they come to actual life. But now they want life outside of Henry. And they'll stop at nothing to complete their emanicipation. It's up to Kathy—with her brother's help—to stop them, and if possible, to save Henry before the Tulpas take him over—and everything else around him.

The Kathy Ryan Series by Mary SanGiovanni

Behind the Door
Inside the Asylum

Also Featuring Kathy Ryan
Chills

Also by Mary SanGiovanni
Savage Woods

Inside the Asylum

Mary SanGiovanni

LYRICAL UNDERGROUND
Kensington Publishing Corp.
www.kensingtonbooks.com

LYRICAL UNDERGROUND BOOKS are published by

Kensington Publishing Corp.
119 West 40th Street
New York, NY 10018

All Kensington titles, imprints, and distributed lines are available at special quantity discounts for bulk purchases for sales promotion, premiums, fundraising, educational, or institutional use.

Special book excerpts or customized printings can also be created to fit specific needs. For details, write or phone the office of the Kensington Sales Manager: Kensington Publishing Corp., 119 West 40th Street, New York, NY 10018. Attn. Sales Department. Phone: 1-800-221-2647.

Lyrical Underground and Lyrical Underground logo Reg. US Pat. & TM Off.

First Electronic Edition: May 2019
eISBN-13: 978-1-5161-0683-7
eISBN-10: 1-5161-0683-0

First Print Edition: May 2019
ISBN-13: 978-1-5161-0686-8
ISBN-10: 1-5161-0686-5

Printed in the United States of America

For my sisters—change is inevitable, and it only makes us stronger.

Chapter 1

March twenty-seventh marked three years since Henry Banks had woken up from the coma. He kept track in a day planner, with new calendar refills for subsequent years, by drawing a symbol he had been taught by his friends in the upper right hand corner of each day's page. Other than therapy sessions, he had no real appointments anymore, but Henry jotted down notes about the day's events, things he learned or discovered, and each night before bed, he drew that symbol of his far-reaching goals. Journaling, even Henry's odd version of it, was encouraged and allowed to continue as a means of reconnecting with one's self and feelings. His was more of an odd, disjointed grimoire of his mind, but that seemed to be okay, too. He never forgot, not even during the trial when his mind was... elsewhere. On days he couldn't get to the planner, Maisie made sure that at least the days were marked. It was important to him. He never forgot, so neither did she.

Every day that passed reminded him that he was drifting farther and farther from the rest of humanity, so Henry didn't think the three-year anniversary was cause for celebration. Dr. Pam Ulster did, though, or at least convincingly pretended to. Every year prior, she had suggested Henry do something nice for himself to commemorate his "return to the world." The irony was not lost on him. He didn't see how he was supposed to do much of anything since the orderlies, who were not big on celebrations, watched him like hawks. Even if he wanted to, what could he really give himself in his current situation? A walk in the sunshine around the hospital grounds? An extra muffin with breakfast? Anything else—anything worthwhile—would be noticed and probably taken away.

Besides, it wasn't like he'd come back from the dead. He'd just come back from...somewhere else.

Henry figured other people would have had reason to celebrate March twenty-seventh if he'd died instead of coming out of that coma. Maybe that should have happened, but it didn't. Maisie, Orrin, Edgar, and the Others made sure of that. They'd come out of Ayteilu and saved him. Or maybe they were right, and he had saved them.

The police and the lawyers and the doctors told him he'd done something bad to the teenagers in his basement right before the coma. He couldn't remember much about that. He was pretty sure he hadn't been the one who'd done it, but it was his fault all the same. He'd seen those teenagers before; they hung around outside the Dollar Tree and said mean things to him from behind the safety of their cigarette smoke clouds when he went to shop there. The girl was pretty, but she was sharp where she should have been soft, like something made of glass or porcelain, something whose temper could shatter her into a thousand jagged, deadly pieces. The three guys were mostly messy mops of hair, black trench coats, and jeans. Their faces didn't matter to him. Their fists did, and their words; they often threatened the former with the latter. Henry wasn't even sure if they'd had eyes, but he imagined that if they did, those eyes were cold.

They made fun of the holes in his t-shirts and the way he walked and the scar on his shaved head. They made fun of the burn marks on the back of his shoulder and neck and the way he growled at them instead of using words. Still, they had always been an away-problem, an outside-the-house problem, like savage dogs on leashes. They were tethered to the Dollar Tree, and if he could make it past them to his car and then to his home, he would be safe.

Then it turned out that they weren't on leashes. They could move anywhere they wanted. And they had chosen to break into *his* house, *his* safe space. They'd brought baseball bats and knives. The Viper and the Others had come simply to protect him.

Sometimes, Henry thought he should have started keeping count in his planner on *that* night.

Dr. Ulster had asked him once during a session why he bothered to maintain such meticulous records of the past three years if he honestly believed everything in his life had fallen apart since the coma. Why approach the planner as a constant reminder of his deterioration, then? Why not just put the past behind him and focus on getting better?

Henry had told her then the truth about the Others, just like he had told the police when they found what was left of the four teenagers in his basement. He told them about Ayteilu and its tendency to swallow up reality. He'd told them about Maisie and Orrin and Edgar and all the Others. He'd even told them about the Viper. Maisie said that was okay. The problem was, he couldn't *show* the police or Dr. Ulster, so they hadn't believed. He couldn't make it all happen on command, not back then. But he was learning, and over the last 1,095 days, he was steadily growing better at it. What he didn't tell anyone was that in three days' time, as set forth by Edgar's prediction, he'd have complete control in summoning the Others at will and opening the way to Ayteilu. The Others hadn't wanted him to share that part with anyone else.

Henry peered through the gloom of his bedroom. His cot was against the wall across from the door, which of course was locked now that it was lights out. On the far side of the room was the door to his simple bathroom—one sink, one toilet, both gleaming white—and next to that door was a small closet in which hung his hospital-issued clothes, soft and harmless. No zipper teeth or sharp metal claws there, not even buttons or laces. Beneath the clothes, like obedient lapdogs curled up on the closet floor for the night, were a pair of loafers and a pair of slippers. Against the back wall near where the head of his cot lay was a small, barred window. The orderlies could open it sometimes to air the room out but they had keys to do that and were allowed to reach through the bars. That night, his window was closed but Henry didn't mind. He just liked having one, and from his, he could see the parking lot. Some people liked seeing the neat, tight little lawns that constituted the hospital grounds, but he preferred the parking lot. It reminded him that there was still a real world out there, with normal people who had jobs and houses and pets, and that those people could actually leave hospitals and move freely through it.

He got up from the cot and shuffled over to the window. The moon was mostly hidden behind clouds, but in the lot below, the arc-sodium lights illuminated patches of asphalt in a soft melon color. Shadows skirted those halos of glow, darting quickly from one spot to another in the dark. It wasn't their shape so much as their movement that Henry caught, but it was soothing all the same to see they were down there. Probably it was Maisie who had sent them. She was thoughtful like that. Maisie always knew when he was sad or angry or just feeling drained.

That night, Henry was exhausted. The geliophobia had been particularly bad all day. He had shouldered the burden of many crippling mental conditions since early childhood, but the one that garnered the least sympathy and understanding was his fear of people laughing at him. Decades of laughter, pressed between the pages of his memories, always found a way to resurface, to grow fat and loud again in his thoughts and even in his ears. When he was stressed or tired, he could hear a chorus of guffaws and giggles, tittering and peals from people who should have kept their damn mouths shut.

The laughter echoed in the back of his thoughts, jarring and ugly like the squawking of angry hawks, and he tried to put it out. Bad things happened in the dark when he couldn't, and he didn't have the strength to make the bad things go away. Not tonight. His limbs felt heavy and his eyes were dry and burning. He shuffled back to the cot and climbed beneath the blanket.

Henry forced each of his muscles to relax, starting with his toes and working his way up to the top of his head, just like Dr. Ulster had taught him. Then he worked on clearing his mind. He imagined the inside of his head as debris on a darkened stage, and with a big broom, he swept away all of them like they were piles of dust.

Sleep came on like a slow tide, lapping at him in waves and eroding his conscious thought. Just before he drifted off, he heard Maisie moving gently through the dark.

"Good night," he mumbled.

A butterfly flutter of lips brushed his forehead, and a soft, cultured voice replied, "Good night, Henry."

* * * *

Ever since Martha's death the weekend before, Ben Hadley had been on edge. He was a nervous man by nature; his nerves had, in part, put him in Connecticut-Newlyn Hospital to begin with. That damned clumsy woman, with her barking, thumping dog in the apartment upstairs from his, had finally compelled him to take action.

This was different, though. He was on meds now; he wasn't supposed to get nervous, not like this. Of course, it was hard not to be a little out of sorts when all around him, people were dropping like flies. There had been the suicides last month—the twins, Belle and Barney McGuinness, who had jumped off the roof of Parker Hall and made a terrible mess on the front steps. How they had gotten up there was anyone's guess; apparently security protocols were "still being looked into," for all the good that would do. And then there was Sherman Jones, who had supposedly died in his sleep. Sure, he was ninety-eight, but he'd been fine all day, alert and active as ever. Ridley Comstock had come as less of a surprise. They'd found him hanging all blue-lipped and bloated in his own closet. Autoerotic asphyxia was the culprit there, according to Toby Ryan, and given Ridley's proclivities on the outside, that was probably true—an accident, but an ugly one, if the orderlies' gossip was to be believed.

But then there was Martha, and hers was one death too many, and with far too many strange circumstances surrounding it.

At first Ben thought Toby had done it. Toby killed women; it was his thing. Of course, he'd sworn he hadn't killed Martha, that he couldn't have. He said he'd been locked in his room overnight, the same as everyone else. Ben didn't argue. Toby scared him.

As it turned out, though, a new and more likely suspect had emerged over the course of the week: Henry Banks.

Of all the inmates at Connecticut-Newlyn, Henry had always seemed the most harmless. Soft-spoken with an occasional stutter, he'd never seemed dangerous before. In fact, he'd seemed so *un*dangerous that Ben had even harbored doubts as to whether Henry had actually killed those teenagers.

That was, of course, before Ben learned about Henry's friends.

The thing about them, Ben had discovered, was that *they* weren't mild-mannered, and they certainly weren't locked down at night. Henry's friends came and went as they pleased, and they mostly answered to Henry. Martha had threatened to tell the doctors about them; she'd said so the day before in the common room. She was going to tell, and Henry had been worried. His friends, after all, were only there to protect him.

Toby had said it was a silly fight; Henry's friends were imaginary and Martha was getting all worked up over nothing. Still, someone didn't think it was too silly a fight to silence her. If Henry didn't kill her, then one of those allegedly imaginary friends must have.

Ben wasn't crazy, despite his lawyer's convincing case to the court. Ben was just nervous. Sometimes, he got very nervous, and he understood that if Henry's friends had gotten nervous, too, about Martha telling on them, they might have felt compelled to take action.

That didn't make Ben any less sad or nervous. There was probably a whole town out there that was glad Martha was dead—Martha, who had drowned her own four children in a bathtub on the advice of an angel—but she had been one of Ben's only friends. He didn't believe she would have told the doctors or orderlies anything.

The doctors claimed Martha choked in her sleep, but Ben had seen the blood all over her room—the walls, the sheets of her cot, her neck. He'd seen her eyes, wide and scared and glazed over. Her mouth had hung open like a small, crooked cave. Her tongue, torn out by the roots, had been on the pillow beside her, close to her ear. He'd seen it all...before two of the orderlies realized he was standing there and roughly led him away.

No, Henry's friends were not mild-mannered at all. And Ben didn't think Henry knew everything they got up to in the night.

He thought all these things as he lay on his cot, waiting for the sun to come up. He'd resigned himself to the fact that he'd be getting no sleep that night. He was too wired for that. Plus, he wanted to watch the door. Henry's room was right next to his, and if these friends, imaginary or not, were moving around the halls out there, he wanted to know about it. They could obviously move through doors and maybe walls. If they could get into Martha's room, they could get into his as well.

The doors to each room had small windows made of Plexiglas, and from his position on the cot, Ben could just see the top of the far hallway wall and a bit of the ceiling through his. It was quiet out there; the dark remained still and the ceiling tiles—twelve in his line of sight—were all accounted for. He'd learned not to try to look outside at night. Shadows had shape out there and moved in deliberate and predatory ways that shadows shouldn't. It was better for his peace of mind just to look out the little window in his door.

Ben might have dozed for a moment but he didn't think so; in the next, however, he saw a hazy, wavering face peer in, followed by an equally insubstantial palm on the Plexiglas. Ben froze, and a moment later, the palm was gone. His heart pounded. Who were they looking for? Would the morning bring another dead inmate?

There was no sound of footsteps. Henry's friends were quiet; he'd give them that. But they were also clearly on the move.

* * * *

Orrin and Edgar sat in the dark, waiting for Maisie. She watched over Henry at night, at least until he fell asleep, and while they waited for her to come out of the hospital, Orrin and Edgar watched over the Others.

Tonight, Maisie would be late. She had taken an interest in some of the other inmates there, who she claimed had special knowledge locked up in their heads that she was certain would prove useful to them. Of course, she made Orrin and Edgar swear never to mention this to Henry, because it would only upset him and Maisie didn't like to see him upset. They had, so far, held to that promise. Edgar didn't like to cross anyone, and as for Orrin…well, he had other reasons for wanting to keep Maisie happy. He couldn't understand what she thought she'd gain by getting to know these other guys, but Maisie was a thinker, and she probably saw a way to protect them and the Others somehow. Most of her plans involved protecting them or making them stronger, and Orrin could get behind that. He didn't trust damn near anybody, not even Edgar and they were brothers, but he trusted Maisie.

So they sat and waited while the Others ran and tore at things in the darkness, a silent show of mad, dancing, light-changing silhouettes. Two of them had set upon an owl and were pulling off its wings while a third extended the fingers of its tendrils into the meat of the bird to explore its insides.

"D-d-do you think she'll b-be out soon?" Edgar asked in that stop-start, jerking way he had. His good eye glowed like an ember in the dark.

"Soon," Orrin said, and gave his brother a reassuring nod.

"They're not easy t-to wrangle when they're this r-riled up," Edgar said, gesturing at the Others. "Henry's g-gonna b-be pissed if he looks out the window tomorrow and sees d-dead b-b-birds all over the parking lot."

"You worry too much," Orrin told him.

"D-do I?"

Orrin didn't reply just then. Edgar's worries weren't without substance. Henry could be pacified, but the longer Maisie spent in that hospital, the greater the chance that someone else would discover him and Edgar and the Others and cause them to make an unpleasant scene. That wouldn't be good for Henry or anyone else.

Finally, he said, "She'll be out soon."

"Then what?"

"Then we find the Viper and see what comes next."

* * * *

As Henry dreamed, the darkness spread in silence. Inside the utility shed about two and a half acres behind the hospital, the darkness pooled in the corners and seeped through the cracks in the floor. Waves of inkiness washed over the detritus of hospital maintenance. Tendrils snaked around and inside the lawn care equipment and tools. Bottles of chemicals were probed and poked until they spilled, and their smoking, acidic contents were drunk and assimilated. The darkness lapped up the shadows and the night itself and made them its own.

As it took the shed's contents, it changed them. It brought the imps through from Ayteilu to claim and reshape them. Orrin had called it "giving land to a country." Maisie and Edgar just called it "breaking through." But the Viper knew it for what it was. He sat on a length of old fence just outside the shed and watched through the open door as a riding lawn mower became a silverbacked beast whose underside contained rows of mouths and bladed teeth. Leathery wings broke through the creature's back and folded themselves neatly against it. Its legs, shaped like a bulldog's only longer and more powerful, grew from its sides, hoisting its bulk a good two feet off the ground. It had no eyes and no discernible nose, but it seemed interested in sniffing around the doorframe of the shed, adjusting to its new surroundings.

The Viper hopped off the fence and strolled over to the shed. Inside, a new shape was forming from a puddle of darkness and industrial cleaner. He watched as the substance traveled upward, dipping in and out of feminine curves as it formed legs and hips, a waist, breasts, arms and shoulders, a neck, a head. The last things to appear were the eyes, which, when opened, focused a cold, bright green gaze on him. Black swirls lifted off her body like steam. This new being, an ebony mist condensed in human form, took a step forward and waited. She and the Others coming through and developing behind her would follow the Viper's orders. Maisie couldn't control them; the mist Wraiths only ever listened to the Viper, even in Ayteilu.

What had once been a rake wiggled off its hook on the wall and slithered by the Viper's feet. The rake head had formed a bottom jaw, and those rust-colored tines grew sharp. The creature's jaws were immense. What passed for the Viper's smile found his face as he watched that snaking tail, muscled though it was, just manage to push forward the large skull in front of it.

The Viper looked up at the sky. It was a clear night; the stars of this universe twinkled overhead like tiny eyes. He supposed that one night, he'd look up and see Ayteilu's familiar constellations…but not tonight.

He took a step back as the shed itself began to change. The wood creaked a little and then stretched, and the dimensions of the building increased. In minutes, it was the size of a large barn. The substance of the wood had taken on the faint red tint and rough grain of the trees in Ayteilu. From within, the newly formed were beginning to find ways to make sounds— little sounds, but new and exciting to them all the same. Soon, they would growl and roar, and find the strength to devour this world. Soon…when the constellations of Ayteilu remapped the sky.

Gently, he closed the barn door. The darkness and its changes would spread soon enough, but there was no sense in letting the creatures inside roam free just yet. Maisie and Orrin and Edgar had to do their parts first to make Henry stronger.

The Viper glanced up at the sky once more, then walked off into the darkness. The shed-turned-barn shuddered with the new life inside it, and the darkness began to spill out from under the door.

Chapter 2

Kathy Ryan had little patience for red tape of the bureaucratic kind. Her work often led her to the outskirts of society, law, and even reality, and jobs were a lot tougher when her intolerance for the maddening delays of protocol and jurisdiction put her at odds with law enforcement. Usually in those cases, it was a balancing act between those who believed and wanted to stop cosmic calamities and those who wanted her to get the hell off their turf.

Still, she worked to cultivate professional if not friendly relationships with various law enforcement agencies and had made several inroads in that regard over the years. She was the kind of woman who got results regardless of the obstacles, and law enforcement liked that.

Actually, she ran into more problems when she was hired by special interest groups or individuals to consult on cases, rather than by police or federal agents. The red tape, particularly in a state-run facility like Connecticut-Newlyn Hospital, was a pain in the ass.

Still, she had ways around it.

Silver Street was lined with birch and quaking aspen trees just starting to bloom. It was pretty, really. Any other person could almost forget, driving through rolling acres of flatland, that the road ended at the visitor parking lot of an insane asylum. Kathy couldn't forget, though. She'd made the drive six times in her life, and it never got any easier. That same knot would form in the pit of her stomach, and her chest would get tight just as she crested the hill and saw the parking lot.

This time was no different, even though she was there to see someone else.

By the time she pulled into a spot just outside of Parker Hall, her palms were sweating. She wiped them on the thighs of her jeans and took a deep breath. Stern and unwelcoming, the red brick building had narrow, barred windows and a mansard roof. From the main building, long, slanted wards, dubbed "halls," stretched out from Parker Hall's administrative offices like wings.

She knew the staff at Connecticut-Newlyn Hospital liked to think of their resident charges as patients rather than inmates, but to Kathy, neither word seemed to fit very well. In many ways, she thought they were like caged animals or sharks in tanks. Her life had taught her that they were not more than human—not the boogeymen so much of society made serial killers, mass murderers, and spree killers—but she found it tough sometimes not to think of them as *less* human.

She'd questioned many of them in the course of her work, mainly in connection with tenuous or substantial ties to the occult. Some remained silent and observant behind their unsmiling mouths, soft voices, and inability to make eye contact. They might have almost struck the average person as painfully shy. Then there were some who charmed and smiled, talked up a blue streak about almost any topic laid in front of them, just glad to have someone to talk to…or at. Kathy's brother fell somewhere in between, one of those quiet, smiling, arrogant assholes that enjoyed making people uncomfortable by alternating silences with sudden, shocking revelations. Different strokes for different folks. They all had some vague idea that the outside world did not see them as patients or inmates, either, but as monsters. And how did they see themselves? Most understood they were killers; some saw themselves as heroes, and even more as victims of their tragic lives and circumstances. A rare self-aware few understood themselves to be the predators they were. The subject of murder, of course, usually made all of them cagey and evasive. Many seemed to find any reaction to their answers to be of interest and importance. There was only maybe one true similarity among them: The residents of Connecticut-Newlyn were dangerous.

Kathy had never visited her brother there when her father was alive. Even if she'd wanted to—and she hadn't—her father had forbidden her to see him. She didn't often dwell on her father, who had never understood how powerful his hands were and how scary his voice could sometimes be. He was a man with limited social skills and resources raising two kids alone, and he'd almost lost one to the other. Every time he'd looked at Kathy's scar, the one that ran unevenly down through her left eyebrow and over her eye to plant itself just below the socket, then down her cheek to her jawbone, he'd get this strange look in his eyes, part horror and part anger, and she'd turn away from him. No little girl wants to see her father look at her like that. It took a long time to realize neither the horror nor the anger had been directed at her, but by then, those looks had formed a kind of scar of their own inside her.

Kathy parked the car and sat a few moments staring at Parker Hall. Toby was in there. Toby, who had once beaten a boy into unconsciousness after he called her a slut when she was in the sixth grade. Toby, who once covered for her and took the brunt of their father's rage over a broken lamp, and a day later, snapped the neck of an injured bird she was trying to save right in front of her. Toby, who had murdered all those women, who had threatened to rape Kathy, kill her, and dump her in the woods. Toby, who had carved his distorted feelings for her into her face.

He was hard to hate, but he was even harder to love. And if any resident of Connecticut-Newlyn could be more aptly described as a caged animal than Toby, Kathy hadn't met that person.

She forced herself to get out of the car, slamming the door a little harder than she'd meant to, and made her way up the long paved walk to the front door. After pushing the intercom button, she gave her full name, then flashed her ID at the CCTV camera mounted above the front door. A click and a crackle preceded a loud buzz that made her flinch. She opened the front door.

Ahead and to the right, Margaret, a middle-aged woman with coiffed blond hair, a tired mouth, and cool eyes magnified by thick glasses, sat behind a glass wall in a small office. She looked up as Kathy approached and gave a little nod.

"Hi, Margaret," Kathy said as she held up her ID against the glass between them, then slid it through a narrow slit onto the wooden desk on the other side.

"Hello, Katherine. How are you?" Margaret returned Kathy's credentials, then handed her a laminated visitor's pass on a lanyard with a clip. Then she slid a small clipboard with log lines halfway down the page through the same slit in the glass. A pen on a chain dangled behind it.

"New protocol. Just sign your name, the time—it's 11:36—and in that space there, who you're here to see. I was keeping track of visitors manually for some time, but now we have to scan signatures, so there you go."

"No problem," Kathy said, filling out the line. "I'm here to see Ben Hadley."

Margaret, whose stoic exterior rarely betrayed her opinions of the residents of Connecticut-Newlyn, shook her head.

"Sad case, that one."

"Why?" Kathy found that sometimes, it was the people in the background of an institution like Connecticut-Newlyn who had more useful information than those she had reason to interview.

"High-strung. Nervous. Lately, it's nightmares."

"What about?"

Margaret shrugged. "Who knows what goes on in their heads? He screams for a while, then cries for a while, then whispers about imaginary friends for a while. Not his, mind you. He claims another patient—our new guy, Henry Banks—has some pretty dangerous imaginary friends."

"Really…this Henry Banks, what's his story?"

"Claims those same imaginary friends butchered a bunch of kids in his basement. Creepy, quiet. You know the type."

"And Ben shares his delusion about these, uh, imaginary friends?"

"Seems to," Margret replied. "Between his screaming and one of them walking about all night—the footsteps echo all down those upper-floor wings—it can be very disruptive. Sad, but unsettling all the same."

"I can imagine," Kathy said. She was surprised any of the patients was allowed to walk around like that at night; she didn't think anyone was allowed outside his or her room after lockdown. She made a note to ask Ben Hadley about it when she spoke to him. "What room is he in again?" Though she often met with interviewees in the visiting area and not their rooms, she'd come to find it helpful to know who they roomed near, who their daily influences were, and what ideas were being exchanged between them and others. Margaret seemed to have caught wise to her methods, and offered the information freely in most cases.

"Who, Henry?" Margaret checked a list on the wall. "He's in 307. Two down from your brother on the right."

At the mention of Toby, Kathy tensed. "No, Ben Hadley."

"Oh, right. 305. Right between them, as it turns out." She offered a brief, somewhat perfunctory smile and returned to the endless signing, stamping, and filing of her ambiguous paperwork.

"Thanks, Margaret. See you in a bit."

Kathy's visitor pass got her through two more security doors. The third was opened for her by a huge rolling snowball of an orderly, Kenny, before she reached the visiting area. Kenny nodded at the paperwork she showed him for her interview, then left her at one of the long cafeteria-style tables to retrieve Henry Banks.

She looked around the visiting area. It was relatively small—few of the residents of Connecticut-Newlyn received visitors—with uncomfortable chairs and bland walls. She understood the common areas were somewhat more homelike, but the hospital maintained an unexciting, professional and objective decorative style throughout. Even within the residents' rooms, there were few personalized touches, other than some simple allowances given to those who worked hard and stayed out of trouble—prints of landscapes, the occasional personal photo, birthday cards, that sort of thing.

The staff at Connecticut-Newlyn believed in breaking down the aberrant aspects of character through therapy and carefully modulated medication and then rebuilding healthier pathways of thought and behavior. Kathy was not involved with the minutiae of the process; her specialty was in the occult, particularly where it became entwined with the supernatural. To her, abnormal psychology was useful only so far as it explained the thought processes behind certain occult practitioners' behaviors and rituals.

A few minutes later, Kenny returned with a man probably in his late forties, with thin-rimmed glasses and a small goatee and mustache. They were graying much faster than his hair, which was vaguely military in style and nearly all black. As he shuffled along behind Kenny, he seemed bent and a little twisted like an old tree, only barely weathering the storms of his memories and whose upheaved roots threatened to send him crashing down at any moment.

He sat heavily in the chair across from Kathy, glanced at her scar, and then looked her in the eye. "Are you my lawyer?"

"No, Mr. Hadley. My name is Kathy Ryan. I'm a private consultant."

"What do you consult in?"

"That depends on the situation," Kathy replied. "Primarily, I work with companies and law enforcement officials to assess the potential dangers of fringe occult group activity. That, I guess, is the easiest way to explain it. It's a specialized field."

"And you're here to talk to me?"

"I am, if you don't mind my taking a few moments of your time. I'd like to talk to you about some of your old friends."

Hadley blinked a few times as if trying to remember. "Which ones?"

Kathy pulled a small notebook out of her purse. "You were a member of the Shining Light of Imnamoun, before your family removed you. And you made some interesting claims that—"

"Oh. That was a year and a half ago. Why are you asking me about it now?"

"Well, Mr. Hadley, while the information you relayed to your deprogrammer was of interest, as is the cult itself, investigation into your claims took some time."

"You had to make sure I'm not delusional, I guess? A product of brainwashing and abuse?"

"You could put it that way."

"And what did you determine? I mean, I'm here, right?" He studied her, his gaze alternating between tracing her scar and the contours of the rest of her face.

"That's not necessarily relevant to the reality of your experience. I'd like to hear about it in your own words."

"Hmm." Hadley shifted in his seat, seeming mildly pleased to be believed for once. "Well, sure, if you want. There isn't much to tell, though, beyond what I told Jerry, my—what did you call him?"

"Your deprogrammer."

"Right, right. Funny. I thought you might be here to talk about Henry Banks."

Kathy sat back. "What about Henry Banks?"

"Well, his friends, for starters. The ones he brought with him."

"Are he and his friends affiliated with the Shining Light of Imnamoun as well?"

Hadley looked confused for a moment. "No, not at all. He's just…some guy. The new guy. But I think his friends are, uh, dangerous." A shiver racked his whole body, and he shook his head slowly. "I'll tell you that much. The drugs, Henry's drugs, don't affect them. They do what they want, when they want. And no one messes with Henry's friends, even Toby."

"Oh?" Kathy chose to gloss over the mention of Toby's name. Given the body language of the man sitting across from her, it didn't appear that Hadley had made the association between her and her brother. "How are Henry's friends dangerous?"

Hadley looked around, glancing at the corners of the room as if looking for invisible cameras. The year of therapy and deprogramming prior to Hadley's being committed to the hospital hadn't worked out nearly as many mental bugs as his family might have hoped. Kathy waited patiently as Hadley squirmed a bit in his seat, checked under the table for hidden microphones, and glanced around the room for invasive ears once more.

"If I tell you," he whispered finally, "they'll kill me."

"Mr. Hadley, we're in a secure facility. No one will hurt you."

Hadley scoffed. "This place can't protect anyone. It wasn't built that way. It exists to protect *you*…from us."

"Do I need protecting from you?"

Hadley thought about it for a moment. "Not from *me*. Not anymore."

"Okay, well, why don't you tell me the names of Henry's friends, and I'll look into it on my own, okay? I'll keep your name out of it."

He considered it. Leaning toward her conspiratorially, he spoke in a low voice. "Well, let's see. There's Orrin. Edgar, too. I think they're brothers. And there's Maisie. She seems to be the one making all the decisions. And...there's the Viper. I don't know much about him other than that Martha and the others were—"

Hadley paled suddenly, his eyes darting wildly around the room again. "Martha? Who's—"

"Shh! They're nearby! I know they are, and I've said too much. I shouldn't've told."

"Mr. Hadley, it's okay."

"Don't tell them! Don't tell them I told. Please!"

"Mr. Hadley, please calm down. I promise I won't say anything about you to—"

Hadley covered his ears and began shaking his head; any further attempt on Kathy's part to induce him to talk about Henry Banks's "friends" or anything else was met with more of the same. He muttered about *tongues* and *hands* and *drugs, the drugs!* until Kathy finally put the notebook back in her purse and signaled to Kenny.

On her drive back to her apartment, she thought about the interview. She hadn't gotten anything from Ben Hadley on the pantheon of interdimensional deities that the Hand of the Black Stars cult—Toby's old friends—and now this fairly new group, the Shining Light of Imnamoun, believed in. Their faith in those entities was powerful...and dangerous. Experiences in Colby, Connecticut, had proved the danger of this other dimension, this place called Xíonathymia, and of the servants of its terrible gods. The problem with interviewing so many of these cult members was that a good number of them were too crazy to be coherent, or too scared of their old associates to talk. The Hand, in particular, was a tight-lipped bunch; once, a girl of about fourteen had cut out her own tongue with a piece of broken bathroom mirror to avoid spilling secrets, and another time, a young man in his twenties had dragged a broken bedspring across his neck. He'd only succeeded in a nasty scrape, but it was enough to get him relegated to special, around-the-clock observation and at least temporarily out of Kathy's reach.

Kathy hated not getting the information she wanted. She prided herself in having both a fair degree of skill and exceptional luck in skirting around, skipping over, or plowing through obstacles that stymied most others in her line of work. She could be persuasive. She could even be a little intimidating. And she got answers nearly every time.

Nearly.

However, it hadn't just been striking out with the interview that had gotten under her skin. Over time, she'd developed a certain instinct for picking up the signs that a problem of an otherworldly nature was gathering momentum. It was part of what made her good at her job, that ability to distinguish between the rantings of lunatics, the fantasies of the desperate, the delusions of the misguided, and genuine supernatural occurrences. The last on that list happened infrequently, to be sure, but more often than the general public was aware of, and Kathy and her colleagues did their best to keep such occurrences quiet and to a minimum. While there was no doubt in Kathy's mind that Ben Hadley was mentally unbalanced, there was something in the earnestness of his fear regarding Henry Banks's "friends" that warranted further investigation. She would have to go back and take another crack at Ben Hadley, and maybe talk to Henry Banks as well. If something was going on at Connecticut-Newlyn Hospital, Kathy wanted to know.

* * * *

What had been a very taxing day was stretching into a very long and uncomfortable night. After the cop lady or whatever she was left, nothing had gone right. In the games room, Robert had undone about a third of the puzzle Ben had been working on for the last month and a half. Nellie kept licking her fingers and trying to put them all over Ben's face, particularly in his ears, which he absolutely hated. Then there had been no Jell-O with the dinner trays. The food at Connecticut-Newlyn Hospital more or less sucked, in Ben Hadley's opinion, and was made bearable only by that small treat. It wasn't the taste, although that was pleasant enough. Jell-O was a comfort food to Ben in a way he didn't quite understand. Maybe it was because it looked like it was giggling when he shook the cup a little, or maybe it was the simple pleasure of vibrant color. Ben's therapist likely would have attributed it to a subconscious connection to some simpler, safer, more ordered, and quieter time in Ben's life, back when there was someone in it to make him desserts. Whatever the reason, the absence of the Jell-O was a small but upsetting void in Ben's evening, a way point between a difficult day and what turned out to be an even worse night.

He'd gone to bed early—right after choking down the gray lumps of instant mashed potatoes and the creamed spinach—just to put an end to the day. They'd wake him later for his nightly pills, but for the next hour or so, he just wanted to blot out the world. He could feel anxiety creeping in, the noiseless din in his mind from which the Bad Thoughts came and the whirlwind preceding that need to take action.

Ben had dreamed about awaking in a desolate street in some empty suburban neighborhood. It wasn't one he recognized outright, but pieces of it were familiar. On one neatly kept lawn sat a little white house with blue-checkered curtained windows. It was Mrs. Merman's house, across the street from where he'd lived until he was eight. A few houses down on the right was another ranch home from another street where his foster parents had lived all through his high school years. It wasn't so nice, nor were the people in it, he remembered. Across the street was the apartment building he'd moved into when he was eighteen, next door to the halfway house he'd stayed at after his very first nervous breakdown. Even in the dream, where the deepest and truest feelings are safe from therapists' questions and group talks and police interrogation, where he could admit the truth behind the curtain of sleep—even there, he felt nothing for any of those places, nor could he muster up even the memories of feeling for the people who had one occupied them.

Ben himself sat in his hospital bed in the middle of the street. It occurred to him that being parked right there in the path of potential oncoming cars was not safe, but he felt no immediate need to move. There were no cars on the street, moving or otherwise. There were none in the driveways. There were no dreamsounds of traffic from adjoining or adjacent streets. In fact, other than the buildings, there were no signs of human life or influence at all—no toys or bikes left on their sides to wait for little hands to retrieve them, no garbage cans by the curb, no garden hoses left uncoiled in the grass.

But then he noticed the chalk scribblings on one of the driveways. The house beyond was not one that he recognized; it was a gray two-story Colonial missing about half of its shutters. The rusting metal numbers 8 and 2 hung askew from the aluminum siding over a dented mailbox near the front door.

Ben's attention returned to the driveway. As he slid off the bed, he noticed that dust had begun to accumulate on his sheets in a thin layer of soft gray. The still life scene all around him was likewise dusted, though Ben hadn't noticed its slow accumulation. He looked up at the sky, convinced dust or ash must have just begun to fall, but the endless whiteness above him was too bright, anxiously bright, and he looked away. He cut a path quickly to the sidewalk, sure as one can only be in dreams that the dust meant deterioration, the decay of a moment time had passed by, a memory that would begin to erode from the edges inward until the mind holding it lost that hold completely.

When he reached the sidewalk with the chalk, he was surprised to find that the dust hadn't fallen anywhere over the markings, and the bright colors—Jell-O colors—stood out against the irregular ring of gray surrounding them. The chalk marks took up most of the middle of the driveway, as if the children of the house had spent the better part of a summer day on them, before both the day and the artists moved on with time. There were stick figure children playing stick figure games beneath crude suns with stick figure dogs. There was a boxy hopscotch pathway along the left side near the dust-frosted grass. There were hearts with initials and cross-outs and more initials. It made Ben smile seeing the innocent graffiti of childhood, those little hearts and figures and games.

Something that caught Ben's eye from a spot on the driveway closer to the house drew his attention. He frowned, though at first it was only because of the incongruous aspect of the symbol. He hadn't quite taken in the surrounding words, relegated to the hazy periphery of his dream vision. It was an eye, and although still crude in its aspects, given the medium, it appeared to have been sketched by a more experienced and steadier hand than the rest of the chalk markings. There was far more detail in the background behind the eye, reminiscent of tapestries from one of his own thankfully eroding memories. His dreamself muttered the Platitude of Okatik'Nehr the Watcher, to shield himself from the Terrible Gaze.

He turned from the eye and saw the other chalk drawings had changed as well—only a little, but just enough to cast a sinister light on the actions performed. The stick figure children weren't running with the stick figure dog, but chasing it with sticks and rocks. The hopscotch path had become a series of broken summoning squares that left open doors and invited in the Myriad. Ben shuttered, turning back to the eye, but it had gone away. In its place was some type of house or barn with a large door, and streaks of bright yellow and green had been drawn as if emanating from beneath.

It was then that he noticed the poem, scribbled in stanzas surrounding the new structure.

Little Benny spent the day
With Edgar, Orrin, and Maisie May
They had a game they said was nice
With cards and boards and glit'ring dice
But Little Benny lost a turn
And felt his muscles start to burn
Edgar, Orrin, and Maisie May

Called the Others to come and play
They laughed at what Ben once had been
And changed his bones beneath his skin

In the dream, Ben Hadley tried to scream, but the shape of his throat had already begun to change. It felt as if a balloon had been wedged into his windpipe, and each time he tried to suck in a lungful of air, he succeeded only in inflating the balloon. He clawed at his throat in a panic and felt it swelling. He tried to run back to the bed in the center of the street and its thick blanket of dust, back to the confines of his hospital bedroom. It looked so far away, that bed, and the dust seemed bound and determined to slow him down. It was only up to his ankles but he could do no more than slog through it, and with each failed breath, his field of vision was growing dimmer.

His collapse just a foot or so shy of the bed brought him out of the nightmare, and he sat up panting, pulling in the dark, stale, semi-sterile air from all around him. He tugged at the neckline of his t-shirt, still caught in the grip of panic, then yanked it over his head and flung it away from him. He couldn't bear for anything to be touching his throat just then, with the dark of his room still mingling with his fading dream vision and the chalk images still floating behind his eyes.

He noticed the sound of footsteps only gradually, only as his own ragged breathing finally started to slow to normal. Someone was walking down the hall outside his door. It might have been an orderly, maybe one heading toward his room. He might have cried out in his sleep, and the staff was coming to check on him.

Ben was sure, though, that those footsteps really belonged to one of Henry Banks's friends. He didn't know how they had managed to manipulate his dream like that, but it had been a taunt, a promise of things to come. They were angry that he had told the cop lady about them. They had heard. They knew. And now they were going to do to him what they had done to Martha and the others.

He began pounding on the walls, the doors, the desks, anything to make noise, anything to stay awake and keep Henry's friends at bay. He paced like a tiger back and forth, back and forth, pounding the walls until Larry came. He was relieved to see the nurse, though not even the meds that Larry brought in could calm him down. The footsteps had been matching his pace, and fists angrier and stronger than his had pounded the hallway walls in answer.

Ben tried to tell Larry about Henry's friends, but it only made him more nervous—so much so that Larry had called Kenny and Joe and they'd had to hold his arms down while Larry injected him with the stuff that made him sleepy.

Most of all that was a blur now. The dream, that *damned dream*, was the only vivid thing in his mind, still Jell-O-colors bright, but everything that followed was blurry, its edges already eroding. Once again, Ben found his ability to draw clear-cut lines between what was inside his head and outside of it to be faltering. He was nervous, and his nerves made things cloudy and uncertain.

Once Larry and the others had left, he rolled off the bed and staggered toward the locked door.

The hospital was old and made strange sounds, some of which sounded like voices, but most of which were not too different than footsteps and pounding on the walls. Just then, though, Ben could hear nothing but the rushing sound in his ears from the drug they'd given him. He pressed the side of his head against the door and listened.

For a long time, the hallway was quiet. Then the rushing in his ears faded to a dull, cottony monotone and he thought he could hear singing. The voice beyond the door was faint but unmistakably feminine, and although Ben couldn't make out the words, he knew it to be the song from his dream, the one whose lyrics had been scrawled out for him in chalk.

It wasn't until the melody grew closer that it dawned on him whose voice was singing. It was one of Henry's friends, Maisie. And although her singing came from just outside the door now, it never really got any louder…

…not until it entered the room.

Ben flinched at the voice suddenly so close behind him. He wheeled around, breathing hard.

Behind him stood a silhouette of a young woman, maybe a foot or so shorter than he was, with the bony thinness of an early adolescent. Her singing had fallen to a soft and almost soothing hum, but that broke off as well. Then she said, "Hello, Ben."

"Are…are you Maisie?"

A little giggle. "I am."

"What do you want?"

She stepped into the moonlight coming from the high window.

Her curtain of light brown hair hung straight and obedient to her shoulders, tucked on both sides behind her ears. Her eyes were doe big, almost anime big, and a sharp blue, with soft lashes. A sprinkling of freckles dusted the bridge of her nose and cheeks. Her skin was winter pale, but she wore a little floral summer dress. She looked like a young girl...mostly. There was something a little off, though. She had no scars, no birthmarks, no lines at all anywhere in her skin, which gave Ben the odd impression that Maisie was what his therapist would have called "somewhat idealized," a doll or mannequin version of a person drawn from imagination and not an actual flesh-and-blood, living person herself. His therapist said that people like him and Henry tended to do that, especially with women and children. Maybe Maisie was what Henry wanted her to be.

Ben thought it more likely that Maisie pretended to be what Henry wanted, but beneath, she was something else. As if in response to his thoughts, he saw that the more he took her in, the more pronounced an unusual feature of hers became: she had a strange patch of glittering, iridescent scales around her left eye and part of her cheek.

After allowing him to study her for a bit, she spoke. "I've come to talk to you."

"About what?"

"Well, about some incantations you have in your head, like those in Toby Ryan's. I imagine yours will be very helpful...but I can get those from you in just a moment. I've also come to discuss with you this pesky little habit you have of talking about us to other people. I'm sorry, but I can't have that, not just yet."

Ben's mind raced. "Did you kill Martha? You killed her, didn't you? And the others..."

Maisie smiled with her perfectly innocent little girl's mouth.

Ben backed away. "No," he said. "No! No! Please don't do this. You don't have to do this!" He stumbled over the corner of his bed and let out a cry.

"Ben," Maisie said in that soothing voice, "let's not be difficult. I just want to talk to you." She took a step toward him. "I just want to protect Henry."

"Protect him?" Ben held his breath for a moment. Maybe she wouldn't kill him after all. Maybe she really did just want to talk.

"Yes. There are many who would hurt him if they could. Hurt *us*. I can't let that happen." In a quick and fluid motion, she lunged forward and put a slightly clawed hand on his chest, just above his heart.

He felt a tugging at first and then a dull ache, but he couldn't pull away. A burning sensation radiated outward under his skin, spreading in all directions beneath her palm and bent fingertips. His heart began to beat faster

"Please don't," Ben whispered. It was all he could manage to say.

She gave him one of those little smiles again but her hand remained rigid. The burning was traveling down his arm now. He felt weak.

She guided him gently to the floor, crouching beside him as he shrank into himself. Her hand remained over his heart. He tried to curl into the fetal position and found he couldn't; his bones and muscles wouldn't comply. Suddenly he didn't bend the right way, and he began to struggle against the rebellion of his body.

"Shh." Maisie's soothing voice came from above him. "Shh, now. I have what I need. You're going to have to die."

Ben heard the grinding of his bones and the red-hot fire of his muscles detaching. He opened his mouth to speak, but all that came out was the darkness in his lungs and head, which turned back on him and swallowed him whole.

* * * *

When Larry Myers turned the corner of the third floor hospital wing and walked down the hallway at 8:00 a.m. to give Benjamin Hadley his medication, his mind was on other things. He'd had a date the night before, and it had gone far better than he could have expected. He wasn't great-looking and certainly not rich, nor was he especially quick-witted or funny. As his father had always told him, he didn't bring all that much to the table. He was smart enough, but suspected that the best way to apply that intelligence was always going to elude him. Frankly, Larry's best asset in the dating world was that he was persistent. He wasn't a stalker, but he was genuinely enthusiastic and his endurance, at least prior to the bedroom, was admirable. He was the kind of guy whose desperation fell somewhere between endearing and pathetic, or so he was told, and so he did all right for himself with those women easily moved to pity.

Linda, the woman he'd been with last night, had a beautiful cloud of chestnut curls, sexy green eyes, hungry lips, and long, long legs. He knew that the social politics to which he pretended to ascribe, to some degree, would have dictated that he notice more substantial and lasting attributes than her breast size or how it felt to grab her ass while she was riding him. However, when the bulk of their relationship pretty much just consisted of her riding him, he didn't see much reason to notice a whole lot more.

Larry's mind was on Linda and her beautiful body; he hadn't been thinking of Ben Hadley as anything more than a perfunctory task that morning, and so when he unlocked and entered Hadley's room, he didn't register the blood stain on the sheets hanging off the side of the bed right away. It took a moment, but then the small dark pool seeping out from under the bed began to spill across his thoughts of Linda and finally register as something wrong. Still, he'd turned and managed to say, "And how are we this mor—" before dropping the little paper cup with the pills in it. Larry took in the scene by the bed with no remarkable change in his expression, but internally, a wildfire of panic had engulfed all other thought.

Hadley's bedsheets had been heaped in a tangle at the foot of the bed. There was a little blood on them, enough to make a brown-ringed stain on that already begun to dry on the part that hung over the side. That in itself wasn't so alarming, except that it drew one's eye to the floor, and there was the real problem.

Blood was coming from under the bed.

The edge of the sheet just grazed the sticky surface of the floor. To get a better look, Larry gingerly drew back the blood-speckled fabric. He couldn't move the bed; in Connecticut-Newlyn, the beds were bolted to the floor. Still, he could peer under, or if he had to, toss the mattress. He pulled out the little pocket flashlight he kept clipped to his belt loop and clicked it on, directing the beam through the dust particles skittering out from under the bed.

The light found an upturned eye, glazed with clouds.

Shit. Oh fuck. Oh shit. This is bad...

Larry had no love for the inmates of Connecticut-Newlyn—most of them were, in his opinion, terrible people, if "people" was even an apt description—but dead inmates meant investigations and interviews and paperwork. Dead inmates meant policy changes and scrutinizing. It was his job to keep them alive until they died of natural causes or became well enough for the state to execute them. Gut instinct, though, told Larry there was nothing natural about the death under the bed.

He rose on shaky knees, took a deep breath, and grasping the edge of the mattress, flipped it up.

"Jesus Christ," he muttered, his stomach lurching. He turned his head and called on his walkie for Kenny and Joe.

"Can it wait?" Joe asked on the heels of a static crackle.

"No. Come now." Larry, bent over, fought to keep the world from swimming away from him.

"But—"

"Drop what you're doing and come now, goddammit!"

He took another look at the mess under the bed and immediately regretted it. Staggering backward, he gagged, trying to force down the rising acid gorge with big gulps of breath. When he thumped against the doorframe, he felt a little more in control but not much, and held on to the walkie and the flashlight as if they were the only things keeping him standing.

Beneath the metal frame of the bed, the body lay facedown, although many of the bones had been broken as if to facilitate the odd new positions of the limbs and head. Some of the broken shards jutted through the skin, but mostly, the body had taken on the appearance of a thin leather sack filled with sharp things. Several fingers of one hand had been removed; two had been shoved into the ears up to the second knuckle. The rest were clutched by the death grip of the other hand. The upper right portion of the head, including one of the eyes, was missing. The other eye lay cradled in what remained of its socket. The tongue lay just outside the lips like an ancient offering at the mouth of a sacred cave. Another offering, the heart, had been removed and placed on the altar of the back.

Larry's gut had been right. Death was not uncommon at Connecticut-Newlyn. Suicides, even homicides happened often enough that none of the orderlies was unfamiliar with it. But whatever that was under the bed, whatever had done that to a human being—*that* was most certainly not common.

Neither was the layer of dust coating the body and its rearranged organs, as if it had been there for years.

Kenny got there seconds before Joe, who slammed into the back of him when Kenny stopped short.

"What the fuck is that?" Kenny muttered, pulling on his rubber gloves.

"That," Larry said in a low, shaky voice, "is what's left of Ben Hadley."

Chapter 3

Ernest Jenkinson had been a custodian for almost fifty-five years. He'd been drafted just out of high school, which was fine by him. He'd never been much for school anyway and had no more of an interest in going to college on the government's dime after Vietnam than he'd had before the war, when he'd have had to pay his own way. What he realized too late was that if nothing else, a degree was a bargaining chip in the workforce; with it, he might have landed a job with decent pay and benefits. Without it, and with no training and the wrong color skin, Ernie Jenkinson learned to scrub toilets. Ernie's dad had raised him to be the sort of man who recognized a job as a blessing, though, and who tackled any job he had with the work ethic of a mule, so when Ernie Jenkinson became a janitor, elevated years later to custodian, he set about becoming the best damn one he could be.

Ernie was popular around the hospital, loved by the unlovable and unloving. He never thought much about it, but if he had, he might have chalked it up to just treating those residents like normal fellas. They didn't get much "normal" in their lives these days—probably never really had, truth be told. And he cleaned up their piss and blood and shit and broken things, the evidence of tantrums and fights and plain good old-fashioned clumsiness, and never once made them feel like anything but regular Joes about it. That was not to say that any of them could pull one over on Ernie or treat him low. Ernie didn't put up with anything less than civility, and the crazy folk at CNH saw something in him worth being civilized to.

It might have been that Ernie was a Vietnam vet. He'd seen some shit and he'd done some shit, and while neither alone would have earned him the loyalty of the CNH residents, both seemed to do the trick. He'd killed and seen killing and didn't judge. He'd cleaned up messes back then, as well, though it had been for his government and, he'd thought then, for his country. One or two of the residents were ex-soldiers, and because Ernie had outranked them during his service years, they saluted him. It could also have been that they thought of him as a protector and guardian. Ernie wouldn't allow mistreatment of residents by anyone— not by each other or the orderlies, and not even by nurses or doctors. He found ways to settle differences and restore what he'd come to call the civilization of the ward. His little forms of justice were accepted, even appreciated by the others. Ernie was fair and efficient and treated people, even them—maybe *especially* them—like human beings. The folks under Ernie's custodial care at CNH never suffered a new resident to show him anything but the utmost respect.

The residents were not above the occasional practical joke, however, all in good fun. That was what Ernie thought the muddy footprints leading down the hall from the rec room were, initially. About halfway to the resident bedrooms, they spiraled up the corridor walls and onto the ceiling, where they changed shape. Though there were fewer toes, those that remained were longer and pointier, with something like a toe protruding from the heel. Ernie had to hand it to the jokester; whoever had made these prints—What was that stuff, mud? Or paint, for God's sake?—had not only managed to plant them in some difficult-to-reach places without getting caught but had worked in all the loving details of an actual animal foot, down to toeprint ridges and everything.

Ernie smiled. The guys around the rec room knew about his interest in what science folks called cryptids. Bigfoot, the Loch Ness Monster, the Bridgewater Triangle creatures in Massachusetts, the Mothman—all that was a light distraction to fill the hours when he wasn't working, sleeping, or drinking beers. He watched all those monster hunter shows on the Travel Channel, all the documentaries about legendary large cats and chupacabras and swamp apes. Ernie had been around a long time and appreciated that there were still mysteries in the world, still answers to get up in the morning and look for. He didn't take much to the alien stuff; sure, there was probably life out there somewhere, but it was too far away for Ernie to ever see in his lifetime. Undiscovered species of animals right here on his own home planet, though, now *that* was something he could get behind.

So, he'd play along. He'd follow the footprint trail and see what the fellas had in store for him. Pushing along his custodial cart, he whistled to himself as he followed the print pattern down the side of the wall again. He reached out and touched one just at eye level, scraping at it with his thumbnail. What *was* that stuff?

He brought the flakes on his fingernail up close to his face to get a good look at them. Not mud, he saw, and not paint, either. He frowned. Actually, it looked like dried blood. He looked at the print again. The stain was certainly dark enough, with just a tinge of red, to be dried blood, but—

He had only a moment to notice that the prints ended at Ben Hadley's room, with one wrapped around the doorframe, when two orderlies, Kenny and Joe, turned the corner and came running down the hall. They pushed past him and buzzed the door to the bedrooms and hurried through, stopping short just in the doorway of Ben's room. If they had noticed the footprints in passing, they didn't show any sign of it.

Ernie left the cart and the footprints where they were and buzzed himself through the same door. His arthritis had been acting up a bit, so it took him longer to reach Ben Hadley's room, but he found the two orderlies, as well as Larry Myers, one of the male nurses, gawking at some mess on the floor beneath a bed frame. It took a few moments to realize what mess was...or had been.

"Good Lord, what happened to him?" Ernie asked.

Larry jumped, turning to notice Ernie behind him. "I—I don't know. I don't—God, what is even capable of doing something like that?"

"Any one of the fuckers in this place is capable of that," Kenny muttered quietly.

No one replied. It was cool in the room, but the air had begun to smell like rot. In the blazing jungle sun of Vietnam, Ernie had become familiar with the smell, but no one ever grew used to it. It was probably hardwired into human DNA not to.

"I'll call the police, then, Larry," Ernie finally said, somewhere between a question and a statement. He didn't need the nurse's permission per se, but there were protocols, meant to protect them as well as the residents.

"Yeah," Larry said. The hand he ran through his thinning hair was shaking badly. "Do that. Joe, Kenny—go get Dr. Wensler. He'll need to be briefed. And Dr. Ulster—I think she was his doctor. I'll stay with the... with the body."

Ernie nodded and headed toward the hall where he'd left his cart. He'd need it at some point, after the police and doctors and crime scene folk had left. This one wasn't a suicide or an accident, so maybe he'd just have to close off the room until the police cleared it. He focused on these things, the practical things, the things that brushed against the fringes of his job description, because his mind wasn't quite ready to tackle Ben's death head-on yet. He'd liked Ben Hadley, despite the man's having murdered an upstairs neighbor. As folks around this place went, Ben was one of the better ones. He was a nervous fella, and he'd admit as much to anyone, but on his medication, he was almost a nice, normal, shy guy. Maybe others couldn't understand Ernie's feeling bad about Ben's death, but he didn't care. He'd call the police and make sure they came. He'd make sure they didn't just brush the murder off as one less sick, crazy killer in the world.

If nothing else, the nature of Ben's death proved that there was something else, a far worse killer, somewhere in the hospital.

Ernie eyed the footprints again, the ones made in blood that no one else seemed to notice, even though they led right to a dead man's room. As he made his way down the corridor, he felt their spiraling pattern around walls and ceiling to be stifling, like a coil pulling tighter and tighter.

For the first time in fifty-five years, Ernie was afraid like he hadn't been since that first night in Vietnam, and he thought he just might have come across a mess he had no way to clean up.

* * * *

If Connecticut-Newlyn Hospital was the domain of Ernie Jenkinson, then lands surrounding the business most certainly belonged to the hospital's groundskeeper, George Evers. Ernie and George had been friends for the better part of those fifty-five years of Ernie's employment, and during off hours, where one was, the other was usually close by. Ernie's wife had died in '92, and George's back in '83, and neither had ever been inclined to remarry. Rather, they were content to drink beers at the Silver Deer Tavern up the road or go fishing when the weather was nice, and trade stories about the war or, sometimes, about the hospital itself.

George was not as well-liked as Ernie around the hospital. To say that people feared him was not, perhaps, entirely accurate, but it was a general unspoken rule that one did not mess with George Evers. With most people, he was taciturn almost to the point of being rude, and he had a nasty temper. Whether the lines in his face had caused the permanent scowl and frown or the other way around, no one could remember. George was like a cliff, worn with time and shaped by decades in the elements. He was immutable and immovable in most instances. Whichever side of the hospital's bars one found oneself on made no difference to George; it was the land he loved, the land he worked for. The rest could be damned. The only exceptions and the only people who had ever known the awful particulars of the hard, tragic storms that had weathered George were Ernie and George's wife, Marian, God rest her sweet soul.

Of course, the domain of George Evers extended to the utility shed some two and a half acres behind the hospital. It was an old shed, worn and splintered like George himself, but it served its purpose. Had George been a younger man, he might have rebuilt it. In fact, he often discussed such plans with Ernie over beers. However, the shed, like the hospital and the men who took care of it, had been standing since the 1940s, and while it wasn't going anywhere, it wasn't going to get rebuilt, either.

It was George who first noticed something wrong with the shed. To be more accurate, his first thought upon hiking the two and a half acres across hospital grounds was that after all those years in the sun, he'd finally started going soft in the head. For decades he'd been taking the same routes through the grounds, past the same trees and boulders and small, decorative benches, and yet somehow, he'd wandered off course and ended up where the shed clearly wasn't. He'd found some type of barn instead, and from the smell of it, one used to store chemicals rather than animals or landscaping tools.

The problem was, there had never been a barn on the hospital grounds before. George was certain of that. As he glanced around his surroundings, he was at least reassured that he was in the right place, where the shed was *supposed* to be. It wasn't the wrong patch of ground he had found; it was the wrong structure.

Ernie complained from time to time that the hospital made changes to things without giving any of the staff a heads-up, but George had never seen it affect him firsthand. He felt nettled—more than nettled, actually—that someone had touched "his stuff," had messed with his equipment and moved things around without telling him, even if it was to move everything into a bigger space. They'd done one hell of a sloppy job, though. The barn looked crooked in a way that hurt the eyes. It offended the human sense of perspective somehow, as if vanishing points and proper angles were alien concepts to the builder, and symmetry a great unknown. George was no architect, but he had always appreciated the fine, clean lines of a well-constructed building, however small, and this barn was wrong in ways it was difficult to pinpoint consciously.

Further, some black and faintly smoking chemical was leaking out from beneath the door.

George swore under his breath as he stomped the rest of the way toward the new barn. If whoever had replaced his shed had also spilled chemicals, there would be hell to pay, and he'd have the devil himself come to collect. Damage to his equipment and tools, not to mention the potential fire and safety hazards.

George threw open the door. Inside, the darkness lay draped over everything. He squinted, waiting for his eyes to adjust. The chemical smell was stronger inside, emanating from the black pool whose center remained hidden in shadow. The opening of the door had sent a fresh wave of the stuff out over the threshold, but there was just enough floor to sidestep it, and George moved cautiously inside.

A silhouetted movement caught his eye, slithering along a shelf behind a dark mannequin shape across from him.

Not only had someone spilled chemicals, but he or she had let a goddam snake into the barn as well. What a fucking start to his morning. He'd have a mouthful of complaints for Ernie that evening.

He felt around in the dark for the Maglite he kept near the door and wasn't all that surprised to find it had been moved. His fingers, rough from work, grazed cans with sticky curves and tools with their sharp sides facing out like claws. He nicked his middle finger and swore into the darkness.

A faint whirring from the black beyond replied. It wasn't quite mechanical nor entirely organic but somewhere uncomfortably in between.

He resumed his tactile search for the flashlight. He brushed against something soft and a little sweaty and instinctively yanked his hand back, wiped it on his shirt, and moved down a shelf. Finally, he felt the familiar plastic handle, and his hand closed around it. At the same time, something closed around his wrist, something thin but strong with thorny protrusions. In the dark, George imagined some type of vine, and he wasn't scared so much as disgusted. Again, he pulled, wresting both wrist and flashlight free of the vine's grasp, and clicked on the light.

What he saw on the shelf did resemble a vine down to jagged leaves, but it, like the barn, was the wrong color, the wrong proportions. It made him think of veins and arteries turned inside out, sprouting serrated leaf-teeth, and George was sure that if he hadn't pulled his hand back when he did, he might have lost it entirely.

Once he found the weed killer, that monstrosity would be the first thing in the new barn to go.

A noise behind him made him jump, and he whirled around, the Maglite arcing its beam across a series of things that wouldn't quite register in his brain. The light landed on the mannequin shape he'd seen from before. However, the rays of light seemed to pour around the thing rather than shine on it. It remained velvety black, like a three-dimensional cutout of a female figure rather than a solid form. It wasn't like any mannequin he'd ever seen, but it wasn't as much a concern as the snake that might have thumped against it.

But then the mannequin opened its eyes. These were all-white orbs devoid of irises or pupils. The cataract paleness provided the only contrast in the face, and although there was something suggestively blind about them, George shivered when those eyes turned on him.

"What the fuck are you?"

A cold hand touched his, and although the figure stood too far away to have reached him, he was sure it was hers. George edged away from those eyes, wishing they'd look away, wishing they'd watch anything else than his retreat, and when the figure took a step forward, he broke into a run.

Just before the threshold, he stepped in the black stuff oozing out the barn door, and before he could look down, the stuff had reached up and coiled around his leg to the upper thigh. It tripped him, and he went down hard, splashing some of that black ichor up into his face. He felt it at the corner of his eye and just under his nose, a sour chemical smell that burned cold on his skin. Without thinking, his tongue darted out to clear it from his lips and he cringed at the bitter taste.

He tried to pull himself up but found he couldn't. The burning cold around his thigh felt solid, like an iron band, and now the stuff had begun to wash over his hands.

George Evers was not a man given easily over to panic, but he let out a moan followed by a few curses born of fear. Panic was for the weak, panic was the extra few seconds or minutes that meant the difference between death and life. George tried to analyze the situation instead. He had to figure out what was happening and thereby how to make it stop. He tried to wrench his hands free of the thick inkiness, but they wouldn't budge. The bands around his leg had begun to squeeze and he thought he heard the sound of denim tearing. He could hear movement behind him in the darkness. Not only was that mannequin thing likely coming up from behind him, but from the sound of it, she was bringing a lot of clinking, slithering, ground-slapping friends.

He knew he was in trouble, and that made it hard to hold on to the rationalizing part of his brain. The smell beneath him had to mean the chemicals in the blackness were burning his skin. He felt no real pain, but that suggested the nerve endings might already be damaged. Chemicals could do funny things to human tissue—sad, awful, funny things.

It didn't cross his mind that the damage might be internal instead, caused by inhalants perhaps, until the sharp rumbling in his gut was echoed by odd ripples from underneath his skin. It wasn't a sensation like his skin crawling, he decided. Rather, it felt like ropy, snaking things were swimming through the lower levels of his skin, slicing through connective tissue and slinking over muscle, flaying him from inside. In a moment, the skin suit he wore would be loose from his body, interchangeable with any other.

It didn't stop at his skin, though; all over, the complex machinery of bones and organs, tissue and systems, was becoming unhinged and detached. The pain was still minimal, but the terrible certainty that he was being dismantled like a junk lawn mower was enough to push him over panic's edge. He managed to mutter a few words like, "Stop! No! I'm losing myself," before falling face-first into the black pool sending a curious, probing tide out onto the grass.

* * * *

When the Viper found Maisie, she was sitting on one of the decorative benches about a half acre away from the shed. A little dandelion-dotted hill stood between the two, and the Viper didn't see her until he had crested it. The faint golden gold from that patch of scales stood out in the darkness. He could see her head was bowed, and as he sauntered within talking distance, he saw she was reading a book.

"How can you see the words?" he asked.

"The words are not for seeing," she said without looking up. "Henry knows the story—he has since childhood. So I know it, too. Of course, I know what the symbols between the folds of the sentences mean, as well."

The Viper didn't reply. The mystical middle ground between what they all had been and what they endeavored to be was Maisie's domain. He was comfortable just providing the muscle. He looked out over the hospital grounds, his gaze following the way the moonlight dipped and glanced off the rolling landscape. It appeared empty at the moment. Usually, wherever Maisie was, Edgar and Orrin were in tow, and beyond them, the teeming chaos of the Others. They were not precision instruments like his mist Wraiths; rather, they were the beasts and berserkers of Ayteilu, Henry's childish and unchecked Id and emotions, and Edgar and Orrin could barely keep track of them, let alone control them.

"Where are the boys?"

"Waiting. Is it working?"

The Viper lit a smoke. A cloud passed in front of the moon, and for a moment, only the light of her scales and the burning ember of his cigarette were visible.

"It is," he said, exhaling a plume into the darkness. "And better than expected."

"So it's possible, then. To make total substantiation, I mean." Maisie closed the book.

The Viper couldn't see the rest of her face and couldn't tell from her voice if her words were an affirmation or a need for confirmation. "Well, it works with the little ones; I can tell you that much. I see no reason why it shouldn't work for us." When she didn't answer, he added, "You keep taking care of Henry, make him strong, and yeah, I'd say it's more than possible."

"Thank you." She stood and the glow turned to him. She had a youngish face, too much like a child's to be more than innocently endearing, but the look in her eyes was hard, knowing, and very, very old. "Time is limited. I'm glad to see things are on schedule."

The Viper shrugged. He wanted her to be pleased, but there were a lot of factors yet to be accounted for. He was about to offer his thoughts on the subject when she broke in.

"A woman came today. Dishy. Scarred. Your type, no doubt."

The Viper flicked the ash off the end of his cigarette. "To see Henry?"

"No. To see Ben. But we can add her to the list of people Ben has told about us. The thing is, she isn't like the other humans, though. She is different. Not a problem yet, but more likely to be one in the future than the staff here."

"And Ben?"

"Taken care of. I didn't tell the others. Henry doesn't need to know."

"So what next?"

"The old brick buildings that they use for file archives and storage nowadays, followed by the electrical station at the back gate and those small residential buildings for staff in the east acres. We should hit those last two at about the same time. Then we'll come around to the northern acres last with the patient cemetery, and then the hospital will be surrounded, and we can move inward."

The Viper considered all of that for a moment, then said, "We can't enter their dead."

"We don't need to," Maisie replied lightly. "We can use the headstones, any wood or bones, that sort of thing. Substance, Viper. We simply need substance."

He nodded. "And Henry?"

Her half-shadowed smile was small and hard. "I'll take care of him. I have always taken care of him."

She turned and left him then without another word. She had, evidently, grown tired with his asking questions, and they all had work to do.

They were going to strangle this hospital and everyone in it, and bring it all to the ground.

Chapter 4

Kathy Ryan had filed her report on the Shining Light of Imnamoun, sparse as it was, both with the clients who had hired her and with the Network, the occult investigation group she was affiliated with, before she'd finished her second tumbler of vodka.

She'd been frustrated with how light it was—she wanted clients to get the most for the considerable money they paid her—but she wasn't going to pad the report. She wrote it up and sent it through all the proper channels to the Institute of Holistic Research. Part of that name, she thought, was intentionally misleading, since so far as she could tell, they didn't work with holistic medicine at all. They certainly did their research, though. The background check on the Institute turned up extensive monitoring of industries and technologies capable of intentionally or unintentionally opening doorways to other dimensions, an objective she could certainly get behind.

The Institute heads had followed her work in Zarephath, Pennsylvania, not too long ago and in Colby, Connecticut, before that, and wanted whatever she could gather on the Shining Light of Imnamoun and its beliefs. It was the Institute's opinion that they might just rival the Hand of the Black Stars for Cult Most Likely to Destroy the World. What she'd wanted—which was also what her employers wanted—was the nuance of ritual and history of their pantheon that all the police and hospital reports on the cult and its reprogrammed members wouldn't contain. She was still annoyed that Ben Hadley had given her so little on them. It was a matter of pride in her work, she supposed. It was personal, though, too. It was a roundabout way to learn what made Toby and people like him tick. To protect against a monster, one had to know the monster, for one thing, but it was more than that. She needed to know a little more about what kind of world (or worlds) had so irrevocably changed her brother, what gods he found so important that he'd embraced blood sacrifices and destruction over family to appease them. She wanted to learn what had killed off all there was to love in him. If that also fell in line with securing future investigative work with the Institute, well, that might be beneficial both financially and in terms of information exchange.

As far as Kathy could tell, the Institute's goals were more or less in line with the Network's. Both the Institute and the Network were interested in keeping tabs on CERN, MK Ossium, the Antarctic Initiative, and other projects globally. The Network sought to keep any one group with power or money from turning such projects into potentially world- or universe-destroying weapons. The Institute's stance on the weapons aspect was a little too vague for Kathy's comfort, but her contacts in the Network had given the okay.

She never trusted all of her clients implicitly, but she trusted the Network. Its origins stretched back through history to 1529 at least, and though their membership was small, their files were extensive and complete, their work was important, and their reach far. Nowadays they called themselves the Network, though Kathy understood there had been other names throughout the centuries. She didn't see it as taking up a mantle or even being part of a legacy, though. To Kathy, there was no other place to go and no other area of work she could excel at. She would never have consciously admitted that some of those ones and zeros on the other end of the internet were friends, but they recognized her worth. They valued the experience and insight that the baggage of her past gave her. To them, she wasn't some old drunk's scarred-up daughter or some serial killer's sister. To them, she was an asset, and she liked that.

What she didn't like was the nagging doubt that, like a small tide, had begun to wash farther into her thoughts, spilling over her annoyance with something more pressing. It was this Henry Banks. She'd included the information about him and his influence on Ben Hadley as a footnote in both reports, but she suspected the recipients of those reports might feel like she did. There was more to Henry's imaginary friends than hallucination; Kathy couldn't prove it, but she knew it in her gut. She knew it.

Reece Teagan, who had been watching what he called "real football" on TV, kept glancing at her. Even from the periphery of her vision, she saw his curiosity and mild concern as he sipped his beer.

"Trouble at work, love? You look knackered. The crazies do a number on you today?" Despite years in the States, his Irish accent was as strong as ever. She found it sexy; he often teased her that he could have looked like a blind cobbler's thumb and still have won her over just by talking. To Kathy, he was the pretty one in the relationship, though she honestly believed him when he said she was beautiful and that he barely even noticed her scar.

Of course, there was more to their relationship than the physical. Kathy had to remind herself of that sometimes, when she found herself wondering what a guy like Reece ever saw in her. He had told her that he had been in love with her for a long time. He accepted her antisocial quirks, her vodka drinking, what was left of her horrible family life, and her staunch refusal to bear children. He knew about her work and accepted that, too, and also knew when not to ask questions about it. She knew she was not an easy woman to love, but he found ways, and she was grateful for that. At first, she had loved him for that. Over time, she had come to find so many more things about him to love—his gentle way of probing for answers without making her feel defensive or afraid, his way of looking at the world, how much fun he had playing with dogs and children. Reece was a good man and a damned good detective, and if there was ever a person to inspire her work, a reason to keep the world safe from the myriad monsters of untold dimensions, it was Reece Teagan.

She wheeled around on her rolling chair, pushing off from the desk toward him on the couch. "It's just something this guy said. I guess it's not really related to the case or anything, but I can't get it out of my head."

"What did he say?"

"He mentioned a guy, Henry Banks. Said this guy had friends, imaginary friends that he didn't believe were so imaginary. I've talked to a lot of crazies, and I think I know the difference between their delusions, no matter how strongly they believe in them, and when there's something a little more. Something more in keeping with my line of work, you know?"

"And you think this bloke might have seen more than a hallucination?"

"Yeah, I do."

"Then follow it up," Reece said, and gulped the last of his beer. "Trust your gut."

"You don't think that's nuts?"

He laughed, and the sound made her smile. "Of course not, love. Not given what you do, or what I've seen, which is only a small part of the bigger picture. Besides, if you're wrong—if he's just mad as a box of frogs, I mean—then no harm done. At least you can rest easy knowing you looked into it."

She considered that a moment, then nodded. "You're right." She leaned over and gave him a kiss, then slid out of the chair and made her way to the bedroom. "I'll be back in a couple of hours."

"Wait, what? Now? It's almost half eight!" His protests were light, though. They both knew that once Kathy had an idea in her head, there was no stopping her.

Changed into jeans and a t-shirt, keys and purse dangling from one hand, she kissed him again in passing on her way out.

"Love ya," he called after her.

"You too." She paused at the front door and gave him a warm, genuine smile. She'd been doing that more since they'd been together. Smiles had never really felt comfortable on her face, but she was finding that she liked trying them on from time to time. "Don't wait up."

He returned the smile, waving her off, and she slipped out into the hallway.

* * * *

Kathy got the call about Ben Hadley's murder just as she pulled into the parking lot of the Connecticut-Newlyn Hospital for the second time that week. Margaret called her personally to tell her.

"You're kidding me," Kathy responded.

"I don't joke," Margaret said flatly, and she didn't. "The crime scene truck just left maybe half an hour or so ago, and it's been barely controlled chaos all day. The patients are very agitated. Ben Hadley's room is taped off and his body, of course, is gone, and they all want to know what happened. It's a mess."

"I'm in the parking lot," Kathy said. "Can you buzz me in?"

"Now? Tonight? Katherine, visiting hours are over in"—there was a pause on the phone—"fifty-three minutes and—"

"I know," Kathy broke in, trying to sound genuinely sympathetic. "I know it's an inconvenience, but I need to see Henry Banks. It's important."

"And Dr. Wensler won't allow it. He's put a restriction on visitation for the next few days, until the police clear the staff and patients."

"We don't have to bother him. I'll be in and out."

"You can't see a patient without that patient's doctor's approval, Katherine. You know that."

Kathy did. She also knew Margaret would be a stickler about the rules and paperwork, too. She tried another tactic.

"Margaret, I may be of some help to the police. I could offer consultation. I spoke to the victim earlier that day, and I believe, based on the conversation I had with him, that I have information relevant to the police investigation. Information involving a connection with Henry Banks."

There was another, longer pause on the other end of the line. "This isn't about his so-called 'friends,' is it?" she asked, but she was weakening.

"What they believe is often a reflection, however distorted, on what they see and what they know. And what they do."

Margaret sighed over the phone. "I can buy you thirty minutes," she said. "Let me know when you're at the front door and I'll buzz you in."

"Thank you, Margaret. I owe you one."

"Nah, don't thank me. Just find out who killed Ben Hadley."

"I will," Kathy promised.

When she got to the front door, Margaret let her in and she jogged to the glass window and quickly scribbled her signature across the paperwork Margaret put in front of her. A uniformed officer stood nearby, giving her the eye. She felt his gaze travel the length of her scar and the parts of her that had been relaxed enough to be soft just a half an hour before at her apartment grew cold and hard.

She approached him and brusquely showed her ID, explaining she was a police consultant who had talked to Ben Hadley the day before and had information to share with the detective. When the uniformed officer, whose uniform identified him as Patterson, tried to take her statement, she reiterated that the information she had was for the detective in charge. She locked eyes with the man, and whether he read something in the tone of her voice or whether he found himself increasingly unnerved by her scar, he finally gave her a nod and let her pass, instructing her that the detective and the doctors were discussing the situation in Dr. Wensler's office.

Kathy got on the elevator and pushed the button for the fourth floor. Kathy had always found the difference in human presence between the third and fourth floors a little disconcerting. The floor below housed custodial offices, examination rooms, group therapy lounges, and even a chapel on the same floor, though Kathy's understanding was that it was seldom used. Some killers found God once they went to jail, looking for salvation, but most of the inmates at Connecticut-Newlyn thought they were gods themselves and beyond the belief in or help of any higher power. And if there was no God in Connecticut-Newlyn, there was no Heaven above. Beyond the administration offices on the fourth floor, there were labs and storage rooms—clinical, harshly lit rooms scrubbed clean of human deficit and insanity. The fourth floor was a locked drawer where the sharp things were kept, the dangerous chemicals, the weapons, the unsafe and unsoothing documentation.

What that said about the majority of people whose offices were nestled in among those things, Kathy wasn't sure.

She was thinking about gods and staring down the hall in the direction of the chapel when she heard a jarring sound she couldn't place. It was reminiscent of but not quite exactly the sound of a loon. It reminded her of laughter, but the kind of laughter the inmates of Connecticut-Newlyn might utter when strung out and withdrawing from their meds. It was the kind of sound that rattled the spine and set hairs on end, but it was more where it was than what it was that got to Kathy.

There were no patient rooms on this floor. There was no reason for an inmate to be down that hall at that time of night. She stood listening for several minutes, but the hallway was virtually silent—so quiet, in fact, that she could hear the hum of the lights overhead.

Kathy crept down the hall toward the chapel and, reaching the open door, peered in. It was dimly lit—a few candles and an overhead chandelier encased in colored glass—and absolutely empty. She followed the burgundy strip of carpet that ran from the door to the nondenominational altar twenty feet away, peering in between the pews as she did so. She found nothing out of the ordinary; it was a pleasant little chapel, faintly incense-scented, but otherwise empty. The only sound came from the *shoosh* of her feet along the carpet.

She retraced her steps to the chapel door. If she didn't get back to the offices soon, she'd lose the opportunity to talk to anyone. Besides, if that noise she'd heard had anything to do with those imaginary friends, she had a better chance of getting to its source through Ben Hadley or Henry Banks. She followed the hall back to the series of offices and put the noise behind her.

As Kathy approached the closed door to Dr. Wensler's office, she braced herself for resistance. If she could have avoided dealing with Wensler and the cops altogether, she would have. They were interested in solving a murder, but what Kathy had to say would likely be little more than a side scribble in their notepads. In a way, she couldn't blame them. If she were in their position, she'd probably find it ludicrous, too, that Ben Hadley was murdered by another patient's imaginary friends. That he was murdered because of them might raise an eyebrow—it was a lead on a suspect, particularly one whose motive might very well have been to protect his delusions. But the idea that the delusions might have done harm themselves wasn't going to sell.

It wasn't her job, at any rate, to convince them that was the case. Kathy's immediate concern was with Henry Banks and determining if said imaginary friends had some semblance of real-world tangibility. Still, in Kathy's experience, the perspectives of doctors and police officers, even when skeptical, were often insightful. Even more so, what they chose not to say with voices but was present in their eyes and facial expressions anyway was illuminating.

Kathy took a deep breath, let it go slowly, and knocked on the door.

The man that answered was in his thirties and not altogether unattractive. His dark hair was starting to grow out of the military buzz cut, at least on the top. His eyes, a cloudy blue-gray, seemed surprised to see her. The way he stood, as well as the way he was looking at her as if trying to piece her together like a puzzle, told her that he was a cop, most likely a homicide detective. His rumpled suit and the faint hint of coffee on his breath suggested he had been there a long time and was fighting work fatigue.

"Yes?" His voice sounded much older, much more tired than his face. Kathy knew the feeling.

"I'm Kathy Ryan," she said. "I'm a police consultant."

The man arched an eyebrow and turned to the assembled group behind him. There was a forty-something woman with an ash-blond updo, black heels, and a business suit. Kathy recognized her as Pam Ulster, a therapist for several of the residents at the hospital. She often had to sign paperwork allowing Kathy to talk to patients under her care. She was seated on the sofa perpendicular to a large oak desk—Dr. Wensler's desk. He sat behind it, a captain at the helm, with his gold name plaque pronouncing him Director of the Long-Term Care and Secure Units. Kathy had had far less interaction with this man from the ivory tower, though she knew that both residents and staff alike thought he was, at best, difficult to like. His fingers were tented in a pretentious show of consideration of the discussion evidently being held with an older, gray-haired man with the scruffy beginnings of a beard standing across from the desk. That older man, presumably a detective as well, wore a suit as wrinkled, if not more so, as the skin around his eyes and forehead. He was, Kathy thought, what the young man in front of her would be in another twenty-five or thirty years.

"We didn't call in a consultant, did we, Holt?" the younger man asked over his shoulder.

"No, we didn't," the older man replied. "Consultant for what?"

Kathy tilted her head to look around the younger man and met the cool gaze of Detective Holt. "I specialize in working with cult members, among other things. I interviewed your victim, Mr. Hadley, yesterday morning. He said some things I thought you might be interested in."

Holt turned to Dr. Wensler. "You authorize this?"

Dr. Wensler flicked a chilly glance in Kathy's direction before responding. "No. I don't see the relevance of her presence here."

"That's Kathy," Dr. Ulster said, recrossing her legs. She wore heels that made Kathy's feet hurt just looking at them. "She's been immensely insightful in dealing with our patients in the past. I would offer that whatever she has to say is worth a listen."

She bore the brunt of Dr. Wensler's glare with grace and poise, no doubt used to it by now, and focused instead on the hesitant expression of Detective Holt.

Finally, the older detective wavered her in. "Let's hear it, then."

Kathy shouldered past the young detective and took a seat on the couch next to Pam Ulster.

"As I said," she began, "my name is Kathy Ryan. Your victim, Ben Hadley, was a former member of the cult known as the Shining Light of Imnamoun. I was interviewing him about his associations and experiences as a member."

"So you think a cult nutjob killed him?" the younger detective said.

"I don't believe so, no, Detective...?"

"Farnham," the man replied. "John Farnham."

"Detective Farnham. No, I was simply stating the nature of my visit. I frequently consult for police and for other government and privately funded organizations with interests in monitoring cult and occult activity. I was gathering information, some of which might be of relevance to you."

"We get it," Detective Holt said with a touch of impatience. "You're a ghost cop. Good for you. What did Hadley tell you?"

Kathy ignored his cynicism. "He believed his life was in danger. He said another patient, Henry Banks, had friends who had hurt other people before to protect the secrecy of their presence in the hospital and their ability to move about it free from the restrictions placed on other inm—I mean, patients here." Before the doctors or police could cut in, she held up a hand. "And yes, I'm aware that the general consensus is that these friends of Mr. Banks are allegedly hallucinations. However, it's been my experience that what patients believe in, or sometimes *who* they believe in, may seem to have no basis in commonly held perspectives of reality—in what you might consider, somewhat inaccurately, as 'objective reality'— but are still indications of very real facts, however distorted the patients have made them."

"I don't understand anything you just said," Farnham said with the kind of helpless frustration only exhaustion can bring.

"What I mean," Kathy said, "is that those friends of Henry Banks may not seem real to you or me, but they do to Henry, and they certainly did to Ben. They may have been distorted to represent someone or something that is an actual threat. Ben believed he was genuinely in danger, and he might well have been—from Henry, who was looking to protect those friends, or from someone else taking up the mantle of a new identity. You can do with that information what you wish, but I would simply caution you not to overlook mention of these friends of Henry Banks. They have evidently caused a stir among the residents here in the past. Whatever details the patients give you about them may have some basis in truth, beneath the delusion."

The detectives turned to the doctors, both of whom shifted uncomfortably in their seats and exchanged glances.

"Further, I would be remiss in my responsibilities if I didn't mention the possibility that the truth I am speaking about may well be something paranormal or supernatural. There is some evidence that points to an unnatural freedom of movement not easily attributable to another patient, given Dr. Wensler here and his no doubt airtight security measures."

Wensler shot her a nasty look. Farnham unsuccessfully hid his smirk behind his hand, and Holt eyed her like he would another inmate at the hospital.

It was Pam Ulster who spoke, though, and it was clear she was choosing her words carefully.

"Patient confidentiality prohibits me from discussing Henry Banks's condition in detail…but he waived the right to confidentiality in regard to what he told me, and subsequently, the court during his trial. If there is anything of truth or sanity in it, I'm happy to share the information with you."

"This is in regard to his imaginary friends?" Farnham reached for the vape pen in his pocket, caught Dr. Wensler's glance, and let it be.

"Please tell us what you know," Kathy said.

"There was eventual talk of Henry's…uh, friends. He claimed they were the ones who killed those teenagers, I believe in order to protect him. As a child, he created a place called Ayteilu, a safe haven in his mind to escape to during the abuse, and he claims these friends are from that place. There appear to be four main entities, among a host of minor ones. I say entities, because he doesn't describe them quite as people, but they are people-like. I believe them to be manifestations of extreme displaced and disproportionate emotions as a result of extensive abuse as a child.

I wouldn't go so far as to say they're dissociative identities; I have never seen Henry manifest any of them as alters, and he seems perfectly aware of them, which virtually never happens in cases of DID. Further, he knows they are, or were once, products of his imagination but believes they became separate, autonomous entities around the time of the murders."

Dr. Ulster added something then that no one quite caught, but it was the way she said it that struck Kathy. Her voice was soft, as if she was afraid of giving sound and thus credence to an idea that had until then been ephemeral.

"Excuse me? I didn't catch that," Holt said.

"He calls them tulpas," she repeated, a little louder, but that tinge of unease was still there.

"Da hell is a tulpa?" Farnham muttered.

"I can answer that," Kathy said. "It's an entity you create with your mind. Theoretically, you give it autonomy—it can think, feel, act of its own free will, establish goals and retain memories."

"That's crazy," Detective Holt snapped.

"That's why Henry is here, Detective," Dr. Wensler replied coldly.

"So your boy Henry thinks his brain gave birth to, what, like, ghost-people who decided to rebel against papa and begin killing random folks?" This time, Farnham ignored Dr. Wensler's disapproving stare and popped the vape pen in his mouth.

"Something like that," Dr. Ulster replied uncomfortably. "I'm sure Kathy would agree that that much is delusion."

They turned to her, but she just shrugged and slowly said, "I've seen stranger things turn out to be true."

"Does this woman need to be here?" Dr. Wensler said suddenly. "This nonsense is just muddying the waters."

Kathy, who'd had enough of this meeting of the minds as well, turned to Dr. Ulster. "Do you think I could sit with Henry? I'd like to talk to him about these friends of his. The ones he said killed the teenagers and that Ben believed had killed other patients."

This started a flurry of protests from both Dr. Wensler and the detectives, claiming violations to protocol and libel about the hospital regarding patient accidents, as well as interference with a murder investigation. Kathy filtered most of it out, keeping her gaze locked on Dr. Ulster. Kathy could help her patient. They both knew that, though it was highly unlikely anyone else in that room would believe what they were both sure of in their guts.

Tulpas. That was the notion that had been nagging at Kathy's subconscious. She had met people before that she believed had the ability to create such beings. Combining that ability with a history of violent abuse, intense escapism, and mental aberration entertained a pretty powerful and dangerous possibility.

"I need to know," Kathy told the doctor as if no one else was in the room. "You do, too. I can see it on your face."

Dr. Ulster hesitated, the veneer of her professional calm beginning to crack under the barrage from her boss and the police.

"Get out," Farnham said to Kathy. "Come on. Out. Now." He took her arm, and she shot him a look that made him hesitate a moment. She pulled her arm free but rose to leave. At the door to the office, she turned back to Dr. Ulster. "Let me find out for both of us," she said, and then a security guard appeared in front of her and escorted her down to the lobby. She and Margaret exchanged shrugs before she was turned out into the darkness.

As she made her way back to the car, her resolve set on returning to see Henry Banks, she thought she heard a howl from someplace far off, behind the hospital. She stopped, turning in the direction of the sound to listen. The air was silent and cool, and although the tiniest hairs stood up all over her, nothing she could see or hear seemed out of place.

Reluctantly, she went back to her car and, with a last glance at the hospital, got in and drove off. She'd come back the next morning, and the next evening if she had to, and every day until they let her see Henry Banks. She had a very bad feeling that things were about to get both bad and strange at Connecticut-Newlyn Hospital—the one place in the world where the security of the normal was the only thing keeping the world safe from what was inside.

She glanced at her phone and saw two text messages waiting for her. The first was from Reece, checking on her, and she replied that she was okay and on her way home. The second had no name attached, only a symbol of a sun, which was how she listed her clients in her phone. She recognized the symbol as the one she'd assigned for the Institute for Holistic Research. She tapped on the text message to open it, expecting some feedback and possibly some disappointment regarding her report.

Instead, it read, *Re: Henry Banks. All the info you can get. Same fee.—GH*

She frowned. The Institute was suddenly interested in Henry Banks, simply from her note? It was possible they were just being thorough; she certainly planned to be, and intended to follow up with the Network for that specific reason. Still, the suspicious part of her made her wonder what the Institute wanted. Had Henry Banks been on their radar before? Did comparing Ben Hadley's records with Henry's lead to an overlap of a word, a phrase, a common acquaintance or location? So far as she knew, they'd never met or had anyone in common prior to the hospital. Maybe the Institute was concerned with their experiences overlapping now, then. But if so, why?

She started the car and pulled out of the parking lot when her phone alerted her to another text message. She pulled it up and saw it was from the Institute again. That one read, *Re: Also, pls send evidence of referenced tulpas if possible.—GH.*

It was strange, to say the least. She had some calls to make and emails to send. It was going to be a long night.

Kathy had just turned the corner out of view when the power from the electrical station of the grounds was cut off, and the entire hospital went dark.

* * * *

The creatures that came across from Ayteilu through the electrical station singed the grass as they walked. Flickering and jittering, they joined the mist Wraiths in the darkness. They brought no bodies with them and made no attempt to bend the circuitry and metal of the station to their will. They needed only the electricity, bundled together in a crackling, sizzling semblance of a humanoid.

The electrical Wraiths had made it across the gulf of Henry's mind and joined their smoky brethren.

One tested out its new form by hurling a small lightning bolt at a decorative bench. The stone cracked in half and the bench folded in on itself in a little pile of rubble. They had no mouths to cheer each other on, but there was a general sense among the creatures of victory. They were free.

The first wave made their way toward the row of residential buildings beyond the next hill, where the Viper said to meet him. Most of those emerging from Ayteilu—the electrical Wraiths, the mist Wraiths, and all their beasts taking on physical forms would be there. So would Orrin and Edgar and their Others, the mad ones. Some of the Wraiths and their beasts would be sent ahead to begin infiltration of the hospital. Ayteilu had already begun to leak through to the top floors, so there would be a little taste of home as well as new places and substances to explore.

All of them had been told they would have an opportunity to try out their new bodies and see what they could do. They could claim what they wanted from the wreckage of each building and build on themselves, choosing a form for this new world. There might be meatbodies in the way to dispose of, and they would do so because the Viper told them to. They did not kill for fun like the Others and they had no interest in pleasing Maisie, but they had less interest in crossing the Viper.

One of the second wave of creatures saw a soda vending machine just outside an old office building. It had long been empty and unused, but the shape and the colors appealed just enough to the creature that it consumed and assimilated the machine, reforming into something new in the shadows. Another absorbed an old pay phone and began reshaping, delighted by the ringing sound it could now make. Two others combined to take on the rusted shell of an abandoned work van, left to rot in the tall grasses. When they discovered the slicing metal edges and small metal teeth they could form along their massive half-van body, they rumbled their approval.

A flurry of sparks erupted as the last of them passed through. The great glass and concrete mammoth at the center of this new land went dark. Immediately, the blue ivy of Ayteilu's Hunger Valley worked its way through the cracks of the hospital façade and grew along the side. The fungal sponges with their thick silvery dust and soft, wet bodies began to eat at the foundation, choosing the main building's basement as their new valley home.

One of the mist Wraiths gave a nod to the last wave of others to follow. There was so much in this world to become and to remake. The excitement among them sizzled like their bodies. It was going to be one long, glorious night.

Chapter 5

Detectives Holt and Farnham had just left Dr. Wensler's office and were making their way down the corridor when the lights all over the hospital went out. They were plunged into total darkness for several seconds, and then the pale blue-white emergency lights came on. These, like the electrical doors and certain pieces of medical equipment, Holt had been told, ran on a separate circuitry system than the usual lights. For the safety of patients and staff alike, Wensler had said, though it certainly didn't seem to Holt like it had contributed much toward the safety of Ben Hadley, nor had it evidently kept Belle and Barney McGuinness from reaching the roof of Parker Hall and jumping to their deaths. Death seemed to be a popular pastime at Connecticut-Newlyn lately. Following the McGuiness suicides, there had been Sherman Jones's death of supposed natural causes, Ridley Comstock's accidental death by autoerotic asphyxia, and an undetermined manner of death (though the coroner was leaning toward suicide) in the violent passing of Martha Lupinski, which Wensler had chalked up to coincidence. Holt, who believed true coincidences were rarer than a decent politician or an honest junkie, thought the deaths might be connected—or at least thought that it was worth looking into a little further—though he couldn't quite see just how. It was a feeling, one Farnham was just a bit too young and inexperienced to trust in himself yet, but Holt knew the younger detective would follow his lead. Police work was an art, as far as Holt was concerned, and not a science, and art was about seeing with more than one's eyes.

For example, a number of murders at a loony bin for the criminally insane had a nice ring of karmic justice to it, with killers killing killers and all, and he might not have thought too much harder about the filth cleaning up the filth except that some of the pieces didn't fit. Holt wasn't going to win any awards for Humanitarian Man of the Year or anything, but he was a good cop; he knew when things didn't fall neatly into place like one hoped a murder investigation would. This one didn't, and despite who the victims were, it bothered him. He'd had a gut feeling something was seriously off about the whole mess just from the preliminary report on Hadley and had grown more suspicious with every evasive answer Wensler and the doc with the nice legs gave him. There were too many Houdini moves necessary to have pulled off a murder like Ben Hadley's in a place where high security protocols and nervous eyewitnesses, however delusional, were the norm.

As they glanced around the eerily blue-lit and exceedingly quiet hallway, warily scanning for signs of trouble as a result of the power failure, Holt picked up his end of the distracted conversation.

"But anyway, yeah, I think we ought to look into her. The name, Ryan—it's familiar. Remember Jack Glazier, over in Colby? I think he used her on a few cases a while back. I'm almost sure of it."

"I'm not sure Glazier's the best judge of character, Mike," Farnham said, taking a tug of that vape pen of his. Since he'd switched to it about a year ago from a pack of Newports a day, he lived quite literally with his head in the clouds, though these clouds were faintly vanilla-scented and, to Holt, reminiscent of his aunt Cordelia's candle-strewn bathroom.

Holt shrugged as they were buzzed through the doors toward the elevator and stairs. "Clearly, the broad's into some weird shit, but like she said, it's about what folks believe. And she believes she has some jurisdiction in this situation. If she's gonna be poking her nose around here, I want to know what she's up to and why."

"Fair enough," Farnham replied in a vanilla mist. They had reached end of the hallway just as the regular lights came back on. He gestured toward the elevator or stairs, deferring to Holt's preference, and Holt nodded at the elevator. Farnham pushed the button to take them down to the lobby.

As they stood waiting, Farnham added, "I guess we could get her number from Scissor-Legs in there."

"You saw those, too? Damn, what I could do with those wrapped around my neck."

Farnham chuckled. "No shit."

"So, yeah, let's get this Kathy Ryan's number from the good doctor and see what's what, huh?"

"Sure, I'm on it," Farnham said. "I guess we could—"

Farnham never finished his thought because there was a *ding* and the elevator doors opened just then on something horrible beyond. Holt instinctively drew his gun on it, backing away slowly. Farnham, on the other hand, seemed to have had his police training shocked right out of him. The thing in the elevator hung from the dislodged emergency escape panel in the ceiling of the car. The arm supporting its weight was ropy with lean muscle, sheathed in a bluish and rubbery-looking skin. Its hands, or maybe they were paws, were too big, their color tapering to black on the backs just before the knuckles. The multijointed fingers ended in great, curving talons of shiny white, almost like marble. Its legs were the same. There was little to differentiate the squarish bulk of the head from that of the torso, and together they were large enough to take up most of the interior space, but it was the familiarity of that bulk that bothered Holt.

The swirls of color and the odd, slotted area where the stomach should have been reminded Holt of a soda vending machine. It was as if the thing in the elevator had swallowed one. No, it was more like the thing had been wearing the vending machine for so long that it had begun to disintegrate and work its way in as a part of the thing's skin.

It dangled a moment from the ceiling of the elevator and then opened its mouth. It wasn't exactly a roar that came out—there was no real sound—but it was the force of a roar, the vibrations, the sound of air whizzing past an ear, and it hurt Holt's head.

Farnham remained standing in front of it, dumbfounded. He'd found his gun holster but the ability to unclip his gun from it seemed to have eluded him. He'd also dropped the vape pen, which had rolled away somewhere. He managed to mutter, "What is that, Mike? What is it?" and then the thing dropped to the elevator floor.

Holt opened fire on it. When the thing screamed again, the vibrations were louder, so much so that the detectives put their hands over their ears, a reaction rather than a reasoned response. They wanted to filter out that horrible soundlessness, that awful pressure in their heads. Holt tried to fire at the thing again but couldn't bear to pull away from his pounding head.

The slot in the creature's stomach area opened, and for one absurd second, Holt expected a can of soda to come popping out of it, the aluminum wet with condensation and maybe some monster goo. Instead, long, black viperous tongues emerged, snapping and swaying in the stale, antiseptic air. One of them shot out and wrapped around Farnham's neck. His eyes bulged and his face began to turn a dark, dark pink.

Holt fired again, trying to stun the creature into letting Farnham go. When that didn't work, Holt pulled a pocket knife from his pants and rushed toward his partner. He began sawing at the tendril around Farnham's neck. That seemed to only make it worse, though whether it was from making the creature squeeze harder in anger and pain or because that grayish liquid from the wounds was burning Farnham's skin, Holt couldn't tell. He just knew Farnham's eyes were bulging and the tip of his tongue, protruding like a grotesque and graying slug, meant the man couldn't breathe.

Holt drew back and was about to charge the thing instead and drive the knife deep into the meat above the open slot when the tentacle made a snapping sound and quickly withdrew, yanking Farnham off his feet and into the elevator.

"John!" Holt cried out, diving for his partner. He managed to grab Farnham's leg, and he pulled hard. The elevator doors closed on it and the car began to rise with only some of John Farnham inside it. Holt let go quickly, hoping John could pull his leg in, but the limb didn't disappear from view. It folded once it reached the top of the floor and then seemed to flatten like a tube of toothpaste. Blood ran down the front of the elevator, and the messy lump that had once been Farnham's leg below the knee thumped to the floor in front of him. Farnham's blood splattered his shirt, warm and wet.

Holt couldn't look at it. He glanced up instead at the arrows above the door and the digital screen telling him the elevator door was going up.

Holt frowned. There were only four floors in the hospital, and he was on the top floor now. There *was* no "up."

He pounded on the down button as if he could somehow stop the ascent of the car to God only knew where. Above him, the digital screen counted off the rise from the fourth to the fifth, the fifth to the sixth…the sixth to 137 and then a jumble of malfunctioning digital pieces of numbers. A cheery *ding* and the sound of elevator doors opening from somewhere above sent Holt scrambling for the stairwell. He had little time to register in the back of his mind that no guards had come to assist, not even at the sound of gunshots only a hospital corridor away, when he skidded to a stop. There was, of course, a perfectly normal staircase going down to the lower floors, but going up…

Holt whistled, his gun hanging helplessly at his side. The part of the stairwell that should have ended in a neat and blandly painted wall was gone. In its place was a mess of gray-green growths that could have been large stones or maybe fungus. Long blades of grass poked out from the spaces between, as did thin trees scraped nearly free of bark, vines that wrapped around them, and strange bowl-shaped and flesh-petaled things that might have been flowers. Set into this odd backdrop were irregular, somewhat erratic stairs partially floating and partially balanced on one another, leading up into the starry night. They turned a corner that led, presumably, onto the roof.

Holt hesitated. This couldn't be happening. He couldn't imagine this was some kind of elaborate joke, but he also couldn't wrap his brain around what had taken Farnham and what he was looking at right now as being real. He wanted someone to explain, either to tell him he was as crazy as the other loonies in the bin or to confirm that what he was seeing had some kind of explanation. Further, it was unbelievable to Holt that no one had heard the commotion, that no one had been alerted by the sight of Farnham's bloody stump by the elevator, but Holt supposed it was no more unusual than anything else that was happening.

Behind him, back in the hospital, there was silence. No one was coming. He had to get to Farnham. He didn't look forward to the idea of doing it alone, though, and glanced back once again as he pulled out his cell phone to call for backup from the station. When he tapped the screen to turn it on, though, nothing happened. It was dead, its little screen dark and silent.

"Fuck," he muttered to himself, then turned toward the doors leading back into the hallway. Maybe he could wake somebody up in there, maybe get somebody to assist.

The doors were locked. Part of Holt wasn't surprised, but he could feel the first flare of true panic setting in. "Of course you're locked. Fuckers," he said, smacking the doors, then turned back to the stairs. He didn't have time to mess with the doors and no backup was coming, apparently. He had to move forward. If Farnham was still alive, he wouldn't be for much longer.

He picked his way up the strange stairs, keeping toward the center. Over the edge of the staircase he could see the grounds below. It was a long way down, longer than it should have been. If one of those stone steps shot out from under him or crumbled away...

Holt pushed the thoughts from his head. He was rounding the corner now, cautious footstep by footstep, and saw that the steps kept rising. They came to an abrupt end about six or seven feet above the solid surface of the roof. The whole area below appeared to be empty, but there were many corners where the Mansard slopes cast shadows on the flat planes below them. Holt couldn't see Farnham or the creature from the elevator but he did see a leg-width trail of blood leading into the dark.

With a clumsy leap, a bone-jarring thud, and an *oof*, Holt managed to land without too much pain on the roof below the stairs. He'd worry about how to get back down later. He had to find Farnham.

He took a mini-flashlight from his jacket pocket and switched it on. It didn't do much to light up the space around him, but it cleared a path of visibility over the trail of blood. All around him, the silence ate into everything. The moon seemed unable to reach certain spots, no matter how close he got to them or how intently he focused the flashlight beam. There was a faint sick-sweet smell that reminded him of a mother's old tampons left too long in a garbage can, or the breath of some new "uncle" at the house whose dental surgery has become infected.

He shook his head. Those didn't feel like his thoughts. He didn't know what those things smelled like, though he supposed he could guess. Dead homeless people and heroin overdoses and old ladies whose souls left for better places but whose bodies lay unclaimed for a summer month—those smells he knew. Those smells, like the one on the roof, got up inside the nose, the hair, the clothes. Those smells followed you home. Smells like untreated cigarette burns festering on bare shoulders or the carcasses of zenner-beasts in the desert after being picked through by the acid flies, or—

Holt blinked as if to squeeze those thoughts out of his head. He was sure that time that they weren't his. But if not his, then whose? Wherever they were coming from, they were products of a head he most definitely did not want to stay in.

"He calls them tulpas," the pretty doctor lady had said.

Holt shivered, though the air was warm and uncomfortably sticky. The blood trail was his best lead to Farnham, so he focused on that, following it several feet until the flashlight beam picked up a pair of scuffed sneakers.

Holt jumped and bit down on his tongue to stifle a shout. Then he snapped the flashlight to eye level.

A man who had begun to turn gray in both hair and skin looked solemnly at him. His work overalls, also gray, were torn in several places, the fringe shredded and sticking up stiffly. The man was staring at him, it seemed, without really seeing him. Holt had seen people before with the thousand-yard stare, people preoccupied with so much that it crowded out everything else behind their eyes. This man, though, was different. This man looked...empty, as if everything had been drained out of him. Even psychopaths, with their shark eyes, didn't look like that. Only the dead looked like that.

Pulling out his badge, Holt approached the man slowly, as if approaching a lion. "I'm Detective Holt," he said in a calm, measured voice. "You need to leave this roof, Mr....?"

For several seconds, there was no answer and no movement, just a gray, dusty thing propped up like a man. Perhaps he was deaf or blind...

though if that was the case, why was he up on the roof in the dark? And could he sense all the horribly weird stuff going on around him? How had he managed to get up here, and had he seen Farnham?

Holt was about to ask some of those questions when the gray man finally responded, "Evers. George Evers."

"Mr. Evers," Holt repeated. "I'm going to need you to come with me, okay? If you're hurt, we can get you some help, but—"

"No," the man said. There was no hostility or malice in his voice. His face remained unperturbed.

"Excuse me?"

"Your friend is dead," Evers said. "The vending machine and the lawn mower got to him. Maybe the rake, too."

Holt glanced around slowly, unwilling to take his eyes off the gray man for too long. The man wasn't making any sense, but then, neither was anything else that had happened that night.

"You saw Detective Farnham? Can you tell me where he is now?"

"Who's to say? They might move his bones around. Or absorb him, maybe. They needed him. They might need you, too."

"Mr. Evers, please, just come with me. I'd like to hear more about this, but I don't think you're safe up here, and—"

"I can't come with you."

"Why not? Mr. Evers?"

The man didn't answer. He tugged at something growing out of his ear, then backed into the darkness and disappeared.

"Mr. Evers? Hey! Mr. Evers!" Holt tried to follow into the dark, his flashlight in one hand trying to split the shadows while his gun nosed around alongside it. There was no trace of Evers or Farnham or anyone else. There was only the roof and the suffocating black of an alien night and smears where the blood trail had ended beneath the gray man's feet.

Holt stumbled on anyway. All around him, the lightlessness had taken on substance and its own kind of volume, so that he felt like he was wading through water. He couldn't make out much, even with the flashlight, and didn't see the lump on the ground until he tripped over it.

"Jesus! Shit!" He caught himself before he fell, but stumbled backward against a wall, breaking the thickness of the air all around him into tiny bubbles of oily black that bumped and floated before his eyes.

Before he could wave all of the bubbles away and get back to what he'd tripped over, he saw something fly over his head and over the ledge of the rooftop. He rushed to the edge and looked down, fighting the lurching dizziness of vertigo as he did so.

In the arc of one of the hospital's streetlamps lay a crumpled heap that made his heart sink. The body below was missing part of a leg.

Holt backed away in horror, his flashlight trembling in his hand. Something had tossed Farnham to the ground like a rag doll. That gray man didn't look strong enough. Likely, it had been that thing from the elevator. But where was it? *Where the fuck was it?*

The flashlight beam caught something and he swung back to the spot. It was Evers, standing near the edge of the roof, and this time, Detective Holt did cry out, a body-racking cry of fear, anger, and confusion.

The old man's eyes had gone as gray as the rest of him, mottled with the white, dry frost of death. There could be no seeing from those eyes, and yet Holt was sure Evers saw everything—in this world, and maybe in others, too. The smile beneath those cloudy eyes was way too wide for a human mouth to make. When he opened wide to laugh, the bottom jaw hung down to the middle of his chest.

It was the teeth, though, that Holt would remember in the long nights to come—those long, horrible teeth, like dirty icicles that should never have been able to fit in that shriveled little man's mouth, teeth that looked so cold that every one of them sinking into the skin would spread frostbite deep into the meat of a man, and just rot all that living flesh away...

Evers waved at him and then jumped over the side of the building.

Holt, dumbfounded, let his gun lead to the edge of the roof again. When he looked down, though, he pointed the gun at the ghoul he was sure must be clinging to the side of the building just out of sight.

George Evers wasn't there at all. Once again, the man had vanished, and Holt was pretty sure he wasn't coming back. Down below, the hospital grounds looked so far away. The real world, the normal world, was so far away. And lying smack-dab in the middle of it, surrounded by a dark halo of his own cooling and drying blood, was what was left of Farnham.

* * * *

During the hospital blackout, Maisie found the serial killer Toby Ryan in his room. He was sitting in a chair, looking out the barred window onto the parking lot. He seemed lost in thought, though unlike with Henry or even Ben Hadley, Maisie couldn't tell what he was thinking about. His thought waves, their patterns and colors and textures, were different. They were cloaked somehow, shut away from her. Maisie didn't like that. He had in his head the secret to substantiation. She was sure of it. He could fill in all the gaps in Ben's knowledge, all the missing symbols and fragments of incantation Ben couldn't quite remember. Those secrets could be adapted; Henry could use them to give permanence and independence to Maisie and all the others. They wouldn't have to be just another man's thoughts, however fully realized they might be, and at the whim of his creation and destruction. They could break the life link with him, and they could be free—free to exercise their own will, free to bring their home, Ayteilu, the sanctuary Henry had created, pouring into this world with them. They could be free to survive...and to create and destroy. Toby was the key to that. Toby had the last of the answers, and Maisie was going to get them.

Toby was a good-looking man, in a rakish sort of way, in his mid-forties, but the years, or perhaps the mileage, had only begun to show around his eyes. His hair, still blond, had grown into little spikes from the military cut he'd worn in his admittance photo in his file. Wiry, muscled arms with various occult tattoos were crossed over his chest. She couldn't see his eyes from the way his head was turned, but she knew his eyes were blue. Sometimes, they were blue. Other times, they were black.

Suddenly he seemed to sense her behind him, a predator's instinct that he was not alone, and he turned to her, his expression placid but guarded.

"So, you're real, then. One of Henry's friends."

Maisie moved into a stream of moonlight and gestured at her cheek. "Scales give it away?"

Toby studied them a moment. "They're no scar, but they're sexy. But no. Rumor has it you have a way of walking through walls, and well..." He crooked a thumb toward the space behind her. "Door's locked, sweetheart."

"Hmm. Attractive *and* smart," she replied with a small chuckle.

Toby let himself smile a little. *If snakes could smile right before they struck, they'd smile like Toby Ryan*, Maisie thought, and knew with some frustration that it was Henry's opinion as much as hers.

Toby said, "Oh, darlin'...you shouldn't tease. I haven't always been nice to girls who tease."

"So I've heard."

"Aww, has old Henry been talking about me to you?"

Maisie strolled by him with dreamlike slowness. Sudden moves wouldn't do in a locked room with a predator like Toby. He wanted her uneasy and uncomfortable, furtive and darting, but that wasn't Maisie's way.

"Ben talked about you. Ben did a lot of talking, actually. Too much, if you ask me. Henry, on the other hand, doesn't care for you. He'd prefer to keep knowledge of you from me, but he can't. I suppose you scare him a little."

"Well, the real question is, do I scare *you?*" In the moonlight from the window, Toby's eyes glinted, and she could see hunger in them, a barely controlled lust seasoned with years of hate. "Are you worried, being in here alone with me?"

Maisie shook her head. "No more than a tiger worries about being alone with a gazelle."

"Oh, you're cute." He chuckled. "You're…that's cute."

"See, poor Henry is afraid a lot. It's why I'm here, why I exist. He doesn't realize that if anything, you're the one who should worry about being in here alone with me."

"Can't say as I'm seeing any reason to be afraid of you, sweetheart," he said with amusement and just a tinge of impatience, giving her a once-over from his chair. The snake was gauging when he ought to strike.

"That's unfortunate for you. You would be, if you were smart."

Toby arched an eyebrow and leaned toward her. "Oh really? You know, I've carved up girls' faces and breasts and stomachs like Thanksgiving turkeys. I've shoved all kinds of things into their tight little spaces and cut them up from the inside out. I've splashed around in their blood and, honey, I still dream about all those screams. And they were all girls like you."

It was Maisie's turn to smile. "No, Toby. I daresay you've never met a girl like me." She sauntered over to him and leaned down until her face was close to his. He seemed both breathlessly thrilled and uncomfortable with her proximity. It had been a long time since he'd been allowed to get that close to a woman. She reached out and touched his face and he grabbed her wrist. She grabbed his and could tell from his expression that he was surprised by her strength. She could feel the faintest glimmer of fear from him at something he saw in her eyes. She could tell that much, even with Toby.

"You think you're a badass monster because you've killed a few girls?" she purred at him. "You have no idea what a monster is. What I am. No idea at all."

When he let go of her wrist, she let go of his. He rubbed his arm where she'd left the beginnings of bruises.

"And just what kind of monster are you?" he asked, looking up at her.

"Just one who wants to pick your brain." She smiled again. "So to speak. Someone who wants the benefit of your experience."

Toby frowned, confused. "You want to hear about me killing all those girls?"

"No, that was not the experience I meant. I want to hear about your time with the Hand of the Black Stars. Specifically, their ways of making things that were not from this world...well, stay."

Toby choked out an astounded laugh. "What? Get the fuck out of here, sweetheart. I'm not telling you shit about that."

"But you will, Toby. You will. You'll tell me everything I need to know."

Toby glared at her, but there was something beneath the glare that made Maisie smile. "I'm not Martha, you crazy bitch," he said. "I'm not Ben Hadley, or any of those other suckers you twisted up in this place. You can't threaten me."

"Oh," Maisie replied. "I don't plan to threaten you. I plan to show you exactly what kind of monster I am."

And Maisie May began to change.

Chapter 6

For a decade or so after Toby Ryan's conviction and admittance into Connecticut-Newlyn Hospital, Kathy Ryan was convinced that if she never saw her brother again, it would be too soon. A part of her—a hard, sharp little ball of hate and shame and guilt compressed and crushed, pushed down and compressed again, layer after layer, year after year—had wanted the state to execute her brother. It wanted him dead, that little part. And every time it tried to rise and bob to the surface, coated with new therapeutic insight or well-meaning sideways opinions, new guilt or flare-ups of anger, she'd squeeze it back down to manageable size and shove it deep into her subconscious like Toby's box of finger bones at the back of his closet and try to forget about it.

Her brother had hurt her in a number of ways on a number of levels. He'd threatened to rape and murder her. He'd cut her face deeply enough that almost thirty years later, the scar remained. And that hard, sharp little part of her jostled around, cutting her insides a thousand little times until even its nesting place was scar tissue, and Kathy Ryan, who couldn't forget the scar or the man who caused it, did manage to begin to forget about how she really felt about both.

Toby hadn't been executed, though. He'd been remanded to a mental hospital for the criminally insane instead, and the gears that turned the wheels in the machine of justice went grinding on by. Kathy had learned to be okay with that, too. He was out of sight if not out of mind, and he couldn't hurt anyone else anymore.

When Margaret called and left a message for her the morning after her last visit to the hospital, Kathy had been hoping it was with word from Dr. Pam Ulster, giving her the okay to come talk to Henry Banks. She intended to talk to the man one way or another, but it was always easier when there were fewer red tape hurdles to jump on the way.

Instead, Margaret had left a message asking Kathy to call back about an incident with Toby. It was a professional courtesy call, because Kathy was pretty sure she wasn't listed as her brother's closest next of kin; to the best of her knowledge, he didn't have anyone listed. Both of the Ryan siblings preferred it that way. But Margaret didn't know about the hard, sharp little ball embedded deep down in Kathy and thought she might want to come down and check on Toby.

Toby, who'd once snapped the neck of a bird with a broken wing with one hand, right in front of her, to "put it out of its misery." Toby, who'd gotten between her and her dad's wrath more times than she cared to remember. She would have liked to believe that when that hard little ball tried to resurface, it had softened a little with sentiment and time, but...she couldn't be sure. She didn't want him dead anymore, so she supposed at its core, the ball was empty now, its layers just accumulated after-feelings, the detritus of trauma. She may not have been self-aware enough to begin healing, but she knew herself well enough to know she wasn't ready to begin peeling back the layers to find out what really was left at the center.

Kathy texted Reece, who had already left for work by then: *Problem with T at hosp. Going to see what's up. Will check in later. Love u.*

He was working the homicide of a teenage boy in Colby and probably out in the field, so she didn't expect him to answer right away. She showered, dressed, took a swig of vodka from the bottle in the medicine cabinet, brushed her teeth, and gathered up her keys and her purse. A text response was waiting on her phone as she picked it up on her way out the door.

Aye. Love you, too, babe. Ring if you need to.

Kathy decided not to call Margaret back but rather just to show up. Whatever Margaret had to tell her about Toby, she needed time to prepare to hear it. The worst of the possible scenarios ran through her mind, and she systematically tried to discount them.

Maybe the administration was thinking of transferring him. They'd never consider releasing him, but they might move him...unless they *were* considering his release. Every time the suggestion had ever come up, Kathy had been there with notes and research from *Psychology Today* and signed statements from mental health professionals. She'd been there with her scar and her story and she'd fought to keep her brother committed. To release him would be a smack in her face. It would also be dangerous to the surrounding community. Toby was relentlessly unapologetic. He'd told doctors on more than one occasion that he would keep killing if released; he was compelled to. They couldn't possibly think of releasing him.

He could have escaped. Except that it wasn't really likely that he could or even would. The residents called it being a "house pet," when one got used to the hospital life, its rules and meds and comforting, familiar schedules. Kathy had come to believe that was the mind-set Toby was in, that he'd adjusted to being a house pet. She supposed it was possible she'd been wrong that he'd been biding his time or that he had changed his mind. Maybe he wanted to be free to experience the sexual thrill of killing and mutilation before he was too old to get an erection anymore...but Kathy just couldn't see it, not with all the deaths happening at the hospital just then. He'd always been fascinated with dead things and he'd enjoy the commotion. He'd want to live through the carnage and the violence vicariously, even if it wasn't a string of girls specifically.

Of course, other people's killing probably wasn't as satisfying to Toby as doing it himself. Kathy remembered his mentioning that his therapist had been trying to find him healthy outlets for his feelings. He'd said none of her suggestions helped much. They didn't scratch the itch, he'd told her—no more than porn really worked as a substitute for real sex. She thought he'd come to accept that something was better than nothing, but a string of deaths at the hospital, at least one or two of which could only be murders, might have gotten under his skin and started that itch going again, undoing whatever flimsy progress he might have made over the last few decades.

Maybe he'd killed someone inside, a fellow inmate or worse, maybe a staff member. Kathy tried to tell herself this was also unlikely. She had been told his urges would probably dwindle with age as his sex drive decreased, and so she'd been content to believe he was getting his fix nowadays from threatening and intimidating people. He was medicated, after all, and although he'd once or twice been drugged to a state of lethargy for a violent outburst, the last time had been at least fifteen years before. He'd hated that. She couldn't see her brother putting himself through it again out of the blue, not after all that time.

Maybe he'd killed someone and then escaped just as they were about to release him. Maybe he was on his way to her house right now. Maybe she'd find him sitting on her couch when she got home, or worse, he'd surprise Reece coming home from work and—

Stop it, she told herself. *Just stop. Toby isn't going anywhere.*

She was finding it much harder this time to talk away the worst-case scenarios. Her frustration showed in the way she cut off the tan minivan to make a right turn. In fact, with each mile closer to the hospital, she found it harder to think of a case that wasn't disastrous.

She felt sick to her stomach as she climbed the stairs and rang Margaret to buzz her in. In fact, she could feel her whole body tightening up, from her muscles outward to her skin, as she crossed the tiled floor of the main lobby.

Margaret looked uncharacteristically sympathetic, almost apologetic. "The doctors want to see you about Toby," she said.

Kathy glanced at the doors and the hallway beyond. "What's it about?"

"They'd prefer to tell you themselves, Katherine. I'm sorry. Let me get you signed in right away so you can see Dr. Wensler. He's in his office upstairs."

Kathy signed the log in a daze, that tightness spreading to her lungs. There was a handwritten sign on the elevator indicating it was temporarily out of order, so she went to the stairwell door and pushed through. She climbed the three flights of stairs, barely registering the smudge of black on the far wall of the stairwell, and emerged onto the fourth floor proper, where the administration offices were.

For the second time that week, she knocked on Dr. Wensler's door. The doctor himself opened it, greeted her with a veneer of practiced warmth, and gestured for her to come in.

She sat in the chair across from his desk and crossed her legs, waiting for him to speak.

"Ms. Ryan, we wanted to let you know there was an incident and your brother was hurt."

Kathy blinked. "I'm sorry...hurt?"

"He's all right, conscious now. He's resting in the infirmary at the moment, but he got beaten up pretty badly. The medical doctor can fill you in on the particulars. I want to assure you that we're investigating the matter and he's receiving complete medical care. He is, however, being... obstinate. He won't tell the doctors everything that happened and he won't tell us who did it. I thought perhaps you might talk to him. What with everything that has been going on lately, with the recent tragedies and all, I thought perhaps he'd tell you what he won't tell us."

The man steepled his fingers just beneath his chin, awaiting her response. His steel eyes seemed to be gauging whether she would challenge or accuse him, and if so, what approach to take. He was a gaunt man whose thin white hair was tamed only by sheer force of his patience and iron will. His suit was expensive, a granite gray complemented by a sharp silver tie. He was, in fact, all sharp lines and hard edges, which made any attempt at empathy or sensitivity, things he no doubt found frivolous but necessary job evils, appear dry and crumbly.

When she didn't answer, he added, "If I may be plain with you, Ms. Ryan, Connecticut-Newlyn is an institution noble of purpose and of great reputation. We offer brilliant therapeutic strategies developed by the brightest leading talent in the field of psychiatry and psychology today. We offer no less than excellence in care for our residents and seek every available opportunity to rehabilitate and safely reintegrate progressed residents into the community as fully functioning and contributing members. I believe you recognize that such a top facility requires funding. That funding is more likely forthcoming if those with their hands on the purse strings believe in the success and viability of the facility. Unexplained deaths look bad, Ms. Ryan, and unexplained assaults and murders even more so. This puts the safety and security of our residents and of the community at risk, and I won't have that. Therefore, any information that would help clear matters up quickly and to everyone's satisfaction before things get needlessly messy—needlessly *public*—would benefit all the residents here at the hospital, including your brother. I trust you see my position here."

Kathy did. He wanted her to talk her brother into helping them clear away these deaths and the potential nastiness associated with them. He was worried about his reputation, about statistics and funding. The patients were killers anyway, and a handful fewer didn't send an uneasy head to its pillow—the numbers did. The residents were not people, not human lives to Dr. Wensler, but tools in the give-and-take trade of hospital politics. In a way, she couldn't blame him; nearly all jobs came down to numbers one way or another. She didn't like Wensler at all, but she could respect that the transparent concern for patients and the very real considerations of running a state-funded facility were part of the job.

"When can I see him?" she asked.

Dr. Wensler brightened a little. "Why, right now, if you like."

"Lead the way," she said.

The director led her down the hall to the hospital infirmary, where Toby was apparently sleeping on one of the beds, a pale blue sheet pulled up to his waist. His left hand and wrist were in a cast almost up to the elbow and cradled in a sling. His right eye and cheek were a thundercloud-purple swelling with tiny veins of red lightning. His lip was busted, and it looked like the corner of a bandage was sticking out from under the loose neckline of his hospital gown.

"I'll leave you alone to visit," Wensler said, then disappeared into the hallway.

Kathy meandered over to the foot of his bed. His hospital chart hung from a wooden pocket there, and she casually lifted it out to peruse it. In addition to the injuries she could see, he had a sprained left wrist and broken ulna, a broken right ankle, a puncture wound to his left shoulder, a broken rib, and some rectal and internal bleeding. Kathy frowned, dropping the chart back into its slot. She looked up at him. He looked so peaceful lying there, his usual cynical glare erased in a painkiller-induced sleep. He reminded her of how he'd looked when they were kids, when their mom was still alive and things were still okay. He used to sleep peacefully like that back then, dreaming good things...or maybe not dreaming at all. Now he looked small. The man who had cut her looked harmless, almost pathetic. He'd been hurt badly, and she found as she crossed around to the side of his bed that she actually felt the faintest stirrings of pity for him.

She knew Toby. He'd have fought like a wolf if some inmate had attacked him. There'd have been at least two sleeping bodies in infirmary beds. Whoever did those things to her brother had to be strong, very strong, and very determined. The residents in Connecticut-Newlyn might have been aberrant enough, but who would have been physically able?

"He calls them tulpas." Pam Ulster's words came back to Kathy, and they were as good an answer as any. It hadn't been who, so much as what. Henry's friends had done that to Toby. And if they were dangerous to someone like him, then they were an even bigger threat to others beyond him.

Toby coughed in his sleep then, and before she realized what she was doing, she had placed a calming hand on his arm. He flinched, waking suddenly, and looked up at her with groggy, half-closed eyes.

"Kitty-Kat?"

Toby hadn't called her that since they were little kids.

"It's me."

"Wha...why are you here?"

"The hospital called me. Told me you were hurt."

He moaned as he tried to sit up. "It's nothing. Coupla scratches."

"Oh yeah? Who scratched you up?"

He gave her a sidelong glance and tried with only moderate success to raise himself up with his good arm. "Right to the point, eh? No talk about the weather, the season the Red Sox are having? How that Irish guy is working out for you?"

Kathy pulled her hand away. She'd never told Toby about Reece.

He tried to chuckle but it came out as a painfully dry billow of air. "Don't get your panties in a bunch. Just like to know what sweet baby sis is up to. No one's gonna hurt'm."

"What happened to you, Toby?"

"Got inna fight."

"With who?"

She could tell from his expression he didn't want to answer. He didn't like direct questions, for one thing. He took them as a challenge to his autonomy. There was more to his reticence than that, though. Toby looked troubled. Beneath that, he seemed...he actually seemed *scared*.

Softer, she asked, "Who did this?"

"I don't wanna talk about it."

She was about to argue that the hospital needed to know, but nothing would have clammed him up faster. She tried a different tactic.

"Does it hurt much? Want me to get a nurse?"

"Nah, I'm fine," he replied. "Or I'm not, if you're offering to kiss where it hurts."

She also stifled the urge to respond that she could make him hurt more, if he didn't knock it off.

"I'd hate to see what the other guy looked like," she said, hoping her voice sounded light.

Toby eyed her suspiciously. "Why are you here?" he asked again.

"I told you, the hospital called. Told me there had been an incident involving you. I came to see if you were okay."

"Came to see if I fucked someone up in here, more like. Maybe slipped out past old Margie down in the lobby so I could come visit?"

Kathy hoped her expression did not betray the worries she'd brought in with her. She'd never been able to lie with her eyes, not like Toby could. "Are you going to tell me who hurt you or not?"

Toby sighed. He suddenly reminded Kathy of a guy she'd met on a case a while back, out on the New Jersey–Pennsylvania border. She'd tried hard then not to make a connection between him and her brother, but staring at the form in the hospital bed now, it was difficult not to see. That other man—his name had been Toby, as well—had been a pedophile, a bad man by all societal accounts. The thing was, when he'd sighed or looked at her the way her brother was looking at her now, there'd been something so human, so vulnerable and almost...forgivable. The good in him—and there was good there—had wanted redemption. She very seldom ever thought her brother wanted or needed something so intangible, except when he looked at her like that.

She knew people like Toby carried a weight on the shoulders that was inconceivable to those who had the tools to manage and minimize their compulsions...or perversions. It made people sleep better at night to relegate men like him to the category of monsters, to boogeymen with superhuman appetites and abilities. And there was no doubt that what they did was monstrous. What troubled Kathy, and what disturbed the sleep of people who knew better, was that those boogeymen had parents, siblings, spouses, and children who loved them. They had vulnerabilities and weaknesses, not the least of which were those appetites and abilities they didn't want and couldn't always control. What was worse was that sometimes, true and often harder to understand monstrosity was in the evil easily and knowingly committed by people others wanted to believe were good, people held up as the best of humanity, with the resources to do and be better.

Finally, he said, "You could say it was a friend of a friend."

"You have no friends," Kathy interjected.

This seemed to trigger some private amusement behind Toby's eyes. "You cut me, sweet sister." He looked at her scar and added, "So to speak."

Her face flushed red, which seemed to please him more, and the last bit of pity she had for him dried up. "Henry Banks's friends...did they do that to you?"

Toby's look of surprised suspicion was all the confirmation she needed. "How'd you—oh, right. That's your job, I guess."

"Tell me about them."

"Ask Henry about them."

"I'm asking you, Toby..."

"I'm tired," he said. He pushed the pain medication button on his IV and turned away onto his side.

"You *will* help me on this," she said through clenched teeth.

The back of his hospital gown was open above the sheet, and she watched the shallow rise and fall of the tattoos on his back. Finally she turned and was almost to the door when he said, "Yeah, it was them. Well, one of 'em. Maisie, I think her name is. They're real. And they're like me."

"Like you?" Kathy asked without turning around.

"Killers. They're killers." Then Toby was mostly asleep and Kathy fought tears and the roaring in her head and she fled back around to the main corridor and down to the elevator.

* * * *

George Evers didn't show up at the Silver Deer Tavern that night. It was the third night in a row that he'd missed his usual meet-up with

Ernie Jenkinson to drink off the remains of the day. Ernie wasn't so sure George had been to work either the last couple of days, and he hadn't been answering his cell phone or land line. The old fool probably couldn't figure out what damned button to push on the cell—Ernie didn't know why he even bothered—but he should have at least answered the cordless in the kitchen. George hadn't been sick more than a handful of times in fifty-five years; it took a lot to keep him down, and even when he was under the weather, he wasn't ever too sick to answer the phone. Ernie thought of going over there just to make sure George hadn't had a heart attack or stroke or some damned thing, but he hadn't had the time, what with all the goings-on at work. He figured if old George didn't show up that night at the Tavern, he'd make the drive over.

At a booth toward the back of the place sat the trio of staff members who'd found the body of Ben Hadley. Ernie caught their attention, they waved, and he nodded back, tipping his beer to them. They'd had a tough couple of shifts, too, since they'd found the chewed-up white boy, what with answering the police's questions, making apologies and excuses to Wensler, and fielding even more from the rattled patients themselves. There was always an uptick of the usual fluids when the residents got rattled—more blood, more urine, a sight more drool—and Ernie was only the physical cleanup crew. Those boys had to deal with cleaning up their fear, their anger, their disconnecting from the world. Ernie thought of buying them a round of beers, remembered his wallet was a little light that month, and decided against it. Beer wouldn't fix up their night anyway. He'd had a few himself already, and still, he couldn't get those damned footprints outside Hadley's room out of his mind.

The door to the Tavern opened and Ernie craned his neck over the heads of the other patrons to check for George. It wasn't him; it was a pretty blond lady with a long scar through her left eyebrow and cheek. She wore it well, he thought, and he smiled at her when she caught him looking. She nodded back, taking a seat three or four stools down from him. She ordered two shots of vodka to start. Ernie chuckled to himself. That there woman, he thought, was what his brother used to call a firecat—a hard-drinking, wild-living hot piece of pussy. If he were a good thirty years younger, he might have bought her a drink, maybe slid a few bar stools down, but even then, he probably would have had to hold on for dear life.

He turned back to his own beer and his own business. Images of those footprints kept playing in his mind. They hadn't been a joke. No one had seen them and no one had known what he was talking about. By the time he could get near Ben Hadley's room again, they were gone—not cleaned-up gone, but never-there gone. He didn't like that. Old codgers imagining things was never a good sign.

Ernie had just finished his beer and was thinking about hitting the head when a familiar thatch of gray hair appeared in the crowd. The man was turned away but Ernie recognized the slouch of the shoulders and the gray overalls as George Evers.

He cupped a hand around his mouth and called, "George! Hey, over here!" George turned and Ernie waved him over, holding up his beer bottle to indicate the plans for the night. George stared at him blankly, as if he didn't recognize the beer bottle or the man holding it.

Ernie's eyesight wasn't what it used to be, but he got the distinct impression something was wrong with George. The man didn't look quite right—a little peaked around the edges, like he was getting over a flu or something. Based on that blank look he was giving Ernie, maybe a stroke was a distinct possibility.

"George! Hey, you old fool!" His voice was snatched away by the drunken laughing and chatting as the night warmed up. The bar had got noisier at that hour, as the young folk started dropping in for the night. That was usually his cue to hit the road.

As if thinking the same thing, George turned and shuffled toward the door. Ernie supposed it was possible his friend hadn't seen or heard him. It could even be that he'd seen Ernie and not recognized him, if he had in fact had a stroke. Either way, George didn't look in any kind of condition to be going home alone in the dark. If Ernie let him go on his way, Marian from the Great Beyond would have both their hides.

Ernie pulled a few crumpled bills from his wallet and tossed them onto the bar, then slid from the bar stool. The world rocked a moment then straightened itself out, and he made his way toward the front door of the Tavern, which George was currently pushing open onto the night.

A moment later, Ernie emerged onto the front stoop and half expected to see George waiting for him there, chomping on a cigar and watching the pretty young things as they went to and fro between bars and restaurants along the street. When he wasn't, Ernie glanced up one side of the street and down the other, trying to make out the shuffling gray form. It had been one of the first springlike days of the year, and that mild weather had only just begun to cool. George liked walking better than driving ever since the eye doc told him his cataracts were getting worse, so Ernie didn't bother looking for George's car. The man only lived two blocks away from the bar, and many nights had found the men stumbling back to George's when they were too drunk to drive. He didn't see George on the street heading toward the direction of his house, though. He didn't see George anywhere. On a good day, George didn't move so fast anymore—faster than Ernie, sure, but not so fast that he could have made it up the street and around the corner in the three minutes between his and Ernie's leaving the bar, and certainly not looking like he had.

Ernie took off in the direction of George's house anyway. Maybe he had taken his car after all, or had hitched a ride up the street. He couldn't think of any other place but home that George would go off to in the night. If he hurried, he might be able to catch up to his old friend.

It took a good ten minutes of practiced weaving up Shale Street and halfway up McCumber to Ashton Road. George's place was a little white and blue ranch on the left about a quarter of the way down. There weren't too many streetlights on that road, but most folks kept their porch lights on the whole night. Not a lot of money flowed along Ashton Road, but it was a mostly white street, and through his growing concern over George, he couldn't help but wonder what folks peeking out from their curtained windows would think of a half-drunk black man stumbling alone down the road. He chuckled. Most of George's neighbors probably recognized Ernie by now, and while maybe not all of them liked a black man wandering their street, they kept themselves to themselves about it. Things weren't like they were when he was a pup. It wasn't like the lynch mobs were going to be throwing rocks and calling cops on him. Besides, it had been a long time since Ernie Jenkinson had looked threatening, anyway.

He was so lost in musing on the neighbors that he nearly plowed into George, who stood partially hidden in shadow from a large oak whose branches reached over the street. George was standing in front of a curbside mailbox that was not his own, with his hand closed over the little flag. He didn't move even so much as to glance at Ernie's approach, and he didn't speak. He wasn't checking for mail, either, but just holding on to the little red flag. That close to him, Ernie could smell the man, a nauseating mix of urine and sickness, rot and toxins from the inside seeping out of his pores, and a kind of charnel mustiness.

"George, you okay? I been tryin' to reach you for days, man. What you been up to?"

George turned his head and looked at Ernie, but for all the recognition there, he might as well have been looking at a brick wall.

"Hey now, you know this ain't your mailbox, right? Can't be stealing other folks' mail, now. What say we go on back to your place and sort out what's goin' on with you? Come on," Ernie said, and took George's arm. He recoiled immediately. The skin beneath the sleeve was so cold that its chill came up through the fabric, and it was way too soft. It felt to Ernie like rotting vegetables, how they got slushy and almost pastelike if they sat too long at the bottom of a trash can in the sun. It had slid all over beneath the pressure of Ernie's touch, so that his fingers seemed to push it out of the way to reveal something chunky and very hard underneath.

"George, we need to get your ass to a doctor, you hear? You ain't right."

"Been at work," George said, but his voice sounded more like an echo than the sound that made it.

"All right, then. Tell me on the way," Ernie replied, and swallowing his distaste, took George's arm again. George let Ernie lead him nearly all the way to George's house. They were in view of the man's lawn when George stopped short. Ernie, who had his work cell phone in his hand and was about to call for an ambulance, looked up.

"Come on, George. We almost there now," he said to his friend, giving the arm in his grasp a little tug. He suppressed a shudder at the way the flesh yielded under the skin, but the meat of the arm remained rigid.

"Can't," George muttered.

"Oh yeah? And why not?"

George turned his head and looked over Ernie rather than at him. "The rake is in there. The lawn mower."

"We ain't goin' in the garage, G. We—"

"Some of them mist folks, too. If I go in there they'll rearrange me again."

Ernie frowned at him. "You ain't makin' any sense. I think we need to get you on over to the hospital." He tapped the cell phone and the screen lit up, casting a faint blue glow on the men. He'd tapped the phone icon and the 9 when George put a cold, hard hand over it. Ernie heard the crunch before the phone crumpled in his hand. When George pulled away, a black hairy thing like a centipede with pulverized metal and plastic embedded in its body crawled over his palm on multijointed legs, while its circuitry eyes, sticking up from random stalks along the back, turned in unison to focus on him.

Ernie, who was not at all squeamish about insects in general, tossed the thing as if it were on fire, wiping his hand on his pants leg. Then he looked up at George in amazement.

"What—what did you do? How...?" He floundered, looking for the words. George had not only crushed his cell phone but reshaped it and set it in motion. Ernie suddenly thought of the footprints, and it occurred to him that he was alone in the dark without a car or phone. The man, if it was a man anymore, wasn't George, at least not most of it. No stroke did that to a man. Nothing the good Lord above or the devil below ever put on this earth did that to a man. Whatever was left of George, it was lost, and what was left…well, Ernie knew in his bones that it was dangerous. He hoped Marian, God rest her soul, would forgive him when he beat feet out of there, and he hoped his old legs would do the job of carrying him out of there fast enough to make it worth the risk.

"You're like the other cop," George said with almost mechanical atonality. "You won't bend. They'll just kill you."

"George, I'm gonna go get help, okay? You go on…go on home," Ernie said as he backed away. All around him, the neighborhood seemed different, and he kicked himself for not noticing it before. The shadow-dappled, tree-lined street of white folk wasn't settled in, quiet and comfortable for the night. There were things in the dark he couldn't see but he could feel, more animated and likely more dangerous than whatever had gotten inside George, and they were watching. Waiting, for now. It wouldn't make any difference, putting space between him and George; it was whatever was skulking around in the bushes or laying low around the sides of the houses he had to worry about.

George made no attempt to go after him, and for that, Ernie was glad. He just wanted to get away from him, away from the tittering, trembling shrubbery lining houses and walkways, the glare of porch lights like angry, glazed eyes, the picket fences that looked like teeth, the movement of charcoal silhouettes in the lightless side alleys between houses.

Ernie couldn't have run if his pants were on fire, but he found he could hustle-jog, and though he knew his knees would have him damn near crippled in the morning, he kept at it. He focused on the stop sign at the end of the road. He thought if he could make it to the sign, he'd be close enough to civilization, real civilization, to be safe. He'd be out of that weird, somehow stained pocket of neighborhood where his oldest friend had been reduced to little more than a sack of sick and broken things and had begun to pass on that sick brokenness to the street on which he stood.

An inky spot near the edge of his vision darted between two shadows, and Ernie stopped. He shouldn't have; he realized that a second later, but he'd been struck with the notion that any movement of his would draw the thing's attention, as its movement had alerted him. Now there were eyes on him, though, a dozen or so little glittering pairs of ice-chip blue light that moved with him as he picked up jogging again. If there were bodies attached to those eyes, Ernie couldn't see them. He could only barely hear them, slipping through the negative spaces, where light and color and normalcy couldn't reach.

To Ernie the footprints on the street materialized out of nowhere, not catching the moonlight at all but seeming to swallow it.

He skidded to a stop, unwilling to touch the deep blue-black that formed those awful marks. He had a crazy notion that the prints were like holes in the earth, punched right through into another reality by whatever ungodly feet or paws had stepped there, and if he were to step on one himself, his leg would fall straight through it. They weren't shaped like a man's footprints at all; they were more like what those prints in the hallway of the hospital outside Ben Hadley's room looked like—three toes, long and pointed, with a shorter fourth toe protruding from the heel. And they were everywhere, crisscrossing each other in a frantic dance pattern running every which way.

"Shit." Ernie's chest ached, and he hoped that if it was a heart attack, it would take him down quickly. The footprints had closed him in, spiraling outward in multiple directions as if a wild, frenzied dance of invisible hooves and paws whirled all around him and into the darkness. From beyond that lightless circumference, he heard a scraping sound like metal tines being skipped over pavement, and behind it, a slithering sound.

The rake is in there...

His knees had begun to throb up his legs and down into his shins. He'd never be able to outrun them, whatever they were. He wasn't sure he'd even be able to walk toward them. The stop sign at the end of the road looked impossibly far away now. Ernest Jenkinson was a dead man.

Then a gray sedan wheeled around the corner and shot down the street. It skidded to a stop a few feet in front of Ernie, and in the sweep of the headlights, he could have sworn he saw various squat, rust-colored, tool-shaped heads and slippery-looking wings pulling back from the sudden light and noise, and behind them, misty silhouettes.

The driver's side door opened and a man swung out. He looked beaten to hell and back, his rumpled suit reduced to a stained and tattered mess of rags. Blood and some of the footprint stuff speckled his beard. He fired a couple of shots toward an encroaching silverbacked beast maybe three or four feet high, with rows of mouths and bladed teeth whirring where its stomach should have been. Its leathery wings snapped when the gun ricocheted with a metal ping off one of its stubby legs, and it gave a guttural little growl like...*Like an angry riding lawn mower*, was the thought that came to Ernie's head, and he almost laughed. They were being attacked by George's gardening equipment.

Another shot landed close to him and Ernie jumped. He looked down to see what might once have been a weed-whacker, looking now more like a bladed scorpion with a long, erect tail, which the bullet had dropped near his feet. Beneath it, that black-blue hole-in-the-world stuff was spreading, and Ernie was almost positive that bits of the pavement were crumbling away and falling into its void.

"This way, old man! Now!" the guy from the car was shouting. He gestured to the passenger seat. "Come on! I'm almost out of bullets!"

For one terrible second, Ernie was sure that his legs had locked from the pain. He was dead certain they wouldn't move no matter what kind of command, plea, or threat messages his brain sent them. Then he found himself moving, his legs propelling him in that hustle-jog toward the car. It was a weird disconnected feeling, his legs reacting without any other necessary stimulation than sheer survival and preservation.

When his hand closed around the metal handle of the door and he pulled it open, the groan it made echoed the last groans in his knees before they gave out and he fell onto the passenger seat. The bearded man dropped in beside him and slammed his door. His arm shot out and he emptied the rest of his gun into a pale, blood-splattered lumbering thing that reminded Ernie of a stewpot filled with a sloshing soup of alien internal organs. It caterwauled in anger but backed off just enough for Ernie to get the door closed.

"The name's Holt," the bearded man said between ragged breaths as he threw the car in reverse. The car shot backward on chirping tires.

"The detective from the hospital?"

Holt slammed the car into Drive and sped back toward the Stop sign. "Connecticut-Newlyn? I thought you looked familiar."

"Custodial Services. Ernie Jenkinson. I went round to check on George... and, and...my Lord. George Evers, he..." Ernie had no more words. All the stress, both physical and mental, finally caught up with him and his body erupted in a series of bone-jarring shudders.

"He isn't George anymore," Holt said solemnly, turning onto the main road.

Ernie watched the stop sign sail by and thought reaching the boundary to the normal world would have made him feel better, safer, than he did. That cop hadn't come out of nowhere by coincidence, and he hadn't been surprised at what he'd seen, either. Which meant the boundary he was looking for was still a good distance away.

"No shit, sir. Don't look like nothing is what it used to be anymore." He shook his head. "If you don't mind my askin', what the blazes is goin' on out there, Detective?"

"Was gonna ask you the same thing," Holt replied, "seeing as how it's bleeding outward from somewhere on the hospital grounds."

"What is?"

"Whatever's changing people into things and things into beasts. I don't have much to go on right now but a name, but I can tell you what I think." Holt glanced in the rearview and frowned. Ernie tried to catch whatever it was Holt saw, but it was gone.

"What's the name?" Ernie asked.

"Henry Banks," Holt replied.

Ernie shot him a quizzical sidelong glance. "Henry? Aww, I know Henry. Boy's harmless. Besides, this can't be no man, even a killin' man, doing this—this…" He gestured toward the night beyond the car.

"I wouldn't be so sure about that."

"But…but how?"

"I don't know," Holt said, "but I think I know someone who does."

Chapter 7

The information on the internet about tulpas had provided Kathy a place to start, particularly with its definition as an "emanation body" and the earliest mentions of it or something like it in the fourth or fifth century CE. In many of the early Indian Buddhism texts, the tulpas were manifestations of other spirit versions of the conjurer. The multiplication miracle of Buddha was said to be a divine ability to project multiple versions of himself into the world. The Tibetan Buddhists believed tulpas—the *nirmanakaya, sprulsku, sprul-pa*—to be creations of or even avatars of deities, though the ability of "unrealized beings" like humans to have or even be divine tulpas was not outside the realm of possibility, either. From what Kathy could tell, there was a slight evolution of the meaning of the word from "emanating body" into "thoughtform" that changed the context. A 1927 translation of the *Tibetan Book of the Dead* was one of the earliest mentions of "thoughtforms" specifically. What Kathy found interesting, though, was that throughout its evolution and despite its fluid definition, the concept of tulpas was an ancient one—that of sentient and more or less autonomous beings brought about by the use of the mind. They weren't just imaginary friends come to life or the fractured multiple personalities associated with dissociative identity disorder, but both of those ideas, or at least covering all that ground in between.

Kathy was waiting on Henry Banks's psychiatry files, but she thought she knew what she'd find in them. She'd seen broken, abused children with an amazing ability to create whole worlds in their minds and disappear into them during times of stress or horror, particularly during a cult's programming or a family's deprogramming phases. She had also seen what the force of will could do in opening doors to other dimensions or summoning entities from other planes of existence. That Henry Banks might be able to do a little bit of both—summoning from the planes of existence in his own mind all his protectors from the most terrifying and tumultuous phases of his life—was not only possible, but probable.

The next bit of research was to find accounts of those who had direct experience with tulpas in action. Belgian-French explorer, spiritualist, and Buddhist Alexandra David-Néel claimed to have witnessed the mystical process in action in twentieth-century Tibet, including the ability of the tulpa to develop a mind of its own. She also found the 1937 account of Francois de Boudiard, a French scientist and philosopher who claimed to have perfected the meditation and deep concentration methods necessary to summon a thoughtform to perform a simple task. Much like with the tulpa created by David-Néel, de Boudiard's tulpa took on a will of its own and was subsequently destroyed. She also found several Western occult magicians claiming the ability to create and command tulpas to serve both good and evil purposes for their masters. Many cases showed a clearly subservient role to their creators. In some, relationships extended to the romantic and even sexual. Creators of tulpas treated them as somewhat real individuals with likes and dislikes, thoughts and emotions separate from their creators. However, in every case she could find, the tulpas, once they had served their purpose, were dispelled or summarily deconstructed. Even the Network's files had little on what to do if those tulpas chose, in their autonomy, to not give up the ghost, as it were. If tulpas were so fully realized and granted so much power by their creators that they could prevent their being sent away or destroyed, what then?

Kathy sighed, running her hands though her hair. She pulled it back and twisted it up into a messy bun held by a pencil, then went back to her searching.

She almost missed the link on one of the poorly designed metaphysical websites, with its clashing fluorescent colors against a pink and turquoise background. Amid the claims of angels' love and guidance and the power of auras and their emanations, she found one sentence that stood out to her:

...takes the will, in the form of **_entities subservient to the determined and hateful_***, to pervert gifts our higher selves are meant to claim.*

The phrase "entities subservient to the determined and hateful" contained a live link, and she clicked on it. A new web page opened that evidently required an approved user name and password to access. Its URL, she noticed, showed it was part of the Hand of the Black Stars member website. The title of the article under lock and key was "Dissipating Summoned Entities—Demons, Elementals, Tulpas, and Ghosts."

The author was Toby Ryan.

Kathy felt sick to her stomach. That son of a bitch knew what Henry Banks was capable of all that time. He knew how dangerous Henry's "friends" were, and he'd done nothing. Well, of course he'd done nothing. He was a psychopath.

His lack of human empathy just then paled next to the bigger implication: Toby knew how to stop tulpas that had become too strong to control, or at least thought he did. She'd take his theories over nothing at all. The trick was getting him to share what he knew.

Kathy hacked into the article, a little trick she'd learned from a fellow Network colleague. When it opened, she saw a black screen. She tried bypassing it, assuming it was some kind of security measure. She tried highlighting over the black in case the article was hidden with black font. She tried pretty much every hacking trick she knew, but the screen remained black. No nonsense words, no symbols, no code…nothing.

"Dammit!" She slammed her nearly empty glass of vodka down on the desk. The file was corrupted. She'd have to ask Toby herself.

The doorbell rang and Kathy heard Reece padding across the floor from the bedroom to the front door to answer it.

"Sure," Reece said. "She's here. Come in, I guess."

A moment later Reece came up behind her in the living room, and she turned to face him. He was holding on to the towel wrapped around his waist, and his hair was still wet from his shower. He hooked a thumb over his shoulder and said, "They want to talk to you. Work, I'm guessing."

She peered around him and saw a worse for wear Detective Holt and an older black man, both of whom looked exhausted and a little beaten up.

"Kathy Ryan," Holt said, "looks like we'll be needing your consulting services now."

Reece nodded. "If you'll excuse me, I'm going to get dressed." He slipped past Holt and the other man and headed off toward the bedroom.

Kathy sized up the rumpled men in front of her, then gestured for them to sit down on the couch.

"You two look like you could use a drink," she said, standing.

"You got vodka?" Holt asked.

"A man after my own heart," she said with a small smile, holding up the bottle on her desk. After retrieving two more glasses, pouring them each a double-shot's worth, and handing the glasses over, she asked, "So what can I do for you?"

She waited for them to gulp their drinks and gave them refills. They seemed to pull themselves together after that, and finally, Detective Holt spoke.

"You were right. About that Banks fella, I mean. About those...what did you call them? Tulpas."

Kathy nodded.

"We seen 'em," the other man said. It was the first he'd spoken since he arrived. He looked pretty shaken up, but he was holding it together admirably.

"This is Ernie Jenkinson, a custodian at the hospital," Holt said, nodding toward the other man. "It's been a tough night. He's had some run-ins with these things. We both have."

"Nasty goddamn beasts," Ernie added. His hand shook just slightly as he raised the glass of vodka to his mouth.

"I'm not sure if you know a George Evers at the hospital? He's a groundskeeper," Holt said.

"I don't." Kathy filled her own glass of vodka and sat back in her desk chair.

"I'm guessing he might have been one of the first to run into these tulpas. I think something got inside him. He looks..." Holt searched for the words.

"It ain't him no more, is what he's tryin' to say," Ernie broke in. "I know George—known him almost my whole life. That shamblin' shell of a man ain't George any more than I'm the Queen of England."

"There are a bunch of different types," Holt continued. "Some look like shadows, like, uh, smoke or something. Others crackle like lightning. And then there are...I don't know what you'd call them. Their hounds, maybe. Things cobbled together from tools and machines, from clothes, even. I saw one that looked like a nightshirt strangle a dog to death in an alley on my way to the car. And so far as I can tell, they travel in packs. Now, I've seen them at least as far from the source as George Evers's house, which is real close to the hospital. Maybe they're spreading out or maybe they only came after George. The way they operate, I suspect there's some organized plan at work, so that means someone is calling the shots. If not Henry, then some King Tulpa. I don't know, something like that. I think the main threat—the ground zero, if you will—is somewhere on the Connecticut-Newlyn Hospital grounds, and I think the hospital staff and residents are in danger. I also think you're the only one who knows enough about whatever the hell these things are to stop them. So what I need is for you to tell me how and why the fuck Henry Banks is making them happen, if you'll pardon my language, and how to stop them."

"Where's your partner?" Kathy asked suddenly. It had taken her a while to notice that the younger detective wasn't with the men. She thought she knew the answer as soon as the words were out of her mouth.

Holt replied, "Last time I saw him, or what was left of him, he was in a crumpled heap just outside the steps of the building. Doubt he's there now, though. These things, they tend to recycle whatever they can to form bodies, including other bodies."

"Why didn't they get you, too?" Kathy asked, although it was more to herself than to the detective.

"He don't bend," Ernie said softly.

"Pardon?"

Ernie looked her in the eye. "That's what George told me. He said they took the ones that could bend, that could be, I think he called it being 'rearranged.' He was afraid to go into his house, that they'd 'rearrange' him again. And he said they'd just want to kill me because I don't bend right. I'm figurin' he meant they couldn't do to me what they did to him."

"Yeah," Holt agreed, "I'd figure that to be about right. Some big ugly took my partner, and I followed them up to the roof. After George tossed Farnham over the side," Holt's voice hitched, "I just kind of stood there for a few minutes, just in shock. And...well, I heard a girl's voice say, 'He won't bend. Kill him.' Just like Ernie says."

"And what happened?" Kathy finished off her vodka and poured another. She offered the bottle to Holt, who declined with a small wave, and Ernie, who held out his glass to her. As she poured, Holt spoke. His voice was low and serious, a fallback to training as a police officer, Kathy supposed.

"Well, this man stepped out of the dark. He was tall, very tall, and he wore a black cowboy hat, black jeans and boots, black shirt and leather jacket. He also wore sunglasses, which I thought was odd because it was nighttime. He had tattoos on his neck, on his hands. And a scar running through his bottom lip, down into his chin." He glanced up at Kathy awkwardly at the mention of a scar. Kathy did her best to hide it behind her vodka glass.

Holt continued. "So this guy whistles and these black-smoke people appear behind him. And *they* bring the lightning people. Next thing I know, these bolts of electricity are whizzing past my head and this black fog is rolling in and I'm running. I couldn't go back the way I came and they were blocking the door to the other stairwell and...and I jumped. I didn't think about it; I saw shrubbery over one side of the building and I jumped. Thought I'd broken something for sure, but..." He shrugged.

"Anyway, that's when they called their hounds on me. I can say in the three decades I've been a cop that I never before tonight had to fight off a vending machine, a lawn mower, a rake, three hospital nurse's scrubs, and flying bolts of lightning. And that smoke—whatever it touched just resurrected the things. I barely made it to the car and off that property in one piece.

"I mean, if what you're saying is right, that these things, these tulpas, are thoughts summoned into being, then I'd bet the farm they don't just want to be thoughts anymore. They want to be living, breathing things free to run amok all over my town. And they're taking what they find here, and I'm guessing molding it to be like the bodies they had, or the bodies they'd like to have. What I *don't* have a fucking clue about is how can one man create monsters capable of...of infecting people—and objects—to create other monsters? How can one man do that with his mind?"

Kathy glanced back at the research file on her computer, minimized it, and sighed. "I can't tell you for sure yet how he's doing all of it, but I agree that Henry Banks created those tulpas. I've seen children disconnect. They create a happy place to escape to when they're being abused. They create imaginary friends to protect them from bullies. My understanding of Henry's childhood was that it was a series of one horror after another— abuse, incest, torture, even a murder right in front of him. And I haven't even gotten his psych file yet—that's just what my own alternative sources have provided on him."

She poured more vodka. Holt reconsidered, holding his glass out with Ernie, and she refilled their glasses. They drank theirs quietly, waiting for her to continue.

"Like other traumatized kids, Henry probably created an elaborate fantasy world to escape to when things got bad at home or school. The thing is, Henry has a kind of ability to actualize what he imagines. It's rare; I've seen the skill before but not very often, and never so intense and all-encompassing. It's a skill that usually only the strongest and most focused practitioners of meditation and magick possess, and only after years of study and practice. With Henry, it seems to be just a sort of natural talent. Unfortunately, I don't even think he knows the extent to which he's lost control of those things. Usually, the one who creates tulpas can simply wish them away, but these particular friends of Henry's seem to have found a way around that. I think Henry imagined them as unstoppable protectors, but he made them too strong. In his mind, he visualized them with almost godlike abilities, and now I think they want their freedom to create and destroy like gods. Further, I believe Henry is in as much danger from these things as anyone else once they figure out how to become physical entities. Then they won't need him anymore. And I don't think he has any idea."

"So what do we do?" Ernie asked. "I know that boy. He ain't perfect— Lord knows none of them residents in there are angels, but it wouldn't surprise me none if the boy'd been tellin' the truth, that his friends actually done the killin' of those kids. Bloodthirsty freaks that they are, it ain't too far a stretch. Maybe he wanted it deep down or thought he did, but Henry ain't no killer, and he don't deserve what those ungrateful sons of bitches are fixin' to do to him."

"You're right," Kathy said. "And I'll do whatever I can to stop them from hurting him. Hopefully, I can stop them from hurting anyone else. But I need you to get us in there, Ernie. Can you do that? We need to talk to Henry about his friends, all the info we can get, and...I need to talk to my brother."

"Your brother?" Holt looked genuinely mystified.

Kathy turned a cold eye on the men. "He's incarcerated at the hospital. He knows how to stop them."

Holt shrugged. Ernie leaned forward in his chair, recognition dawning on his face. "Wait, Ryan...Toby Ryan, he's your *brother*?"

Kathy nodded stiffly, looking into her glass.

"Well then, woman, you just might be the toughest young lady I ever met. Good on you." He raised his glass to her and finished off the vodka in it.

A tiny smile crept over her lips. "Hope I'm as tough as you guys, up against these things. So you think you can get us inside? Even past Margaret?"

Ernie held up his massive key ring and jangled the keys. "Challenge me, pretty lady."

She smiled warmly at him. "Good. Let me make a few calls, gather up some things, and we'll go."

Chapter 8

While Ernest and Holt were tracking down Kathy Ryan, and George Evers was lost to the blight spreading down his residential street, the Connecticut-Newlyn Hospital was settling in for the night. The overnight staff at CNH was a skeleton crew, to say the least. Budget cutbacks and restructuring had left the administration, beholden to shareholders' interests, with something of a fluid plan for the hospital coffers. After the nightmare at Bridgewood up in Massachusetts and the ugly rumors about Haversham down in New Jersey, Dr. Wensler was careful about where he meted out the funding and why. There was never a shortage of meds to calm the residents, nor the latest medical technology to impress the mayor and councilmen and women. There was, at times, simply a shortage of personnel to hand out said meds or use said technology.

Officer Luis Vargas always took the post in the lobby, standing guard as the administrative secretary, Margaret, finished up her paperwork and gathered up her things to go. In all the years they had overseen the setting of the sun at CNH, she had only ever asked him to walk her to her car once, and it had been earlier that very night. Something had spooked her prior to his arrival, though she was a tough old nut and not one to share such frivolous feelings with the night guard. It didn't seem his place to ask, and she didn't answer, but seemed grateful and honestly relieved when she unlocked her car and slipped inside.

As Vargas had crossed the dark parking lot back to the front door, some lone bird chittered into the night. It sounded like hysterical children laughing; that was the thought that came immediately to Vargas's mind, though he couldn't remember ever having heard such a thing before. Vargas was from the city, and though he'd spent the last ten years in Newlyn, the variety of odd sounds nature made all around him still perplexed him. What night birds sounded like that, like children laughing, their fragile sanity thin to the point of cracking? He didn't know. It came again, carried on a light breeze, and it gave him chills, and he walked a little more quickly back to the lobby.

Two other guards on Vargas's night team, Ted Luftan on the third floor and JoAnn Reuger on the fourth, were already at their posts. Reuger was new, and new guards unnerved the inmates as much as inmates unnerved the newbies, so he'd put her up in the administration area. Teddy Luftan, on the other hand, was a power-tripping dick. He insisted on handling both the second and third floors while they were short-staffed, though not through any sense of protection of the inmates. When those "baby killers" got out of hand, Luftan smacked them back down into place. The guards couldn't have guns on the hospital grounds, but Luftan didn't need one. What he was going to need, sooner or later, was a good defense lawyer; the cops had already questioned him a few times in the last day or so about his distaste for his charges. Still, what Vargas didn't see wasn't his problem.

Vargas buzzed in the orderlies working that night's shift, nodding and offering a tightly polite little smile as they walked by, laughing with each other about some private experience among them. He didn't know their names and didn't much care to, but they seemed okay enough. At least one of them was big enough to keep Luftan from getting too rough, and Vargas appreciated that. They grew quiet, though, as they passed through the doors into the corridor leading toward the hydrotherapy room. Vargas watched them. Even their body language changed; he'd seen it in cons when he'd worked as a prison guard at Endleton State. It was like a light frost of uneasiness had settled on them. People who worked closely with inmates, he found, could sense when things were out of whack with them. Lord knew he could feel it, and he wasn't even near them. From the reports of inmate anxiety, though, that Luftan was sending over the walkie from the second floor (*"Must be a full moon, man, 'cuz the baby killers are fuckin' howlin' and jibberin' tonight"*), there was certainly something in the air.

Nighttime lockdown hadn't been without its ugly incidents the last few weeks, and that was on Vargas. He, Reuger, and Luftan had been given a pass so far, but the hospital couldn't be racking up any more bodies on his time. Until Hadley, Wensler and the other admins had been content to write off the last few deaths as accidents and suicides, and after all, why not? Those inmates, in their plain prison beds dreaming of kiddie diddling or whatever they thought about, were violent and unstable. That was why they were in CNH in the first place. Now, the last guy, Hadley…a few of them had jumped him on Vargas's watch, and that was sure to bring some heat—not just to Luftan, who had been assigned to his floor, but to Vargas himself. He couldn't quite believe that Luftan had heard nothing that night—Vargas had *seen* those crime scene photos of the body, and a man screamed when someone did things like that to him. As if Hadley wasn't bad enough, apparently some nutjob had walked through a locked door and kicked another inmate's ass badly enough to put him in the infirmary. Luftan swore he'd heard nothing then, either. It didn't seem to be washing with the cops any more than it was with Vargas, but that was the story Luftan was sticking with.

He wasn't surprised when Reuger radioed down that someone had pushed the emergency stop on the elevator—an inmate shirking the lights-out rule, she suspected—but he was uneasy. He shoved off the wall on which he was leaning and walked over to the elevators and sure enough, one of them was stopped on the fourth floor.

"No problem," Vargas called back on the walkie. He pulled the key ring from his belt and pushed through the door to the stairwell. "I'm on my way up. I'll bring the keys up and we'll manually open it."

"Okay," Reuger said. She sounded nervous. "Just hurry, okay?"

"You scared, Jo?"

There was a crackling of static that might have been a huff. "No, of course not," she replied. "But the noises the guy's making in there are just kind of freaky, you know?"

Vargas smiled as he climbed the stairs. "What kind of noises? Like 'oh, oh, oh baby, ohhhh, oh JoAnn, do me!'" He laughed.

"No," she said, sounding flustered. He could almost feel her blushing over the walkie-talkie. "Like...like animal noises."

"Like I said—"

"*No,*" she repeated more firmly. "Like whip-poor-wills, kind of. Like if they could laugh. Long, eerie whistle-laughing. It reminds me of..." Her thought, wherever it was going, trailed off. "It's just creepy. Why would he make noises like that? Can't you hear it? I'm holding the walkie up to the door."

Vargas listened for a few seconds, then radioed back. "Can't hear it, Reuger. Sorry."

"You can't hear that? Are you fucking with me? You've got to be fucking with me, right?"

"Sorry, I can't," he protested with a chuckle. "Look, I know it can be a little unsettling walking around a nuthouse at night, but I really think—"

"Wait, the door's opening," she said, her voice nearly a whisper. "It—" Then she began to scream.

"Reuger? Reuger, what's going on? Reuger!" He bolted up the stairs, taking two and three at a time. He nearly took a spill on the second-floor landing but caught himself and leaped toward the next flight of stairs.

He was breathing hard when he broke through the stairwell door into the fourth-floor corridor. He skidded to a stop just before the blood. It was everywhere in front of the elevator—on the closed elevator doors, the walls, the waxy leaves of the plastic potted plants to either side of the elevator…and the floor. It was thick on the floor, its heavy, coppery taste coating the back of Vargas's throat.

Vargas pulled out his Taser. Slowly, his gaze panned the hallway. The silence was as thick and cloying as the smell of blood. The office doors were all closed. Small droplets of red had managed to reach the nearest ones, dark against the polished honey oak. There was no sign of Reuger anywhere—no sign other than the blood, assuming it was Reuger's blood. Even her walkie was gone.

Vargas glanced up at the digital window over the elevator. It reflected back a frozen red 4. The elevator was still on this floor…and whatever had been inside, whatever had made Reuger scream, was just behind those metal doors.

Should he call on the walkie? Try to use the silence to his advantage? He wasn't sure.

"Shit," he whispered to himself. "Shit, shit, shit."

He decided to back out into the stairwell and call Luftan. He was pretty certain prying open the door was the way to go, but he sure as hell wasn't about to do it by himself.

"Luftan," he said into the walkie in a hushed voice. "You there?"

No answer.

"Luftan," he said, a little louder. "Ted, where are you?"

The walkie didn't so much as chirp. Vargas was about to head back down a floor when a crackle of static made him jump. It was all he could do to keep from tossing the walkie in surprise.

"Yeah, Yeah, I'm here. Checking out the solitaries on two. What's up?" Luftan sounded guarded…not quite afraid, but on alert for sure.

"It's Reuger. She's gone."

"Like, took off?"

"No, like missing. There's blood everywhere. I think she…I think whatever took her is still in the elevator. Up here."

"Whoever."

"What?"

"Don't you mean 'whoever'?" Luftan asked.

"Yeah, sure. Just get up here, okay? It's a mess."

"Well, shit," Luftan responded. "Gimme a minute. I'll come up."

A few minutes later, he heard Luftan's footsteps echoing through the stairwell and saw his tall, lanky shadow jogging up the wall. He appeared a second later with a club in one hand and a Taser in the other.

"So what's goin' on, boss?" he said in a low voice, joining Vargas by the stairwell door.

"I don't know," Vargas whispered back. "She called me on the walkie and then started screaming, and I came up and found…that." He gestured toward the door.

Luftan looked at him a moment, then eased open the door. "Jesus," he breathed. "One of the baby killers did that?"

"I don't know," Vargas repeated. "I've never seen anything like that before."

The two crept into the corridor, inching up to the blood on the floor. It had begun to congeal, though instead of turning a rusty brown, it looked threaded through with stringy veins of blue so dark it was almost black.

"What is that shit? The blue shit in the blood? Is that some kinda chemical or somethin'?"

Vargas didn't answer. His gaze was fixed on the elevator doors. They kept opening just enough to flash a large, bloody pile of rags and then closing. Open and close, open and close, open and close, each time with a cheery little *ding* that ratcheted up Vargas's unease.

The rags inside were the same color as a night guard uniform.

"Gotta get those doors open," Luftan said. As he crossed through the blood puddle, his boots made sticky crackling sounds on the floor.

"Luftan, man, seriously?"

Luftan looked confused, then glanced down at his shoes. "Oh. Yeah. Right." He turned back to the elevator doors and shouldered them open a little farther, then worked on wedging his nightstick in between them.

He happened to look down into the car. "Oh, fuck!" He stumbled backward, nearly slipping on a still-wet spot on the floor. Luftan, whose face never wore any expression but vaguely sadistic amusement, looked genuinely scared. His chest was hitching with deep breaths and he'd lost both the Taser and the nightstick. His wide eyes were staring at the elevator doors, now completely closed, as if he could see right through them, and what lay beyond was getting worse.

"What?" Vargas took his shoulder and shook it a little. "What did you see?"

"That was Reuger," he said. His voice had taken on a simple, amazed quality, like a child's.

"Teddy, is she alive?" Vargas asked calmly. He didn't feel it, but he was afraid if he lost it, Luftan would go careening over some unseen edge into a place where whatever was on the big screen in the theater of his mind's eye would keep playing over and over on a loop for the rest of his life.

"That was Reuger," Luftan repeated. "That was her head. Where's the rest of her, Vargas? *Where the fuck is the rest of her?*"

"I don't know, buddy," Vargas said.

"We have to find the rest of her..."

"We will. We will. First, we have to get everything on lockdown. And right now, I need you to go down into the lobby and call 911. Tell them we have a staff death here at the hospital, okay? Can you do that?"

"Of course I fucking can," Luftan muttered, but there was no fight in his words. He looked somehow shocked soft, shocked thin. He shuffled toward the stairwell and paused so long at the door that Vargas thought he might have forgotten where he was supposed to be going.

"Ted?"

"There's more in there," Luftan said. He turned to look at Vargas. "Moving parts...that aren't JoAnn. I don't know what they are."

"Parts?"

"They were wearing her head."

Vargas frowned, shaking his head. "I don't understand."

Luftan turned back to the door. "You have blood on your shoes," he said softly, then pushed through into the stairwell.

Vargas watched the space where Luftan had been for a few seconds, listening as the echo of the guard's footsteps faded. Then he turned his attention back to the mess in front of him.

The digital number 4 still reigned over the elevator doors. Whatever lay behind them waited soundlessly for his next move. He circumvented the blood as best he could, inching his way toward the doors. That close to them, he could hear faint singing, punctuated by loonlike laughter. Reuger had been right; they did sound like whip-poor-wills. They also sounded like hysterical children laughing. They sounded like strings of nerves untangled from the body and stretched so tightly that they were on the verge of snapping.

Suddenly remembering the row of offices just down the hall, he glanced in their direction, their own doors like cool, polished oak shields against the horrors just a few feet away. There was always someone working late—Wensler, Dr. Ulster, *somebody*—so why weren't they poking their heads out? They had to have heard the commotion, and Dr. Wensler would never have put up with such a ruckus on his nice, quiet floor, sufficiently removed from the unfortunate and unavoidable dregs of his workplace.

He made his way back around the blood and moved down the hall toward the offices, stopping at Dr. Wensler's first. He did not relish the idea of reporting yet another messy death to the director, but it had to be done anyway. Taking a deep breath, he rapped on the door, then waited.

"Come." Dr. Wensler's command, even muffled through the door, had authority.

Vargas opened the door, words of apology already on his lips.

"Dr. Wensler, I—"

Dr. Wensler wasn't there. Confused, Vargas scanned the room. It wasn't that big, though it was, of course, the biggest office. It was tastefully decorated in muted modern furnishings and bland water paintings representative of nothing. The oak desk dwarfed nearly everything else in the room, including the expensive leather chair, the throne from which Dr. Wensler asserted his dominion. The gold plaque on the desk informed visitors of the director's position. To the left was a door that Vargas believed led to a small personal employee bathroom, and behind the desk chair was a large window looking out over the hospital grounds, but there was otherwise no place for a grown man to have gone.

Vargas slipped into the office. "Dr. Wensler?" he directed toward the closed bathroom door, in case the director had stepped inside. "You in here?"

This time, there was no answer. Vargas crossed around behind the desk to make sure the man hadn't fainted or found himself in the sudden grip of a heart attack. The floor was bare, other than the tidy carpeting. Just to be on the safe side, he peered out the window. The ledge outside beneath the window frame was two, maybe three inches wide. There was no way Dr. Wensler in his expensive shoes could have stood on it, and there was, to Vargas's relief, no body on the ground below, either.

He headed to the bathroom door and opened that, flipping the switch on the wall just inside, but the little room was empty. It was, in fact, a bathroom, and bigger than he'd imagined. It even had a small shower stall next to the sink. Vargas had no time to admire it, though. He flipped off the lights and closed the door.

"Dr. Vargas?" he asked the empty room, but it didn't answer. Whatever he'd heard, or thought he'd heard, either hadn't come from that room or wasn't there now.

Vargas emerged into the hallway again and looked at the elevator. A trail of footprints followed him down the hall. They didn't look like blood, at least not human blood; they were a dark bluish-black, with three foretoes and one on the heel, like some large bird.

Like a bird, maybe, that made horrible child-laughter whip-poor-will noises.

His gaze followed the trail, which appeared to have paused before the room he had just been in and then turned off and disappeared under the door of an office across the hall. The name by the suite number read "Pamela Ulster, MD, Developmental Psychology/Psychopathology."

Vargas's stomach dropped. Not all of the doctors were friendly with the non-medical staff at the hospital, but Dr. Pam had always offered warm smiles and friendly interest in Vargas's well-being. He liked her and hated to think whatever had gotten to Reuger had gone after her, too.

He stepped around the footprints and eased open Dr. Pam's door. It was dark inside, and as light from the hallway spilled in, Vargas thought he saw movement.

Vargas flipped on the switch and poked his head in. Dr. Pam's office was like a smaller, less ostentatious version of Dr. Wensler's, with tidy desk and chair, some soothing prints of non-things hanging on the walls, and a soft-looking couch and big easy chair. Dr. Pam wasn't there, and neither was anyone or anything else living, so far as he could tell, except for a little potted plant in one corner.

Confused, Vargas closed the door. Where was everyone? And where was Luftan with the damn police? When he turned to the hallway, the footprints had multiplied, creating frenzied spirals and crisscrosses all over the floor, walls, and ceiling. They were everywhere, including the doorframe right next to where his hand was resting. He jerked it back.

"Fuck this," he muttered to himself, and took off for the stairwell. He had made it just about halfway when the elevator doors opened. He skidded to a stop.

A thick black mist streamed into the hallway, spreading out without really getting any thinner or lighter. It moved quickly, pouring itself onto the floor as if filling up invisible people-shaped glasses. When the smoke had resolved itself into four distinct human silhouettes, each of them opened their eyes. Four pairs of glowing almond shapes bored into him, watching him.

From the elevator car behind them, beyond the open doors, he could hear metallic grinding and soft rustling, something that might have once been an end table sidling out alongside an odd lamp-shaped bird. He saw an arm in a dark blue sleeve waving what Vargas thought was a thick piece of fabric at him until he recognized one of Luftan's chest tattoos.

The source of the arm was out of view in the elevator, but a fleshy tendril where a head might have been dipped and wavered around the door.

"What the fuck are you?" Vargas whispered.

The mist people tittered and giggled, and the sound was very much like the way children must sound as the breath is being squeezed from their tiny little throats.

It was, in fact, the way Vargas's screams sounded, once the mist people and their odd furniture descended on him.

* * * *

Dr. Pam Ulster had finished her therapy appointments for the day—eight individual counseling sessions with her regular patients, as well as three group therapy sessions, two of which she covered for Dr. Wensler. He had left early that afternoon, around 4:00 p.m.—a descent from on high to attend some board meetings or some such thing. She didn't really care; the hospital as a whole breathed a collective sigh of relief once he'd left the premises. He wore about him like a vampire's cloak an air of constant scrutiny, fringed with disapproval, which Pam found exhausting. She had once harbored a hope that the old man would retire, but she knew now he would not. They'd have to pry the hospital out of his cold, dead, iron grip.

She'd had therapy sessions until eight that night and then she'd spent the next few hours catching up on paperwork. There was always a lot of it—session notes to type up for the file, billing and insurance paperwork, treatment forms. It seemed to multiply like rabbits on her desk, and she was glad for those few quiet hours in the evening when she could get it down to a manageable and acceptable level.

It hadn't been so quiet that evening, though. During the last of the individual therapy sessions, around 7:30, it had sounded like the walls were groaning, and the lights flickered, threatening for several seconds to plunge her and her patient, Gina Maldonado, into another blackout. Around 8:15, Pam had heard footsteps, which in itself wasn't unusual except that they sounded like they were climbing the walls. At 9:00, she'd heard a shout in the corridor outside her door. Frowning, she pushed back her desk chair, slipped those murderous heels back on her feet, and went to the doorway to investigate.

The sound was unlikely to have come from a patient; they were all in overnight lockdown on the floors below. A security guard, then? If the security staff were screaming, that was probably not a good sign.

She peered up and down the hallway over her thin, fashionable reading glasses, but it was empty. Its unearthly quiet had settled again like a layer of dust on the place. Whoever had shouted was gone now.

She returned to her desk and the file lying open on her blotter:

BANKS, HENRY
Age: 28 years
Birthdate: November 2, 1990
Height: 5'8"
Weight: 185 lbs.
Eye Color: Blue (left)/Green (right)
Hair color: Blond

Former Residence: 82 Crownwell Street, Newlyn, CT

Family
Father: Joseph Orrin Banks (deceased)
Mother: Eleanor Maisie Banks (deceased)
Grandfather: Marcus "The Viper" Banks (deceased)
Aunt: Lydia Banks (deceased)
Uncle: Frederick Edgar Banks (deceased)

Diagnosis: Undetermined. Psychotic features, possible DID. See Abuse and Family History, p. 7.

Pam sighed, pulling off her glasses to pinch the bridge of her nose where a headache was forming. She was at a loss as to what to do for Henry Banks. She took pride in the fact that while many of her patients couldn't get much better, they didn't really get any worse. Henry, on the other hand, seemed to be steadily declining. His delusions were taking on more import in his mind, more substantiality. The delusions in particular about a trio of friends and an outlier entity who he claimed had been responsible for the killings were very strong; in fact, they seemed to be having a mass delusion effect on some of the other patients, as well. She hadn't wanted to put him in isolation just yet because they felt it really benefitted Henry to interact with other people and she didn't believe in her gut or in her professional opinion that Henry was a physical threat to anyone. She had no doubt the police were right and someone had murdered

Ben Hadley and Martha and maybe even the others, but it hadn't been Henry who had done it.

That it had been his delusions was a notion so laughable that she'd naturally dismissed it when the other patients first brought it up, but now, after Kathy Ryan's visit and a thorough review of Henry's file and her own notes...

Well, the truth was there. It was between the lines, but it was there, and once she'd seen it, she couldn't *un*see it. Delusions, by their very definition, weren't really there. Henry's friends, on the other hand, most certainly seemed to be. In that context, he was a danger to others, but only if those...things...were doing what Henry commanded, and not, as Kathy Ryan suggested, taking the initiative to kill on their own.

If Kathy was right, then Henry was just as much in danger as everyone else in the hospital.

Pam got up and wandered to the window. It was dark already. Those pre-summer evenings when the end of the workday meant crossing a dark parking lot alone after leaving a mental hospital for the criminally insane always set her on high alert. She wasn't afraid per se, but she certainly kept an eye out for anything unusual, even before she left the building. It was, maybe, that awareness that drew her attention to the odd pulsing glow a couple of acres away, over one of the hilltops. She tilted her head, surprised. What was out that way? Utility buildings, she thought. Maybe an old toolshed the landscaper used. She supposed he might have been burning leaves or other yard debris, though she couldn't imagine why the fire glowed green like that, or changed color. Green pulsed to blue, blue to purple, purple to white, white back to blue, blue to red, red to yellow, and back to green again. It was kind of pretty, how the glow slipped and slid over the hilltop like liquid light, like dripping paint in a pastoral landscape. She smiled...until she noticed that the glow was flowing toward the hospital.

She blinked her tired eyes and slipped her glasses back on. The glow broke into pieces, and those pieces resolved into figures, but they still glowed, some yellow-white and some faint blue or green. Some, she saw, didn't glow at all. Rather, they seemed to suck all the light and even some of that pastoral landscape into them like humanoid black holes. Among them were packs of strange beasts that looked kind of like furniture and appliances in some nightmare funhouse. The pulsing colored lights she had seen, alternating hues and intensity, she could tell now were massive clouds of brightness from which myriad appendages waved and flopped, some tentacle-like and others very much like human arms and legs.

All of the things were swarming the hillside, moving like a small army toward the hospital.

Part of Pam Ulster—the logical, scientific, A-type personality part—knew she should be worried. Something very strange and very bad was happening down there, and it was moving closer every second she stood there gaping like an idiot. She couldn't will her body to move away from the window, though. All she could do was replay the same thought-loop over and over in her head: *They're in my notes. The light clouds are the Others and the black holes are the Wraiths and the beasts are the Little Ones and they're all in my notes. Henry told me about them and they're all in my notes.*

She began to laugh. It came on her suddenly, and that worried, logical part of her felt trapped and helpless. This wasn't her. It felt more like the laughter was seeping into her as opposed to coming out of her. She kept laughing, though, and laughed hard, too, and for what felt like a long time. When that crazy mirth had died down to a giggle, she looked out the window again. They were gone. The rest of the laughter in her died at once.

A phantom hand came to rest on her shoulder...or perhaps it had been there the whole time.

They were here. They'd made it to the hospital. They were *in* the hospital. *And they're all in my notes...*

She turned away from the window. She was alone in the office, or at least, she thought she was. But there were noises in the hallway again, chirps and tweets and a low keening that reminded her of some strange, sad bird.

Slowly—she couldn't make her body move as quickly as her mind wanted—Pam moved to the door and locked it. Whatever was out there, she wasn't about to let it in while she had any control of herself left. Scanning the room for something she could use as a weapon, she kept an ear on the noises in the hallway. They were getting closer. That low bird wail sounded like it was right outside the door now.

She scooped up a heavy glass paperweight and turned back to the door. A dark smoke had begun to pour in from the crack underneath, and at first she thought maybe the hallways had caught fire, that they were trying to smoke her out or get her to jump out her office window. Then she realized that the smoke was not formless; it was pulling together, stretching upward as if being poured into a humanoid mold, and when everything from the feet to the top of the head had taken shape, it opened its eyes.

Pam wanted to scream, but the mist was holding out its arm, its hand closed into a fist, and the gesture seemed to be pulling the air out of her. Her hands flew to her throat, clawing at the invisible pressure there. It was coming from the inside where that alien laughter had been. It felt like her vocal cords were being tied in knots, and each knot was squeezing acid down her throat. Pam's arm flung out in an attempt to grab something, anything, the corner of the desk even, to pull herself away from the force intent on killing her. Objects fell from her blotter, but she barely noticed. Her vision grew fuzzy around the edges.

By instinct, she hurled the glass paperweight at the mist, and as the glass shattered against the far wall, the figure dissipated.

Immediately, the pressure inside her throat withdrew, and she could breathe. Her vision cleared, then grew wet with tears. She leaned over her desk, coughing, gasping, and wheezing for several long minutes.

Finally, her breathing returned to normal and she wiped the tears from her eyes. Her throat still felt a little sore, but she thought she was all right. She went to the small water cooler in the corner of her room and poured herself a small paper cup of water from the cold side. After emptying it over the hot coals in her throat, she felt better, steadier. She crumpled the cup and threw it in the trash. She could think again, and her thoughts, she was sure, were her own.

She had to get out of there. That was all there was to it. Either Henry Banks's mass delusion was starting to affect her as well, in which case, she might as well pull up a residential bed right alongside him, or...

...Or Kathy Ryan was right, and Henry Banks had been telling the truth, and everything in her notes was fact and not fantasy.

She wasn't sure which would be worse, though she suspected before the night was through that the latter would prove to be the greater evil.

Pam grabbed her purse and headed for the office door. The sounds had died away sometime between when she was choking and that moment when she stood with her hand on the doorknob; probably when the smoke thing had disappeared, so had the sources of those awful noises. Right then was probably the best and maybe the only time to escape.

She eased open the door as quietly as she could and peered out into the hall.

It was empty. It was also utterly silent, but she thought that wasn't unusual for that floor at that hour, until she realized she wasn't sure what hour it actually was.

Stepping into the corridor, she was uncomfortably aware of the echo her high heels made on the tile floor. It sounded thunderous to her, and she tried leaning forward on her toes as she hurried down the hall toward the elevator. The button, it seemed, had already been pushed, and the elevator car was on its way up. Although it made her feel vulnerable to be standing out in the open like that, the elevator seemed like a better option than the stairs.

Or was it? Wasn't there some sage advice about using stairs rather than an elevator during times of emergency? No, that was in a case of fire or power failure.

"What was that?" she suddenly asked the solitude. It didn't answer. "What *was* that thing?"

It occurred to her as she stood there waiting for the elevator, still waiting as if it was ever going to come in her lifetime, that she'd been in close proximity to Henry so many times. Countless times, really. She'd been his therapist since before his trial. That meant she had probably been in the room with those things, those friends of his, before they were strong enough to show themselves. She knew Maisie and Orrin and Edgar and even the Viper almost better than Henry did. She knew about the lives and histories of those monsters all the way back when they probably were still fantasies. They had probably touched her shoulder just like some had in her office earlier. And if they could do half of what Henry had ascribed to them over the years...

It was all in her notes. She remembered the way Henry described Maisie's ability to get into people's heads, how Orrin was razor sharp, fast as the wind and possessed of a temper like a storm, and how Edgar only had one eye, but he could shoot laserlike fire from it. Henry always seemed to sympathize with Edgar, whom he'd once sketched as being small and gaunt, almost birdlike, with all the earmarks of a fringe outcast. Edgar, Pam believed, was as close to how Henry saw himself as any of those creatures got. Maisie was his dream girl, one who would love and mother him and take care of him while simultaneously needing him in her life. Orrin was in wit and charm, body and soul, who Henry wished he could be. Along with their collection of misty Wraiths and shapeshifting imps and miasmic living light clouds he called the Others, they were an army of defenders in a world so vastly different from the tragic, brutal one in which Henry had grown up. She'd always been amazed by his creativity and attention to detail. She'd even suggest he write and draw comics with his ideas.

He'd laughed at the time and told her he didn't want to give them a reason to take over the world.

She shivered. Frustrated with the elevator, which clearly wasn't working (the digital screen above said it was on the sixth floor now, and there *was* no sixth floor), she turned to the stairwell and headed for the stairs. In that narrower space, her clicking heels reverberated at an almost deafening volume, but she couldn't wait out in the open any longer. *That Wraith*

thing could come back at any moment and crush my insides, she thought,
or the Others could come.

They would come and turn me inside out.

That's what Henry said they could do. The Others could reach inside
like the Wraiths, but they weren't content just to flatten lungs or crush
hearts or squeeze minds to jelly. The Others *rearranged* people. They
moved bones and organs, cells and tissue, rerouted blood. They made
bodies never meant to change shape into new and horrible things. It was
something Henry had spoken about with awe and tinges of both fear and
satisfaction. He claimed it was what had become of his grandfather in the
end. It was why they'd never found all of the old man's body—only what
was left, what the Others didn't need after he'd been rearranged.

She'd reached the second-floor stairwell landing when a glow from a
floor below made her heels chirp as she stopped short. The light pulsed
different colors, hypnotizing and almost soothing in their hues. She could
almost imagine she heard a soft heartbeat with each color change.

She shook her head, her thoughts returning to her original concern. Her
proximity to Henry and thus to these creatures might mean she was more
susceptible to them. How much of herself had she shared with Henry in
an attempt to reach him? How many careless things about herself had she
let slip in simple casual conversation? And what did they need to know
about her to gain control? She didn't think it was much. They certainly
seemed to be able to come and go inside her head that night almost as
freely as in Henry's.

The glow beneath her seemed to pulse delightedly in response
to her thoughts.

She couldn't go that way. One of those Others was in the stairwell with
her. Could it sense her? Smell her? What had her notes said about how they
found prey? All she could remember was that Henry thought they were
crazy. She'd even helped him find the word to describe them: *berserkers,*
like those wild warriors of old. Manifestations of Henry's psychopathic
anger and desire, she'd thought at the time—his Id-beasts.

Now the glow was rising up the stairs. Within minutes, maybe seconds,
she'd be able to see the tips of those waving tentacles, the stiff fingers of
those mannequinlike hands...

She turned and ran up the steps. The exploding echoes of her heels were
like a gunfight all around her. The alien sedation that had been weighing
her down ever since the first odd noise in the hallways that evening was
finally lifting, and true panic was setting in. Those things were coming
for her, coming to rearrange her, and there was no way out.

Once she had burst through the stairwell doors and back into the fourth-floor hallway, she kicked her heels off toward the reception desk and then bent to catch her breath, her manicured nails resting just above her knees. Her panting was loud like the echoes of her shoes had been, and she was sure it was only a matter of time before that glow ascending the stairs engulfed her in its blinding, pulsing colors and—

"Pam," a soft, sexless voice said behind her. She cried out, nearly falling over in her attempt to stand up straight and turn at the same time. No one was behind her. She felt tears of panic and frustration gather wet and hot in the corners of her eyes, blurring her vision. She staggered away from the sound of the voice and toward the offices again, unsure where to go or what to do next. That haze of thought invasion, that sense of someone else's calm being forced into her brain, was beginning to return. It made her feel weak, confused, and ineffective. Maybe it was the first step in the rearranging process.

Instead of collapsing through the doorway of her own office, she sagged against Dr. Wensler's. He always locked up before leaving, and so when her resting hand turned the doorknob and it moved inward behind her into the dark, she was surprised. She caught herself, flipped on the light, and slipped in, locking the door behind her. The last was a reflex, a taught behavior to establish safe boundaries. Locking the door wouldn't do any good and she understood that intellectually, but it made her feel better to have done it.

She managed to make it to the sofa before her legs gave way, and she sank onto a soft cushion and began to sob. Then she began to laugh, thinking about how annoyed Dr. Wensler would be to learn she was getting tear stains all over a $6,000 sofa there just for show.

The she began to cry again, squeezing her eyes shut tightly. This wasn't going to end well. She didn't need the alien thoughts to tell her that. They wanted her, maybe because Henry liked her or trusted her, or maybe because she knew too much about him and his thoughts and feelings. Maybe they wanted everything back that he'd ever shared with her, or maybe…maybe they were angry that it was her professional opinion that had confined Henry, and them by extension, to the Connecticut-Newlyn Hospital for the Criminally Insane.

She felt the pulsing colored light before she saw it even through her eyelids. "Pam," the sexless voice called to her. "Oh, hi there, Pam."

She opened her eyes. A cloud of light and wispy fog about five feet across hovered at eye level in a far corner of the room. It had turned off the office light; she hadn't noticed that behind her closed eyes, either, but now, the glow was casting red then blue then greenish-yellow light over Dr. Wensler's desk and over its softly waving tentacles, which she saw now were about a half foot thick and made of a smooth, rubbery gray skin. A human leg dangled from the cloud, and Pam got the absurd image of a naked man trying to climb out of the endless source of light. An arm, just opposite, waved upward like that of a drowning woman, its long fingernails translucent.

"What are you?" she whispered to it. "How can you be?"

"I am all the things," the sexless voice responded, and laughed. The sound reminded her of a loon or whip-poor-will, or the broken laughter of a child with all the sanity beaten out of him.

"Are you going to kill me?" Pam wiped the sweat from her palms on her skirt. She was glad to be out of those terrible, painful shoes. No one wanted to die in shoes like that.

"Eventually. After I play." A lunatic giggle.

"Why do it?" she asked.

"For fun," the voice said, and the colors pulsed more brightly. "Because I can."

"Okay," she said. "Will it hurt?"

"Only until you die. Then the hurt stops...usually."

"When will you do it?"

"Now, if you're ready."

She closed her eyes. "I am."

"You were his favorite," the sexless voice said cheerily. "The one who mattered."

"That's nice," she said, and her hands clenched, gathering her skirt in bunches.

"Yes, nice."

Then the light got bright enough to turn the black behind her eyelids red. She could hear her bones grinding and shifting, actually hear it from inside her own head, and the burning began as tissue ripped and organs stretched. She might have bled, but the sensations on her skin were too strange to classify. She would have screamed, but by then, nothing was left of her mouth.

The last thought she had as Dr. Pamela Ulster was that she was going to leave one hell of a mess on Dr. Wensler's expensive couch.

Chapter 9

It was almost 11:00 p.m. when the Wraiths and the little mechanical ones were called back to the hospital. They could forget for now about retrieving the human George Evers and the other two who had gotten away. The mists silently called to each other and to the little ones, who had found myriad items from aluminum cans to skateboards to umbrellas and were delightedly trying them on.

They found the Viper waiting at the hospital gates. He motioned for them to follow him. As they crossed the large front lawn, they were joined by more of their kind from every corner of the property, and finally, by the Others, led by Orrin and Edgar.

The Viper led them all to the front door.

"It's time," he said, and then gave a nod.

The creatures of Ayteilu swarmed past him and into the hospital. When Orrin and Edgar moved to follow, the Viper held up his hands.

"The ones on their way here must be dealt with. They will try to stop us."

"Who are they?" Orrin asked.

"Your brother knows," Viper replied. From the corner of his eye, he could see Edgar tugging on his older brother's sleeve, his one eye searching Viper's face uneasily. He would not find what he was looking for.

"Humans," Edgar said. "They know. About us, I mean."

Orrin shrugged. "Well, shit. Let's go kill us some humans."

* * * *

Inside the hospital, curled into a fetal position on his bed, Henry dreamed he was in a car, but he wasn't driving. The Viper was, and Maisie, Orrin, and Edgar were in the back seat. Outside the windows, the trees blurred as they sped down a highway toward sunrise.

"Where are we going?" Henry asked.

"We're going home," Maisie replied.

"We're going to Ayteilu," Orrin said.

"You're c-coming with us," Edgar said.

Henry couldn't remember the accident that had caused the coma, but the conversation had a vague hint of familiarity to it of a real-life car ride from long ago. He had taken such trips with his friends many times before, and he seldom drove, though the doctors told him when he'd finally woken up that the day of the accident, it appeared he'd driven his car into a tree. He was lucky, the doctors said, that he hadn't been killed. He was lucky he had only ended up in a dreamless coma for three weeks. He couldn't remember any of that. He did remember the blood all over his kitchen and basement, and Maisie telling him everything would be okay, and the Viper wiping blood off his own cheek and telling them to get in Henry's car, that he would drive. The rest was lost to him. The time after he'd first awoken was a blur, too. Cops asking questions, pre-trial and arraignment, sessions with Dr. Pam Ulster. He didn't have Ayteilu to escape to then, because he'd brought his friends over from there. Maisie said that he'd spent his time in the coma there, and now it was time to come back.

Henry was losing time, and he was scared. Ever since he'd brought Maisie and the rest over to his world, people had been getting hurt, and he was often confused. Days were often a blur, and sometimes, he wondered if he'd ever actually woken up from that coma at all.

It was only when he slept that things were simple anymore. Only in dreams were things okay.

In the dream, the sky was getting darker, not lighter.

"What's happening? Where's the sun going?"

"There is no sun," the Viper told him. "Not until we finish what we started."

"We need you to be the one," Orrin said.

"To be what one?"

"The one who sets us free," Maisie cooed in his ear.

Dream Henry felt sad. "I don't want to die," he said.

"We don't want you dead," Maisie replied. "We want you to sleep, like you did before, after those intruding little dogs were put down. Sleep, and let us do the rest."

"You don't want me to wake up?"

"Sleep, Henry…"

And so Henry did.

* * * *

With Henry asleep, Maisie could think.

It had been quick work infiltrating the building once the outer structures had been subsumed and their employees and inhabitants disposed of. They were a small army now: Maisie, Orrin, Edgar, the Others, the Viper's mist and electrical Wraiths, and their mechanical beasts.

Still, there was much to be done, and a number of obstacles to overcome.

One issue was the expansive quality of Henry's imagination. Ayteilu had been a fully realized place for a long time, with a myriad of wildlife that adapted with varying levels of difficulty to substantiation. It was one thing to pour it all out of Henry's head but another entirely to help them find independence. The little ones, the beasts, had an easier time of controlling and reshaping small objects, so their incorporation with solid, stable physical bodies had gone much more smoothly than it had for the rest. The mist people and their electrical kin, the Wraith-folk of Ayteilu, had tried to repurpose some of the humans on the hospital grounds but hadn't expected the human bodies to take rather than give, absorbing Ayteiluan energy and changing the host rather than being absorbed. So the Viper's Wraiths had succeeded in little more than infecting the humans and changing their physical structure in a series of painful rearrangements progressing toward crippling deformity. Their attempts at manipulating the building materials, tools, machinery, and appliances they came across, like the little ones had done, only bled Ayteilu into them rather than giving them something to work with in putting together their own bodies.

The Others were too crazy and too unfocused to understand the concept of substantiation. They were Orrin's, and so Maisie intended to let them run their course, wreaking havoc in their soupy, half-substantial way and dissipating once they all broke ties with Henry. Orrin would be disappointed, but there was nothing else to be done about it. They were chaos and muscle sheathed in sharp claws and teeth and serrated tentacles, and once they'd served their purpose, Maisie would in truth be a little relieved. They were one less factor to worry about.

That left Maisie, Orrin, Edgar, and the Viper in much the same boat as the Wraiths. Fortunately, Maisie had a plan. She also had three very powerful incantations that Toby Ryan, at least, believed were an irreversible and potent solution to their problems.

Toby Ryan and Ben Hadley had belonged to groups that seemed to understand the nature of summoning something into the world and then keeping or dismissing it. The more she understood about the words and the actions involved, the surer she was that she could make it work for them. Sure, they were usually used on entities that already had independent existence, but the idea behind them was applicable. The Infection Invocation of Xixiath-Ahk the Bloodwashed had already boosted their ability to absorb and integrate objects in this world as well as some of the people in it. The Floodgates Spell of Thniaxom the Traveler, which she had learned first, had been instrumental in helping to bleed the flora and fauna and the rest of Ayteilu onto this world and consume it.

The World Caller Ritual and the Essence Substantiation Spell of Iaroki the Swallower of Suns were going to make them free. She knew it.

Then Henry could sleep as long as he wanted. Forever, even.

* * * *

The car ride to the hospital was grim and mostly quiet. Kathy had called a few friends, but none of them had been able to offer anything to help her situation beyond convincing the conjurer to banish the tulpas. Kathy didn't think Henry was utterly beyond convincing to do just that, but it wouldn't be easy. For better or worse, the tulpas had protected Henry through some pretty terrible things, and he trusted them. Talking him into letting them go for good, forever, was going to be a tough sell, especially from a stranger. And even if she could, it might very well not be enough to wish them away. If the guesses of her friends had been right, the tulpas were already using a number of occult spells to not only hold them in place but to increase their power and ability to spread. The Floodgates Spell of Thniaxom the Traveler, the Infection Invocation of Xixiath-Ahk the Bloodwashed, and the World Caller Ritual of Iaroki the Swallower of Suns were powerful and catastrophic in the hands and mouths of even the most rudimentarily trained; someone like Ben Hadley might have known of them from his cult days or maybe even participated in some rituals for a show of power. The tulpas might well have learned them from him.

If they had learned such things from Toby, who was a far more experienced practitioner in a cult much more powerful, then there was a good chance the tulpas would be far beyond anything she or even their creator might do or undo. Given Toby's condition the last time Kathy had seen him, she thought the tulpas had learned way more from Toby than just how to kill.

When she relayed this information to Detective Holt and Ernie Jenkinson, she could tell she had overwhelmed them and possibly dismayed them a little. She was supposed to be an expert consulting other experts, and the general consensus had been "convince a crazy man to give up his crazy or else you're screwed." The men took it well, if taking such information inside themselves and ruminating on it could be considered "well." From time to time, Ernie would ask a question or offer an idea. Holt just sat brooding, looking out the window. He was homicide, after all, and he knew death when he saw it coming. Now he was about to go back into a den of killers who themselves were in danger of predators higher up on the food chain. The prospect scared Kathy; she could only imagine how the two men in the back seat of her car felt.

"If this hospital's under attack, then can't you call in the cavalry, Holt? I mean, what says we gotta tackle them things all by ourselves?"

"Their guns and training won't work," Kathy broke in. "If we involve backup, it's likely we'll just end up with a bunch of dead cops."

She glanced in the rearview, and from the sharp look Holt gave her, she could tell she'd struck a nerve. She felt a little bad, but there was no sense in sugarcoating the situation. Swarms of cops flashing lights, SWAT, and the like would create panic and havoc. Panic and havoc would bring news crews and cause hospital lockdowns. Those things would, in turn, cause delays, and valuable time was exactly what the tulpas needed to finish what they had started. They'd never get to Henry unless they went in quietly and alone, and avoided everyone and everything they could until they reached their target patient.

"Besides," she tried again, "the people I talked to agree that what little protections I can bring in there with me are limited in their scope. I can protect us for a time with what I have, but...well, time is of the essence."

"I hope you know what you're doing, woman. I mean, I got you, I got your back, but I don't want to see no hospital gurney slicing off the front of you."

Kathy couldn't help a small smile. "I'll do what I can to keep my front intact, Ernie."

"Would be much appreciated, ma'am."

After Ernie punched open the security code on the touchpad lock and opened the big gates, they turned down the tree-lined road and Kathy got that same tight feeling in her gut. She had begun to hate Connecticut-Newlyn Hospital for the Criminally Insane. She pulled into a space in the nearly empty parking lot and glanced at the digital clock on the dashboard. It was 11:43. Only the night shift would be working, and that would be a small crew; no Wensler or Ulster, no Margaret. Most of the inmates would be locked down for the night in their bedrooms, and anyone not on patrol would most likely be on the third floor.

The three sat in the car for a few minutes, staring up at the building. It was not completely surprising to see that an odd, spidery ivy, faintly glowing blue and pink with dark red veins, was growing off the rooftop and had taken over some of the upper corners of the building. Odd, bulky creatures, boxy in shape as if made from old mattresses, clung to the side of the building. They navigated the façade in quick spurts on long, spidery legs made probably of window glass, climbing around the ivy. Occasionally, they sniped at probing, leaf-lined tendrils with glassy pinchers, and coils of throbbing blue glow snapped back at them like whips.

"After everything I've seen tonight, that shouldn't surprise me, but…" Holt shook his head.

"You never get completely used to it," Kathy muttered, taking a snubnose .357 out of the glove box. "Ready, gentlemen?"

"No time like the present," Ernie said.

They got out of the car.

"Move slowly," she told them. "If they can see, they may be attracted to sudden movement."

"And if they can smell us?" Holt asked, drawing his own gun out of the holster.

"If they start to move quickly, you move more quickly."

They crept toward the front door. Ernie, who had no weapon himself, clung to his keys like brass knuckles, doing his best to keep them from jingling. Kathy's focus was so intent on the mattress-spider things that she jumped when a voice said, "Well, hey there."

She turned to the source of the voice, a boy in his early twenties slouching against the double doors. He had blond hair sticking up in tall-grass spikes. He wore a white retro-1970s Atari t-shirt whose hem was splattered with blood. He had a nice-looking if someone bony face. His eyes were a clear and icy wintergreen color, and when he smirked, Kathy thought she saw at least two pairs of fangs. His hands were shoved into the pockets of faded jeans, but knife blades protruded from his wrists like spikes.

Another boy limped out of the shadows to join the first. This one was smaller, dwarfed both in height and muscularity by the first boy. He looked younger, too—maybe sixteen or seventeen. One of his hands looked shriveled or burned nearly to scar tissue, its fingers long and fused together to make a kind of crab-claw. He wore all black, including a long trench coat, and the thatch of black hair on his head hung in his face. He tossed it back and Kathy could see one of his eyes glowed like a small fire in his skull. The other eye was completely black, a void of unearthly cold.

The alien ivy swayed in the night breeze, muttering and whispering as the three of them faced off against the two boys. For several seconds, no one spoke.

Finally, Kathy said, "Are you Henry's friends?"

The blond shot the other boy a small, knowing smile. "Henry has lots of friends now."

"I'm sure he does. Henry sounds like a good guy. Not someone who'd want to hurt anyone."

The blond boy's smile faded. "You don't know Henry, then."

"I know guys like Henry. I know the terrible suffering he went through." Kathy had received his medical and psychological file from a Network contact just before the three of them had left the apartment. It was, sadly, much as she had expected, and a lot of what she hadn't. Henry's mother had tried to smother him as an infant. Only his father arriving home in time and pushing her off the baby had saved his life. At three, she tried to leave him out in the backyard in the snow overnight to cleanse him of demons. Again, his father intervened. At five, her untreated paranoid schizophrenia caught up to her for good, and all the screaming of obscenities and pounding of fists couldn't make the voices go away. They told her to shoot her husband and son and then herself, and she listened. The bullet for Henry missed him. The one for his dad exploded red in his chest, and the one his mom had saved for herself gave her a halo of red like an angel, little Henry reported, before the big hole in the back of her head made her fall down.

He was alone with their bodies a day and a half before a neighbor, unused to the sudden silence over there, peeked through a window and saw a sticky, blood-spattered baby in soaked clothes curled up next to his dad's cooling corpse.

Henry Banks was sent to live with an aunt, uncle, and grandfather in Ohio. The file indicated he made it another eleven years in that house. At sixteen, the murder of his three relatives by intruders would have resulted in his being sent to a group home, but he'd run away and never looked back. Kathy did her best to read through the years of abused heaped at the feet of the three adults tasked with caring for a small, traumatized boy. She couldn't get through all the details, but she got the gist of it: sexual abuse at the hands of his aunt and uncle until he was eleven, usually following beatings, burnings, and the occasional cuts from a knife at the hands of his grandfather. That Henry Banks survived as long as he did was a miracle. That he made up an entire world peopled by powerful, fearless beings to protect him like the two facing her right now was not only understandable but almost endearing. It had moved her to tears she had taken some trouble to hide from the men in her company, and it had made her all the more determined to get Henry out of this situation and someplace safe.

"Orrin, we d-don't have much t-time," the smaller, fire-eyed boy said to the blond.

"Orrin, is it?" Kathy said to him.

The blond boy smiled. "Yes, Kathy, it is. And this is my brother, Edgar, and he's right. All this talk is boring. You know we're gonna fight. I know we're gonna fight. So let's get to it." He peered around her shoulder. "Edgar, take the old men. I want me a piece of Ms. Ryan, here." He looked her up and down with a small, hungry smile not unlike Toby's, and it made her skin crawl.

Kathy raised her gun and fired once into Orrin's chest. He looked down at the bloodless hole the bullet left in his shirt and whistled. "Oh wow, that was intense. What is that, pain? Damn, honey. Do it again!"

He pushed off the doors and began walking toward her.

"Just checking to see if you're solid yet," she said calmly, and holstered her gun. She quickly pulled out a talisman on a chain instead. Made of silver, it was shaped a little like a letter "S" speared through with arabesques. Its name was long and difficult to pronounce and most of its history lost to time, but it was powerful. If the tulpas had been using Toby Ryan's occult spells to achieve some kind of permanence, then the symbol in her hand could allegedly do what no gun could.

Orrin, who she supposed didn't know what the talisman was, kept coming at her. When he got within about five feet of her, though, he staggered back, clutching his head.

Edgar, who had hung back, almost cowering against the double doors, strode forward. "Orrin?"

"She's got head magic," Orrin said. "I can't cut her."

"Got it," Edgar replied, and descended the steps. His furtive demeanor had gone. His one eye glowed deep red in the dark, and just as Kathy was about to speak, a bright beam of red shot out of the socket. It hit Kathy in the shoulder and the pain was immense, a burning that traveled down her arm and up toward her neck, her lungs, her heart. She cried out but managed to hold on to the talisman. If she dropped it, she was dead.

Shaking off the pain, she glanced at Holt and Ernie. They, too, had their talismans out, shoving them toward Orrin like ID badges. Orrin growled, swiping the air in front of them with his wrist-knives. Edgar turned to the men as well, and this time when the light came from his eyes, it went from red to white hot, so bright it hurt their own.

Kathy threw an arm up to cut the glare and shouldered past Orrin toward Edgar.

He turned back to her just as she reached him. Up close, the talisman seemed to hurt him, too. The fire in his eye dulled to an ember and he cried out.

Then Orrin was on her, with an arm around her neck. The crook of his elbow pinched her windpipe and squeezed, and explosions of dry, panicked pain went off in her head. For a thoughtform, he was surprisingly strong—neither entirely solid nor entirely ephemeral, but some liquid, fluid sliding scale in between.

She raised the talisman to his forearm, and the skin there began to smoke and flake away. Orrin growled behind her and squeezed more tightly. She thrust the talisman over her shoulder toward her best guess at his face, and the pressure on her neck broke. Kathy gasped for air, coughing, as Orrin howled from somewhere behind her.

She looked up just in time to see Orrin charging her again when Ernie flew across her field of vision, tackling Orrin to the ground. He shoved his own talisman in Orrin's mouth, and the boy began to turn blue. Kathy glanced at Edgar and saw the eye gearing up again with a deadly red glow.

"Ernie!" she shouted, and the old man looked up as a red beam burst forth from the boy on the stairs and shot out toward him.

For one terrible second, the beam lit Ernie's face in a blood glow, and she thought she smelled sizzling flesh. Then Holt was behind Edgar, springing at the boy with his talisman. He reached around and plunged it into the fiery eye. Edgar screamed and crumpled to the ground.

Orrin was on his back convulsing, coughing up blue-black ichor onto his own chin, his t-shirt, and the ground around him. Ernie lay motionless next to him. Kathy's heart sank.

Then Ernie coughed and sat up, rubbing his ear. Kathy and Holt rushed to him, yanking him to his feet and away from Orrin. When Ernie took his hand away, blood and a few shreds of what was left of his ear came away on his fingers.

"You okay, Ernie?" Holt asked.

Ernie looked too dazed to speak. He let them drag him up the stairs past Edgar's still form and to the double doors of the hospital. Kathy fished for the key ring on his belt.

"The key card with the blue label," Ernie mumbled.

"Hang in there, buddy," Holt said. "You just hang in there."

"I ain't goin' nowhere," Ernie said, and tried to chuckle, but it came out as a cough. "Just a little banged up, is all."

Kathy found the key card with the blue label and ran it through the electronic door lock. A second after, the familiar buzz let her know she could open the door, and she ushered them inside.

The front lobby was quiet, even for the night shift. Margaret had, ostensibly, gone home for the night, though it was strange to imagine her having any sort of life out from behind that desk. Kathy knew that the night crew had at least three security guards, and one of them usually took up a post by that first set of doors, which led to the bedrooms and hydrotherapy room. No one was there at the moment. She supposed it was possible that he might be patrolling the second floor—Margaret had mentioned something about their being short-staffed—but the conspicuous absence of a guard gave Kathy an uneasy feeling.

She and Holt got Ernie over to one of the chairs in the lobby's tiny waiting area, and he waved them off that he was okay.

"Much obliged for the help, folks, but I seen worse than that in the war," he said with a smile. "It'll take more than that to kill old Ernie here."

Holt took a look at the side of Ernie's head. "You're a tough old dog, Ernie. Looks like the boy's laser cauterized the wound a little, at least. Bleeding's mostly stopped. We can get that ear bandaged up, though, if you want."

"Not much of an ear to bandage, I imagine," Ernie said. "Can't hear none outta that side." There was no expectation of reassurance in his voice. He might not have been able to see the charred tissue, but he obviously knew enough about the damage. "Nah, let's just get to Henry, take advantage of the moment's quiet, okay?"

Kathy nodded. "You saved my life, Ernie. I owe you a huge debt of gratitude."

Ernie waved it off, blushing a little. "Nah, woman, I was just relivin' some old football days, is all."

She grinned. "All right, All-star, let's get moving, then."

Ernie rose. Kathy could tell from the pained expression that flickered across his features that despite his bravery, he had an old man's bones and an old man's aches and pains to go along with them. He had too much pride, she imagined, to let it show, but he was hurting. Kathy just hoped he hadn't cracked any of those old bones trying to save her sorry ass.

The three of them headed toward the elevator. Henry, she knew, was on the third floor, near her brother.

"I think we should take the stairs," Holt said, eyeing the elevator doors suspiciously. Kathy glanced up at the digital screen above the doors, which displayed "4."

She shrugged. "Okay. Probably faster anyway."

In the stairwell, the silence grew thinner, somehow tinnier and hollower. The echoes of their steps and their occasional words were strange, coming too soon on the heels of their noise or too long after. Holt seemed distinctly ill at ease. He had his gun drawn, even though it would do little good. She figured it was a kind of security measure, a product of police training that made him feel less helpless. Neither he nor Ernie had their talismans now; they were essentially going into a firefight without a bulletproof vest. She kicked herself for not reminding them to reclaim theirs from the tulpas outside.

They reached the third-floor landing with a little huffing and puffing, and emerged onto the corridor by the elevator. The now familiar surroundings still spawned that slick weight in her stomach that greasy lump of discomfort. It was not so easy to bury as that hard little hateful part of her, maybe because it lifted once she left the hospital. It was there now, though, and the total quiet, the empty nurse's station and the lack of a patrolling night guard so far as she could tell made it feel much heavier.

"What room's he in?" Holt asked.

"307," Kathy and Ernie said in unison.

"Okay, lead on."

Ernie led them to another set of reinforced glass doors. He opened these with a yellow-labeled key card, and gestured for them to go first. Their footsteps thundered, despite every effort to be quiet.

Room 321, 319, 317... The walls felt narrow and slanted at unnatural angles there, and in many cases, the numbers next to the doors to each room hung slightly askew. That same ivy on the roof extended out from under some of the doors, waving and reaching for their shoes as they passed. Kathy wondered about the other inmates, and where the ivy was thinnest, she tried to peer through the windows. She couldn't see much, but what she did see wasn't encouraging; mostly, shadowed masses more ivy than person groaned in the corners or from the beds.

Room 315, 311, 309... One of the doors had a rust-colored handprint on it, and a blood smear like a comet tail trailing toward the wall. Beyond it, something that was once a man had been bent backward, and it crab-scuttled on its toes and fingers toward the door. Where the head had been was a ghoulish mask of distorted features. Only the eyes remained human, and in them was a glazed terror that made Kathy flinch.

On the right, Room 307's door was closed. Kathy did not look at the door next to it. She didn't want to see her brother's room just then, or whatever personal effects he thought made him look more human. Instead, she stepped aside to let Ernie unlock it. Then she slipped the talisman chain around her neck, and without knocking, she went inside.

The man on the cot was asleep. The room was uncomfortably cold, but Henry slept in a short-sleeve hospital-issued pajama set with no sheet or blanket on him. He didn't stir as she, Ernie, and Holt approached. Kathy looked around the darkened room. Other than the cold it was, so far as she could tell, untainted and untouched by the alien infection happening elsewhere in the hospital.

Maybe Henry genuinely didn't know what was happening. She'd said she thought he didn't more than once, and had thought she believed it until she took in his room. The poor guy was sleeping away his own creations' rebellion.

"Henry? Henry, wake up."

Henry stirred but his eyes didn't open. Kathy looked back at the men and they shrugged.

"Hey. Hey, Henry," she said, gently shaking his arm. "I need to talk to you. Wake up."

"Not just now, he can't," a sweet, cultured girl's voice said from the shadows. "Henry's taken something to help him sleep."

Startled, Kathy turned toward the voice and saw a girl with a patch of iridescent gold scales around one eye. She could feel energy from this girl that the other tulpas didn't have and a kind of barely reined-in anger. If Orrin and Edgar originally had been manifestations meant to guide him, then this one was clearly meant to protect him, and if Ernie was right about Henry's not being a killer, then Kathy was willing to bet a good bit of his murderous rage was standing right in front of her.

"You think you're taking care of him," Kathy said, keeping her voice even.

"I'm keeping him safe and out of the way," the girl replied. Her eyes were snakelike, full of subtle defiance and predatory cunning. It occurred to Kathy that the talisman she had just might not be strong enough to protect her, let alone all three of them.

"That's what I'd like to do, too," Kathy said.

"What you'd like to do," the girl said, eyeing the talisman as she came closer, "is to convince dear Henry to make us go away."

"I can't convince him of anything he doesn't want himself," Kathy said. She held still, her body tensing to move quickly should the girl strike. "Although I can't imagine he'll be too thrilled that you want to leave him."

An odd expression Kathy couldn't quite place passed briefly over the girl's face, and then that imperturbable calm held sway again. "After all we have done for Henry, he's delighted to do something for us. He's willing to help us in any way that he can."

"He isn't willing because he doesn't know, does he?" Kathy asked. "You've been going around behind his back, gathering your spells and rituals to grant yourself life—real life, not just a shade or reflection of life. You want what he has. And when you're done with that, Henry will be of no use to you."

The girl tilted her head and studied Kathy. "You almost sound as if you think we don't care about him. That's not so. We've sheltered him his whole life. We've protected him against the things that would have killed him."

"And you killed for him. That's why he's here, isn't it? Because you killed those kids?"

"Don't you know? We're not real," the girl said with a small laugh. It was an ugly sound, much older and more jaded than her young throat seemed capable of making. "We're just Henry's imaginary friends. He's a sick boy. A lost, broken boy. And we're just the parts of him he can't resolve or let go of." The last part sounded bitter, and Kathy was struck by how Henry's personification of anger was as much directed inward as it was outward.

The girl glanced at Henry, then focused her golden gaze on Kathy again. "How did you get past Orrin and Edgar?" she asked suddenly.

"We put them down. Just like we'll put you down, if you won't and Henry can't."

"You can try," the girl said with an amused smile.

"We intend to do more than try," Kathy said.

"You can't undo what's been set in motion. No one can, not even sweet little Henry. Not now." The girl sized up Kathy again, as well as the men standing mutely behind her. "Go ahead. Try to wake him up. He's drugged pretty heavily. You won't get what you're after, but give it a try. You can't stop us now. It's no matter."

She backed up into the shadows from which she came, and for a few seconds, all Kathy could see were her eyes and glint of her scales.

"It's our world now," the girl purred, and the last of her Cheshire Cat glow winked out.

"Was that…one of them?" Holt asked from behind her. "Why didn't she attack us like the others?"

"She doesn't think she needs to," Kathy replied, "or doesn't want to take the chance. Help me wake Henry up. We have to get to him before she finishes those rituals or she may very well be right."

Chapter 10

Outside of Henry's bedroom, the hospital began to change more rapidly. George Evers had returned and was tasked with infecting Dr. Wensler and the night guard, Vargas. He was also told to pile the dead bodies in the art therapy room on the third floor, where those who could absorb them would.

In the bathrooms, green water began to flow hot enough into the sinks to steam the mirrors above them. The ivy liked that and snaked its way down the hall to toward the smell of the waters of home.

In Wensler's office, the big polished oak desk shook itself free of the junk on its back and joined one of the lobby chairs in the hallway. The chair wore the head of a blond woman in a security guard's cap on its seat, and through the head's eyes, it took in its new world.

The waxy artificial potted plant from one of the fourth-floor offices had grown legs and taken a walk to the pharmacy closet. It had outfitted itself with syringes in every new plastic tendril, wrapped in every leaf, until it looked more glass and needle than plant. It couldn't talk, but it waved its branches in delight, and the soft tinkling of glass and metal against each other sounded like music…or laughter.

The television in the recreation room on the third floor came alive, crackling with energy as it unplugged itself from the wall with newly grown arms the shape and power of a gorilla's. It cheered on the chess table's transformation in the stolen voices of faraway broadcasts.

The floor tiles all over cracked and split upward as the things taking root beneath began to grow. The ceilings dripped rocky stalactites of crystal.

In the infirmary, Toby Ryan's bed was empty, the sheets thrown back in a rumpled ball. The IV for his pain meds dangled beside it. There were no night nurses to notice, nor any doctors to wonder. The entire floor was empty.

It wasn't quiet, but it was empty.

Toby knew what was happening, probably better than most. And as he limped painfully down the stairs toward the third floor and Henry Banks's room on a stolen crutch from the supply closet, he hoped to hell his only living relative knew, too.

* * * *

It took a long time to wake Henry Banks. It had taken a lot of shaking and some smelling salts from the nurse's station supply cabinet to bring him around, and then even then, he was groggy. He rubbed his shaved head with overlarge hands bound to skinny wrists. As he sat up, he glanced at each in turn, though he avoided meeting Kathy's gaze for too long. He seemed uncomfortable with her in the room; if he'd even registered her face, he hadn't let on. She saw the boy had scars of his own—on the back of his neck and the underside of his jaw. She guessed them to be part of his painful collection of burns and deep cuts, and she felt a kind of empathy for him.

He didn't seem surprised to see them there in his room at night, though beneath his increasingly sullen expression, he looked worried. He stared at his lap and yawned. His breathing was slow and shallow, and his posture was so tightly cringing that it seemed he was trying to collapse inward.

When he seemed sufficiently awake, Kathy tried to talk to him. "Henry Banks, I assume?" She was aware that often, her voice grazed people like a blade across the skin, just enough to put people on the defensive, and the boy looked like he'd spook easily. She tried to keep her voice soft. "I'm Kathy."

"I know who you are," the boy mumbled.

"You do?"

"You're Toby's sister. Kathy Ryan."

Kathy forced a smile at the top of Henry's head. "I am."

"He says you fight monsters."

"I suppose I do, from time to time."

Henry glanced up, but only for a moment. "Not monsters like us. A different kind."

"Many different kinds."

"He said you'd be coming eventually. I think he was hoping you'd visit him, too."

"I'm here to see you tonight." Kathy tried to switch gears. "It's very important. I've brought your friend Ernie and Detective Holt with me if that's okay. Do you mind if we ask you a few questions?"

Henry finally looked up at her. "About what?"

"About your friends."

A brief flicker of emotion, a mix of both fear and relief, crossed his face. "The doctors don't believe they're real."

"I know," she replied. "But I do. I'd just like to know a little about them—what they're like, where they're from, that sort of thing."

"I…I don't think that's a good idea."

"Why not?"

"Well," he replied, scratching at his arm, "something bad always happens when people hear about them. After I told the doctors, they medicated me. After I told the cops, they arrested me. After I told the lawyer and the judge, they put me here. And after I told the shrinks here, they told me I couldn't go home. They all said they'd listen, that they'd be fair, and they lied. They weren't fair. They think I'm crazy."

"I don't think you're crazy."

Henry looked startled. "No?"

Kathy smiled. She thought it came across as warm and reassuring enough. "No. But I do think it's important we talk about it."

"Why?"

"Well, I think you have a very special gift. Not only can you picture things so vividly in your head that they seem real, but you can actually take it a step further and *make* them real. It's an incredible talent. Like, I know your friends maybe once were imaginary, but you've made them real. Am I right?"

Henry nodded, but he looked at her with suspicion.

"I think you wanted to create a beautiful place, a place to escape to, and people to take you in…to protect you. Shelter you. Love you."

Henry looked back at his lap again. She was losing him.

"Do they scare you sometimes?"

That got his attention. "What do you mean?"

"Are you ever afraid of what they'll do? What they can do—without you, I mean? Like when you're sleeping?"

"I know people think they killed the others in here, but they wouldn't do that. They wouldn't hurt people who aren't hurting me."

"Well, Henry, what if they believed those other patients were going to hurt you, or get in your way?"

Henry shook his head vigorously. "No. No, they wouldn't do stuff behind my back." He tried to turn his expression away from her, but despite his protests, she thought he secretly very much believed what she was telling him. "They come from me. That's what Dr. Ulster said. They're reflections of my feelings. Pieces of my personality. Their thoughts are my thoughts and their actions are my wishes, but they…" His voice trailed off.

"Aren't real," she said softly. "But we know that's not true, don't we?"

Slowly, Henry nodded. After several seconds of silence, he said, "You want me to wish them away, don't you?"

"I know how you must feel about them, but they *are* hurting people, Henry. I just don't want to see them hurt you or get you in any more trouble."

"I don't know how to wish them away," he said. His voice sounded very small.

"Maybe you could try to do whatever you did to wish them to be," she offered.

Henry looked up at her and scoffed. "So I should go suffer another twenty-five years of abuse and torture to get up enough juice to undo them?"

"No," she said quickly, "I didn't mean—"

"I can't stop them," he said, "even if I wanted to. If all they want to do is be people, why not let them?"

"Because that isn't all they want. They're changing things, changing people. They want to bring that place you made up in your head outside of it, to drop it on top of this world."

"They're undoing reality out there," Holt said, "for everyone."

"So now you know how I feel," Henry mumbled.

"Henry, we're going to stop them. They may have been good to you once, but they're not good for you now. Surely some part of you, whatever part is still connected to them, sees that. You don't want them to hurt anybody else, do you? You're not a killer like they are."

Henry's eyes flashed anger. "They never killed anyone I didn't want dead!" he shouted. "Bad people who deserved to die. Bad people who hurt me. They saved me! They were my friends when no one even wanted to know me. No one's ever been there for me like they have!"

"I admire your loyalty," Kathy said patiently. "But you need to ask yourself if, once they're free to be their own entities, they will be as loyal to you. After all, they *have* been doing things behind your back whether you believe that or not. I know because I've seen it. I've seen them. And they've been up to an awful lot. What they've accomplished so far, they've done using the words and rites of bad people…and your girl, well, she did some bad things to get that information."

"Don't you dare talk about Maisie like that! She loves me and she takes care of me and she'd never do anything to scare me or hurt me."

"I'm sorry, Henry, but I think she's done with all that now. Done with you," Kathy said softly.

"No! You're lying! You're fucking lying!"

"I'm not. And I need your help."

"Why should I help you?"

"Because your friends are looking for the kind of trouble that has your name on it this time," Ernie broke in, clapping a hand on Henry's shoulder. "They plan to do you wrong, son. I think you know that deep down, too." He pointed to the mangled remains of his ear. "Your friend Edgar did that. The boy with fire in his eye."

"Edgar did that?" Henry reached out to touch the damage but changed his mind and pulled his hand away. "Edgar usually just sees what's going on, or what will happen, or what already did. He never hurts anyone, not unless—"

"Unless Orrin or Maisie tell him to?"

"No…no, not unless the Viper tells him to," Henry said, dazed.

"Who's the Viper?" Kathy asked.

"The only one I'm not sure is one of mine," Henry said.

The door behind them opened. Kathy tensed and could tell from the body language of the others that they, too, were ready for a fight. The bowed blond head and the silhouette of the figure as it leaned against a crutch and limped into the room were familiar. The figure paused just inside the doorway and looked up.

"Well," Toby said, "looks like I'm late to the party."

* * * *

"Toby, how—what are you doing here?" Kathy asked, surprised.

"Looking for you," he said. He was a little out of breath, and despite his reptile grin, he carried a faint grimace of pain on his features. How he was managing to stand on those swollen, purple ankles was, Kathy supposed, simply a testament to his force of will. He didn't just *want* to find her; he believed he *needed* to, though why was beyond her. She would have thought he'd have been enjoying the chaos.

"You found me," she said flatly.

"So I did."

"Toby, they want me to make them go away—Maisie and the others." Henry still sat on the bed, his hands fidgeting in his lap, his head slightly bowed, but he looked up at Toby with earnest desperation.

Toby sighed and slumped against his crutch. "Yeah, kid. This one time I think they may be right."

Kathy and the others turned to him with sharp surprise. Toby was agreeing with them?

"But…I don't have anyone else. Only them," Henry said, unshed tears glittering in the dim moonlight of the room.

"I know it feels that way," Toby said. "I know you feel alone. But you're not alone. You're surrounded by people who care. You've got Pammy Ulster, right? Good old Dr. Pam. And you have Ernie, here. And my sister. If she says she's here to protect you, you can trust that. It's her job, Henry, and she's good at it."

Kathy gaped at her brother. He sounded sincerely concerned and honestly sympathetic…but she knew he wasn't capable of sympathy or empathy. He either didn't understand that people really did have feelings or couldn't imagine such feelings as having any real significance compared to his own. He no doubt had an ulterior motive in manipulating Henry into thinking he cared, but still, he did genuinely seem to want what she did—to stop the tulpas. For the moment, their goals were aligned, and just then, Kathy didn't care what her brother's reasons were, so long as he could convince Henry to make the monsters go away.

Henry took some time to consider what Toby was saying, and then replied, "I told her I didn't know how. And it's true. I don't."

"That's okay," Toby said with that small smile that made her skin crawl. "I do."

Chapter 11

Kathy and her ragtag team made it to the recreation room on the third floor without incident. They had heard some banging around in the art therapy room, but Ernie had been quick; he'd locked the door from the outside before anything in the room knew they were there. Although they crept past the door as quietly as those echoing halls would allow, Kathy couldn't help feeling that the things beyond the locked door could feel them. A partly mechanical appendage slapped the little glass window, and ivy-like tendrils hissed and wiggled at them from beneath the door.

In the rec room, they barricaded the double doors with what little furniture was left. One or two of the couches were missing, as were the chess and checkers tables. Gone, too, was the vending machine that had once delivered candy bars on a credit system to patients who maintained good behavior. Kathy thought there might have once been a pinball machine and an arcade game against one of the far walls, but they were both gone, as well. The thought of having to go toe to toe with a *Space Invaders* cabinet was so absurd and so surreal that it was both laughable and terrifying.

They set up folding chairs in a small circle—like group therapy, Henry commented—and sat down, with Toby at the head of the circle. He probably would have enjoyed holding court like that, but his face was etched with pain and he talked through gritted teeth. He grunted as he shifted forward on the chair.

"As I was saying, the best way to dispel tulpas is for their creator to deconstruct them. However, as my dear sister pointed out, we might just be beyond that point now. These tulpas have used very powerful spells to assure their place in this world. And these spells aren't easily undone, I can assure you. Still"—he leaned back stiffly in the chair—"there are ways."

"And you," Holt said with equal measures of incredulity and distrust, "you know these ways?"

Toby fixed a stare on Holt that spoke of his own mistrust of police. "It was once my job to know, so yeah."

"What do you need from us, Toby?" Ernie appeared to be genuinely interested.

That hard, black hole of a stare loosened a little on Toby's face, and he said, "First, Henry needs to be on board with making them go away."

The others turned to Henry. Kathy could see he looked genuinely scared. They were asking a lot. She knew that. From a psychological standpoint, what they wanted Henry to do could very well break his mind irrevocably. Kathy struggled with that, but not nearly as much as she thought she should. It made her more uncomfortable to imagine she shared even the slightest sociopathic streak with her older brother.

Henry took in the expectant faces around him and with a sigh, finally nodded. "Okay. Yeah."

"You can't back out no matter what they say to you," Toby warned. "I'm serious, man. If you hesitate even for a second, they'll know and they can take advantage of that."

"I know," Henry said with a defensive twitch of the shoulders. "They have to go. I know."

"Okay," Toby said, accepting Henry's acquiescence. "Then we're going to need some of the usual things. I assume you brought the usual items?"

Kathy held up her bag. "Orgonite with black tourmaline, white sage, a black candle, chalk for the triangle, and a lighter. And I figured some more exotic items might be useful—a Key of Thniaxom the Traveler and an Artifact of Iaroki, in particular."

Toby looked impressed. "Way to think ahead, little sis. Now, we're also going to need sleeping pills, a sharp knife or dagger—or maybe a scalpel if that's all you can find—and that small black bag behind the loose piece of wall in my room. Anything else we may need is in there."

"Okay, so pretend half of us in the room don't have any idea what you two are talking about," Holt said. "What exactly are we doing?"

"We're going to create a way to fight back. An egregore."

"A what now?" Ernie asked.

"A manifestation of our own collective will—a kind of tulpa, only less conscious, less aware of itself. Think of it as our creating, say, an arsenal and not a being. I'll show you how to do it. We're going to use the arsenal to...well, to strengthen us, for starters, and then to weaken and destabilize Maisie and her friends. Then Henry is going to wish them away, right, Henry?"

"And if that doesn't work?" Henry asked.

"Then we move on to plan B. If we can't make them disappear on their own, we'll force them to go someplace else."

Holt shrugged. "I know I'm out of my depth, here, okay? I don't know anything about this voodoo shit, but if Kathy is okay with everything, then just tell us where to stand and when."

Kathy thought he looked clearly uncomfortable at having to put any of his trust in a serial killer. Holt, of all people, wasn't about to forget what Toby was.

She tried to allay the man's fears. "From what I know and what I've researched, I think this is the way to go."

"Then we'll get you what you're missing, so we can start," Ernie said. "The dispensary beyond the double doors out by the nurse's station has some aspirin, maybe a box or two of Aleve. You want narcotics or even something like Ambien, we gonna have to go upstairs and get it out of the pharmaceuticals closet. Your bag ain't no thing; that's right next door. But for something sharp, you can either go down to the kitchens on the first floor or the med center on the fourth. I'm guessing you less likely to run into those things out there moving up a floor rather than down two."

"I agree with Ernie," Holt said. "I think Ernie and I should head up to the fourth to get the scalpel and the sleeping pills and, Kathy, maybe you pop over to your brother's room and get his bag?"

"Works for me," Kathy said.

"I'll watch Henry," Toby offered.

"Someone needs to watch Toby," Holt said, casting a quick, undisguised glare at Kathy's brother.

Toby shifted uncomfortably in the chair. "Detective, I'm not in much condition to get into trouble. I think your worry may be a bit misplaced."

Holt regarded him coldly and seemed on the verge of saying something when Kathy took his arm.

"They'll be fine," she said, ushering out the men and closing the door behind her. "I'll only be gone a minute, and then I'll be right back here to watch them both." However, she also felt a flash of unease at leaving her brother alone with Henry. She still didn't completely understand his motivations in helping her. Ever since the day she'd found his trophy box of finger bones in the back of his closet, she'd made it a point to learn his tells, to figure out what he was after long before she agreed to even continue speaking with him. It bothered her that she couldn't tell what he looked to get out of helping in this situation. It bred a quickly growing bad feeling that she was only trading on a lesser of two evils, and only temporarily.

"We'll meet you back here as soon as we can," Holt said. "If we don't run into trouble, it shouldn't take us long."

"Okay," Kathy said. "Be careful, guys. If you can avoid letting them touch you in any way, do it. If they touch you, they can feed on your auras and get inside your head."

The men gave her grim nods and moved off down the hall. She turned to her brother's room.

In all the years that Toby had been confined to Connecticut-Newlyn, she had only ever seen his room three times. The first had been when he was first committed. The second had been when she'd come to get him for their father's funeral. The third had been for his thirtieth birthday. They had been three distinctly uncomfortable moments in her life, and she didn't look forward to adding a fourth.

She took a deep breath and went to the closed door next to Henry's. Her hand paused on the knob. It was just a door, and not even a very impressive one at that. She'd dealt with worse doors, and worse things behind doors than old ghosts and sour memories. She could handle this.

Kathy pushed open the door, and as she stepped across the threshold, a flood of feelings came back to her.

"Oh, Kat. Silly, stupid Kat. You should have stayed out of my room."

It had been hot that night, hot and miserably sticky. She'd just wanted a t-shirt. She'd gone rummaging in his closet and found an old Metallica shirt…and his little box of human finger bones. She would have given anything to believe those bones were anything else, *meant* anything else other than trophies of the women he'd killed.

She remembered how one minute she'd been thinking she had to put the box back before he found out, that he'd be so angry, and the next minute, he'd been pulling her hair hard and dragging her to the floor. She remembered the box flying out of her hand and Toby straddling her, reeking of whiskey. She remembered the storm of hate in his eyes and the shiny new knife.

"You know, I could do you right here. I've thought about it, you know. I could fuck you and stab you to pieces and drag whatever's left of you out into the woods. I'd hide you better than the others. Dad would neeeever find you. No one would ever find you."

She'd felt sick to her stomach.

"But you're my sister. I don't want to kill you—really, I don't…"

He was so heavy on top of her. His erection cut into her hip. He was so very heavy.

"But damn, do I ever want to cut you."

Then he'd pressed the blade into her skin just above her left eyebrow and pulled the blade down, skipping over her eye and landing on her cheek just below the eye socket. Then he dragged the blade down farther, all the way to her jawbone.

All that screaming, an echo in the chambers of her mind now, sounded like it was coming from outside her head. Everything had blurred. Toby had done that. The pain and tears and the screaming had made everything blur. She remembered being sure he was going to kill her, that one of her fingers would end up in that little box with all the others. She had been afraid to die back then.

She wasn't so afraid of death anymore. Death was quick. Death had no memory. Scars, on the other hand, got to be really heavy to carry around after a while.

Kathy closed her eyes and counted her breaths. When she'd let the seventh breath go, she opened her eyes again, and the echoes were gone.

When they'd been kids, long before he'd ever cut her, Toby used to hide things from their dad in a hole in the wall in his bedroom. Mostly it was cigarettes or porno magazines or the occasional bottle of booze. There had been a loose piece of Sheetrock behind the headboard of his bed, and he'd gotten pretty good at stashing things there. Kathy knew about it; Toby had always said it was their little secret, and sometimes he'd share a smoke or a sip of the bottle he was hiding when their dad wasn't home. It had been exciting then, a special string of moments the two of them shared, when he wasn't teasing her or growling at her or looking at her in that way that made her uncomfortable. He was just Toby, her big brother, and she probably loved him more during those moments than any other time.

Their dad had caught them, and Toby'd made it look like it was only him smoking and drinking. He'd covered for Kathy, and for his trouble, their dad had beat him pretty good. He'd had the beginnings of a black eye and bruises all over his back after that, but he'd wiped the tears away and winked at her after, as if to let her know it had been worth it, and nothing was ever going to change those moments or take them away.

Kathy was pretty sure it was after their dad had plastered and spackled the wall that Toby had taken to hiding things in his closet, but it wasn't the same. After a while, Toby wasn't the same.

She went to his bed and bumped the corner of it. It didn't move. Margaret had told her once that after several incidents of inmates tossing their beds in fits of rage, they had begun bolting them to the floor. Kathy figured that in order to get to the wall behind his bed, Toby would have had to find a way to loosen the bolts without the orderlies who changed the sheets and made up the beds noticing. Nudging one at the head of the bed with the toe of her boot, she saw that it was, indeed, loose. She bent and unscrewed the bolt on that side, then went around to the other side and undid that one. After unscrewing a third at the foot of the bed, she was able to pivot the frame enough to get to the wall behind it. Sure enough, there was a hairline crack outlining a patch of loose Sheetrock about the width and height of a laptop screen. She dug her nails into the crack and wiggled it loose. It was a messy job and if the hospital was still standing in the morning, the staff was sure to find out about it, but she wasn't too concerned with protecting the integrity of Toby's hiding places just then.

Tossing the Sheetrock aside in a small white puff of dust, she reached into the hole in the wall. She half expected her hand to graze smooth, stringy, slimy things, the innards of a hospital beginning to change into something else. Instead, her fingers closed around a canvas strap, and she pulled out a small black backpack. On the front zippered pocket was the symbol of the Hand of the Black Stars, a black silhouette of a palm-up hand against red and white, and six black stars, between and surrounding the fingers. It looked like it had been painted on or colored in marker, but applied with careful reverence. Kathy looked at it with disgust.

She gave the backpack a quick shake, and the contents returned a muffled thump. She'd certainly open it before handing it over to her brother, but first, she wanted to get back to him and Henry. The air in the room where he had been imprisoned for almost three decades was starting to get heavy, and she needed to get out of there.

Slinging the little backpack over her shoulder, she nudged the bed back in place and headed for the door. Then she noticed the glow out in the hallway.

She frowned. All over the third floor, it was lights out as usual; the floor was dark, aside from moonlight through some of the bedroom windows and the small oblong lights between the ceiling tiles that ostensibly had been installed in case staff needed to see down the hallway. What glowed just outside Toby's door now, in that hall space between his room and Henry's, was too bright for either of those things. The way it pulsed colors was unusual, too. She'd seen those colors before in the ivy outside the building and in Edgar's eye. These were colors that Henry's imagination had attributed some meaning, and that meant whatever was in the hallway was going to be a problem.

As if in answer to her thoughts, a sexless voice said, "Kathy, come out. I want to show you things. Beautiful things."

Kathy didn't answer. She stood motionless, soundless, with Toby's backpack on her shoulder and her gun in the holster on her hip.

"Kathy," it said, "I want to show you Toby and Henry. They're mine now, and they can see such lovely colors. The colors of Ayteilu. Come see."

She hoped that was a lie. Whatever was out there might be willing to hurt Toby, but not Henry, not yet...not unless Maisie's plan was working faster than Kathy thought.

She let the backpack slide down her arm until she could slowly unzip the top.

"Kathy, come out or I'll kill them."

"No, you won't." She rummaged around, feeling for an object she thought might be in there.

The thing in the hallway laughed. At least, Kathy assumed it was a laugh, although it sounded to her more like the cry of someone about to break.

"You're feisty," it said. "You'll be fun to pull apart."

She felt something cool and smooth and pulled it from the backpack. She allowed herself a small huff of relief; it was an artifact she had been hoping Toby had. It looked like it was made of shiny black glass or porcelain, but it wasn't. That substance didn't come from anywhere in this dimension, nor did its shape, which was something like a three-dimensional, symmetrical kind of arabesque. It was a word in a language no human tongue would ever pronounce, and it was powerful. If Maisie had used certain spells to anchor herself and her army to this world and bring her own bleeding through, then the artifact in Kathy's hand would most likely be the best weapon Kathy had against that army.

At least, she hoped so.

"Kathy?" The glow waxed closer. "I'm going to hurt your friends. I'm going to break them into little pieces. Come out and watch."

"I have a better game to play," Kathy said. The artifact was growing colder in her hand. "How about you come in here and see?"

A hand, stiff and waxy like a mannequin's, came around the doorframe, its fingers bending with some effort. The glow pulsed a bright blue, then green. A moment later, the lower half of a leg dangling from a useless knee appeared just below the hand, its foot jerking around.

"I like games," the sexless voice said, and it giggled in that horrible high-pitched, hysterical way again.

"You'll like this one," Kathy said. She took several cautious steps closer to the door, raising the artifact like a weapon.

A second later, the glow came into view. Its source was blindingly bright, a cloud of light, threaded with the veins of tiny soundless storms and fog. The light burned Kathy's eyes, but she couldn't turn away. The cloud had been right; there *were* beautiful things to see—endless star-sprinkled space painted with nebulae, black holes swirling into infinity, fountains of blood and shards of bone shooting up into sunset-streaked skies over alien worlds, bodies arranging themselves as they pleased, over and over for eons, the cycle of creation and life, death and deconstruction, and over again, forever...

Before the light could swallow her mind, Kathy thrust the artifact into the midst of it.

At first, she felt nothing. Then a biting cold clamped down on her fingers, her hand, her wrist. The pain was sharp, a hundred ice shards and splinters shot under her skin. She held on to the artifact even though her fingers were growing stiff and the pain was eating into her arm. The cloud suddenly screamed, a piercing wail of pain and surprise, and Kathy was able to turn her head away. Just when it felt like her hand had crystallized and was about to shatter, she pulled back her arm and the cloud exploded.

The force knocked her backward and she fell onto the floor just before the bed. All around her, glinting rainbow particles hung in the air, millions of tiny fragments that had made up cloud and tentacle, hands and legs, and then those particles fell to the ground with an almost musical glasslike tinkling sound. In seconds, the confetti that had been a monster winked out and was gone.

Kathy rose shakily and inspected her hand. The whole area that she had plunged into the cloud's light was bright red and raw, her knuckles split and bleeding, but otherwise, her hand seemed okay. Her joints were locked, though, and it took a few seconds to work enough feeling back into her fingers that she could pry the artifact out from their grasp and return it to Toby's backpack.

She was just zipping up when she heard slow clapping from behind her. She turned and saw Orrin stretched out on Toby's bed. He was still a pale shade of blue, and that black stuff he'd coughed up had dried on his chin and t-shirt. His forearm a few inches above one of his wrist knives had bubbled and peeled some, but otherwise, Orrin looked fine.

"Impressive," he said. "You killed one of the Others. I was starting to think they were indestructible in this world."

"No," Kathy replied, "they're not. But you're still going. A little worse for wear, pretty boy, but still holding up, huh?"

"Holding up is what I do," Orrin said, leaning forward. He fixed his gaze on her. "I'm tough to kill. Maybe even impossible, by the time Maisie's done with us. Not like the humans here. They don't bend so well, but wow, how they break!"

"Some people are harder to break than others," she said.

"Breaking people is also what I do," Orrin replied, and rose from the bed. "Let's see how hard you are to break, Kathy Ryan."

Chapter 12

"So which way are the pharmaceuticals?" Holt asked in a low voice as they emerged from the stairwell.

"This way," Ernie replied, hooking a finger to the left. "Down past the offices and on the right."

The two men moved as quietly as they could down the hall, past empty offices and blood-streaked doors, until they came to a corridor veering off to the right. While the first- through third-floor wings of the building were used for patient rooms, therapy rooms, and bathrooms, the fourth-floor wings beyond the administrative offices were set aside for medical and pharmaceutical storage, labs, and maintenance. They had once housed the isolation ward before the restructuring of the hospital, and those rooms that couldn't easily be converted to accommodate the modern changes were either used for file storage or left empty. Ernie never liked being in those fourth-floor wings if he could help it; there was something not right about them. Maybe it was age or neglect that clung like shadows to the walls, and made folks jumpy, but Ernie didn't think so.

The door to the pharmaceutical and medical supplies storage room was unmarked, other than a yellow and green sticker by the room number, to keep any patients who might be wandering where they shouldn't from accessing medications. It was always kept locked, as the small sign on it indicated, for the same reason. He'd had no reason over the years to ever unlock the door, other than to assist the occasional scatterbrained orderly who had locked himself out and/or the keys in. His boss, however, had granted him keys to every locked spot in the hospital, and he'd marked the key to that door with the same colors. Ernie wondered briefly if Wensler would show up and give him grief about him and Holt breaking into the hospital's supplies. Years on the job had trained him to be leery of such things. Given the state of the hospital just then, though, he supposed Wensler showing up and firing him over stolen drugs and scalpels was the least of his worries.

He found the key quickly on his big jingling key ring and let himself and Holt inside.

Metal shelves had been erected under the fluorescent light, which came on as soon as they crossed the threshold. Hundreds of white and nearly translucent orange bottles lined the shelves, many of which had long chemical names he couldn't pronounce, even if he could see the labels clearly without his reading glasses.

"Any idea where the sleeping pills are, friend?" Holt asked, throwing up his hands at the sheer volume to look through.

"Not a clue," Ernie said.

"Looks like the shelves are marked, at least by drug type. Let's see here...opiates, anticonvulsants..." Holt peered at the shelves' different labels.

"Look for benzodiazepines, then," Ernie said, "or NB hypnotics."

Holt gave him a questioning look.

"It's not whatever you're thinking, boss. The orderlies call them benzos and NBs. Short for benzodiazepines and non-benzodiazepines, they told me. Words just stuck in my head."

Holt shrugged. "Okay. Benzos and non-benzos it is, then." He found the benzodiazepines two shelves over and one up from the bottom, in boxes marked Klonopin, Valium, Restoril, Xanax, and Ativan.

"These...aren't these anti-anxiety meds?" Holt asked.

"I guess so. Grab a couple of boxes of those and a couple of NBs. One or the other has to be right."

Holt grabbed a box of Xanax and another of Restoril, tore them open, and shoved the bottles into the pockets of his trench coat, then turned to the shelf of non-benzodiazepines below it. "Oh, hey—Lunesta. I've heard of that stuff. That's the moth stuff, right? From the commercial, the glowing moth?"

"I think so." Ernie was starting to feel very anxious in that supplies room, and not because of Wensler and his policies. The room had gotten smaller somehow, like the shelves were pressing in, and the low hum of the fluorescent lights was starting to unnerve him.

Holt grabbed two boxes of Lunesta, tore those open, and shoved those into his pocket as well, then straightened up again. "Think we can grab a scalpel from here?"

They moved through the shrinking shelves toward the sterile medical supplies and found a scalpel still in its packaging. Ernie grabbed it and stuffed it into his pocket.

"Let's get out of here," he said. "I have a bad feel—"

"Help me!" a man's voice called from down the hall. It sounded furtive, desperate, as if whoever it wanted help from could return at any minute.

Ernie and Holt exchanged glances.

"I thought nobody was housed in the isolation rooms anymore," Holt said.

"Nobody *is*," Ernie said. He grabbed another scalpel package and ripped it open with his teeth.

The two threaded their way through the shelves until they got to the door. Ernie had a strange sensation that they had somehow gone the wrong way, that the doorway in front of them was a different door, the wrong one, but he shook off the feeling. There was only one door in or out of the room, the one with the yellow and green sticker above the room number and the sign reminding people to always keep it locked. The feeling persisted, though, as they brought their gathered supplies into the hallway, so Ernie glanced at the wall. The room number was there, and it was the right one—456.

The sticker was gone, though. There wasn't even that grimy-looking little residue left behind. Frowning, Ernie closed the door. It was blank from top to bottom. No sign.

"What? What is it?" Holt asked, puzzled.

"Something's wrong," Ernie replied.

"Hey! Hey, you down there! Please, help me! I locked myself in!" The voice was indeed coming from one of the old, unused isolation rooms, down at the end of the hall. Ernie thought he recognized the voice, too, but that made him feel more rather than less suspicious of it. The owner of that voice shouldn't have been there.

"Who are you?" Holt asked.

"Myers! Larry Myers! I'm an orderly here. Please, let me out before those things come back!"

Ernie nodded with grim satisfaction.

Holt started down the hall but Ernie put a hand on his arm to stop him. "Myers only works day shifts," he said in a low voice.

Holt nodded.

"Please," Myers said. "I've been stuck in here since three this afternoon and I have to piss like a racehorse.'"

"How'd you get locked in there?" Holt asked.

"I ran in here to hide from one of those, whatever the fuck they are, those glowing cloud things. When I pulled the door closed, it locked. Look, I'm not one of those things. Are you going to let me out or what?"

Holt looked to Ernie, who shrugged. "Your call, boss," he said to Holt.

The detective led the way past the isolation rooms. The glass windows on those doors were barred, and the doors were made of metal. They required special keys; Ernie kept them on a separate ring attached to the main key ring and was fairly sure he'd never used them, nor had the guy before him.

Holt pressed as close as he could to the dust-streaked glass, trying to peer through, but seemed to have no luck. Myers pounded on the door. Both men jumped, and Holt backed away from the window.

"For God's sake, let me outta here!" Myers cried. "Please! I don't want them to do to me what they did to Joe. Oh God!"

"Let him out," Holt said to Ernie. He looked almost apologetic. "We can't leave him in there."

"If that's a 'him' at all," Ernie muttered. Holt didn't answer, but he drew his gun. Ernie searched the jangling mess of keys and found the smaller ring with the isolation room keys on it.

He let out a breath. "Here goes," he said, and unlocked the door.

It squealed loudly as Holt pulled it open, the sound disproportionately loud, its echo ping-ponging longer and farther than it should have. A musty smell of sedentary stone and stale air wafted out to them on a puff of dust that Ernie waved to clear away. Then the two men looked into the gloom inside.

The isolation rooms had no proper windows, but there was a tiny, heavily barred slit near the top of the high ceiling. It was no wonder the medical community had discontinued use of the rooms in the name of humanitarian progress; the little cell in front of Ernie struck him as a questionable step up from a medieval dungeon. If there was a man in there, then the gloom had already begun to stick to him like sweat.

"Myers?" Holt called into the room.

"Yeah," the shaky voice replied, sounding relieved. "I'm here. I'm here."

A figure stumbled out of the darkness. It certainly looked like Larry Myers—curly black hair cut short to minimize the contrast of his receding hairline, the beginnings of a paunch just starting to hang over his belt, hairy arms ending in hairy knuckles, and bright, earnest green eyes. His scrubs were torn across the chest. A cloudy bruise was forming over the outer corner of one eye, and a thin stream of dried blood had left a crusty trail from his left nostril to his upper lip.

Holt put his gun away to help Myers into the hallway, but Ernie caught a look from him that seemed to say *keep an eye on him and keep the scalpel handy.* Ernie did; he watched the orderly as the man panted, his wild-eyed gaze darting up and down the hallway.

"Where are they?" he asked in a near whisper. "Those things, those cloud things—where did they go?"

"Haven't seen them up here, buddy," Holt replied gently. "Haven't seen or heard anything on this floor but you."

"Are they gone?" Myers asked.

"Looks that way, son," Ernie said. "How about we get you out of here?"

Myers turned to Ernie, and the bright fear in them dulled to confusion. "What are they? What the hell are they?"

"It's a long story, Mr. Myers. Let's get you out of here first."

"I have to go to the bathroom," Myers said.

"Okay. Let's take care of that." Holt led the man, with Ernie in tow, to the far end of the hall. A sign for the men's room indicated a door on the left, and Holt drew his gun.

"Just in case," he told Myers, whose empty stare was fixed on the weapon. He pushed open the door and they slipped inside.

Holt checked the stalls while Myers fidgeted impatiently by the sinks. When he gave the okay that the place was clear and holstered his gun, Myers ran to the nearest urinal. While he was relieving himself, Holt sidled up to Ernie and said in a low, confidential voice, "So, is it him?"

"Larry Myers?" Ernie responded in the same tone. "Don't know the man all that well, but I...I think so. Seems like him. No little, you know, quirks, like with George."

"If we turn him loose at the front door, he'll never make it off the property. Look at him."

"Take him back downstairs, then?"

"That's my thinking."

Myers zipped up and went to the sink. The water took a moment, then spurted suddenly from the faucet, as if the pipes had been turned off and on again. Myers flinched when the water hit the porcelain but managed to do a serviceable job of washing his hands.

"Okay," he said. "Okay, now what?"

"Now you come with us."

"Where? Are we leaving now?"

"We can't do that just yet, Larry. You're gonna have to trust us, okay?" Ernie clapped a hand on the orderly's shoulder.

"What? Why? That's crazy! We have to get out of here, we—" His eyes grew wide. "What was that?"

Ernie hadn't heard anything. He turned to Holt, who shrugged.

"What was what, Mr. Myers?" Holt asked.

"It's one of them," Myers whispered. "Can't you hear it? It just—there, it just said my name again."

"We don't hear anything," Ernie said. Under normal circumstances, that might have made a man feel better; he could chalk up Myers's voices to delusion. After what he'd seen lately, though, all it meant was that Ernie was at a disadvantage. He was essentially deaf to whatever was threatening Larry Myers.

"Let's go," Holt said, evidently thinking the same thing. He drew his gun and led the trio out of the bathroom. "Which way is the voice coming from, Mr. Myers?"

Myers pointed down the corridor from which they'd come.

"Good," Holt said, gesturing for them to follow in the opposite direction. "Stairs are this way."

Their passage down the corridor was tense and mostly silent; Ernie's joints creaked so badly he could almost hear them inside his head, but the rest of him held it together. Larry Myers flinched from time to time, stopping short in front of him, and Ernie had to nudge him to keep him going. Holt drew his gun on shadows. Ernie was relieved when they reached the corner.

They turned onto a lightless void, an end of the earth into which the rest of the hospital seemed to have fallen. That's what it looked like to Ernie's tired old eyes, just for a moment, before he realized that the lights had gone out.

"Fuck," Holt said. "What happened to the lights?"

"They like the dark," Myers whispered. His whole body was trembling noticeably now.

Holt ignored him. He rummaged through the inner pockets of his trench coat until he pulled out a very old cell phone. He flipped it open and brought up the flashlight app, then shined it down the hallway. It did little good; the beam of light was too thin to make out anything more than shapes, and it didn't reach too far.

"Come on," he grunted, leading them into the blackness. Myers snatched at Holt's trench coat like a child, and Ernie held on to his shoulder, an uneasy train rolling slowly through a dark tunnel that groaned and mewed all around them. Just like on George's street, he felt things watching him, jostling with each other to get closer, grazing close enough to him to just miss touching the raised hairs on his arms and the back of his neck before gliding back into the black again. When the little red digital elevator sign proclaiming the fourth floor came into view, Ernie relaxed, but just a little. That meant the stairs were close by.

He was about to point that out to Myers and Holt when something passed in front of that number four for a moment, and the train stopped short. Ernie bumped into Holt, who he could now make out as a silhouette with a reddish halo.

"You okay?" Holt asked.

"Yeah, but…" Ernie frowned. Holt's was the *only* silhouette in front of him. He was sure he'd never let go of Myers's shoulder, but the middle man was gone.

"But what?"

"Myers. He's gone."

"What? How?" Holt sounded genuinely perplexed. "Where could he have gone?"

They heard Myers laughing from somewhere beyond the light, although he sounded hysterical enough that he could have been crying, too. A few seconds later, it was joined by more lunatic laughter, as if every crazy person in the whole damned hospital was laughing with Myers.

"Larry?" he called above the laughter. "Larry, where'd you go, son?"

"Mr. Myers? Mr.—ah, fuck it. Let's go, Ernie." Holt grabbed Ernie's leave and ushered him to the stairwell.

Suddenly, the red glow behind them got much brighter, and the stairwell door started melting around the edges. It fused to the doorframe, sagging at an odd angle but effectively blocking the way.

"I'm a-f-fraid I c-can't let you leave," a voice from behind said.

The men turned to find Edgar leaning against the wall by the elevator doors, his one eye socket glowing brightly and casting a bloody tint to his face and neck.

Holt gave the boy a bone-weary sigh. "We ain't about to let you stop us, kid."

Edgar considered that a moment, then said, "Sounds like an impasse, huh?"

"It does indeed."

"Guess we'll have to fight it out," Edgar said with an almost wistful smile.

"Guess so," Holt replied, and he and Edgar charged each other.

* * * *

Orrin grinned at her, and that double set of fangs pressed into his bottom lip. As he sauntered closer, he dragged his wrist blade against the wall, leaving a deep furrow that, having pierced the skinlike paint, split the wall open to reveal alien flesh and muscle underneath. The way he was looking at her reminded her so much of Toby that it made her skin crawl.

"But damn, do I ever want to cut you..."

And Orrin would cut her, too, if given a chance. To get close enough to use the artifact on him meant getting close enough to get cut.

Again.

She unzipped the backpack.

"Where's Maisie?" she asked, stalling.

Orrin shrugged. "Who knows? Maisie does her own thing."

"So I've heard."

"We all do."

"Now, on that point, I've heard differently."

"Oh?" Orrin paused.

"I heard you and your brother don't take a proverbial piss without Maisie or the Viper signing off on it."

Orrin's grin faded, but he said nothing.

"Sounds to me like Maisie and the Viper are running the whole show," she said, pulling the artifact out of the backpack. "She must trust him an awful lot to give him so much power over the rest of you...expendable types. Maybe she'd got a thing for him, or—"

Orrin suddenly slashed out at her, his wintery eyes flashing. She lunged backward, managing to dodge his wrist blade by mere inches. Evidently, she'd hit a nerve. He glared at her and dove at her again, but she knocked his incoming arm away from her face.

She shoved the artifact at his face, but this time, he was ready for her defensive strike. He tilted his head out of the way and backed off, but just a little.

"Your toys are a joke," he said through gritted teeth. "I'm going to carve you up so bad even your crazy butcher of a brother won't recognize the pieces."

"Oh, that's good," she replied tersely. "That's a good one. Did you come up with that on your own, or do you still get all your thoughts from Henry?"

"This is all me, bitch," he said, and plunged one of the wrist knives into her shoulder.

The pain was staggering. It knocked the wind out of her, and for several seconds she just held on to his arm. He was pressed close to her, so close that she could see ice storms swirling through his irises and an uncontrolled hate in the depth of his pupils. He smelled like nothing, felt almost like nothing, and though his face was inches from hers, he had no breath. She observed and held on to these things to keep from passing out. She clutched his elbow to keep from sinking to the ground. And with her other hand, the one holding the artifact, she reached around him as if to give him a hug and plunged the artifact into his back.

"You...you..." The ice storms in his eyes suddenly stopped moving, but that hate grew fathoms deeper. There was something else there, too, swallowing the hate like a black hole. Kathy thought it might have been fear.

Orrin opened his mouth either to say something or to scream, but no sound came out. Instead, the opening that was widening in his back like a vortex started to pull at his insides. His tongue and then his teeth were sucked down his throat and he seemed to be getting shorter. His face distorted and then crumpled in on itself. Just before the eyes were vacuumed up inside the head, they grew wide, that frozen ice storm splintering into a million tiny pieces of despair.

Then the whole of the creature that was Orrin folded in on itself and disappeared. The artifact clanked to the floor. She scooped it up, put it in the backpack, and tossed the strap over her good shoulder.

A moment later, a sharp cry from the adjacent room sent her running. As she burst into Henry's room clutching her injured shoulder, she saw the young man on the floor. Toby leaned over him, not quite able to get to him on the floor with his injuries. It looked like he was trying to prod Henry's shoulder with his crutch.

"What did you do?" she yelled, tossing the backpack to her brother. She rushed to Henry and crouched beside him.

"Nothing!" Toby protested. "One minute he was fine and then he grabbed his head and screamed and fell over like that. I didn't do anything to him."

Kathy looked up into his eyes and saw he was telling the truth—or at least as much of the truth as Toby was able to tell. He hadn't done anything to Henry...

...*she* had. The thought dawned on her with awful clarity. The tulpas weren't entirely removed from their connection to Henry, not yet. It was possible that hurting one of them might hurt their creator as well.

"What happened to your shoulder, Kat?" Toby shifted uncomfortably in his chair.

"Orrin happened. It's fine. It's not that deep. Henry, are you okay?"

"He's gone," Henry whispered, shaken, as Kathy helped him sit up. He looked up at her with frightened eyes. "Orrin...what did you do to him?"

"I…I think I undid him," Kathy said. Truthfully, she really wasn't sure *what* happened. She hadn't thought the artifact would kill Orrin, only slow him down. She still didn't think it would affect the tulpas with greater power, like Maisie or the one Henry called the Viper, but if it could be used to thin out their army some, she was all for it.

"How?" Toby asked. "I don't understand. You shouldn't have just been able to—wait." Toby thought about it for a moment, and a small smile crept over his face. "That sneaky little bitch," he said finally.

"What?" Kathy asked. "What are you talking about?"

"The spell she did to keep them here, it has certain…clauses that can be finessed. In the event, let's say, that you summon a number of entities to fight, and you give them each a certain degree of staying power, you can include a part that allows the most powerful entity to siphon off strength and substance from lesser entities around it to ensure victory. It's only a little bit from each, not enough for any of them to notice, but given the number of things out there…" He shook his head. "That artifact should only have hurt this tulpa, Orrin. But she pulled just enough of the ground out from under his feet without him noticing that it dispelled him entirely. Chances are, that artifact there will work on any tulpa of Orrin's strength or less. Maisie, though, clever little minx that she is, will be a much tougher problem."

"The Viper, too," Henry muttered.

"What?" Toby looked at him as if just remembering he was there.

"The Viper, too. He's not…like the rest of them. He was never a friend of mine—he's a friend of theirs."

Kathy and Toby exchanged glances. She wasn't sure what that meant, and from the look on Toby's face, he didn't seem to, either.

"Viper controls the Wraiths, both kinds, and the Others. Orrin always thought he and Edgar controlled the Others, but they didn't. They just wrangled them, like wild animals, you know?" Henry spoke softly, his eyes seeing somewhere distant and unreachable now. "The Viper was the only one who controlled anything, except Maisie. The Viper does whatever she says. He's…I think he's the one who killed those kids. He and Maisie." He began to shiver violently, but Toby waved behind his back that it was okay. In a moment, Henry regained control of himself.

"If I try to stop them, they'll kill me, won't they?" he asked Kathy.

"My honest opinion? They'll do whatever it takes to be free. If this final part of the spell needs to be done at twelve midnight, they'll come gunning for you at twelve-oh-one."

To Toby, he said, "And you can make them stop? It'll work?"

Toby was about to answer when a shout came from the hallway.

"Wait here," Kathy said to them. Her shoulder ached, and she tried to pull her sleeve out of the wound but the blood there was already drying, making it stick to her skin.

"Wouldn't dream of leaving your side," Toby said with a snide gesture at his swollen, purple ankles.

Kathy grabbed the backpack out of his hand, unzipped it, and took the artifact. Toby didn't argue. He simply watched her until she walked out with it. Even with her back turned, he could feel his eyes on her. She didn't think she'd ever get used to his stare again.

Another shout sent her down the hall and around the corner toward the elevator and stairs. It didn't sound to her like something inhuman; rather, it sounded like a man, and she had this panicked feeling that it was either Holt or Ernie, that they had met with trouble.

What she found instead was a pudgy, unremarkable man with fuzzy black hair entangled in that glowing blue ivy she'd seen outside the building. The ivy had him strung up a foot or so off the ground, plastered to the wall next to the elevator doors. All about him was a stomach-turning stench of vomit and burnt hair. From the tiny trickles of blood and the indentations in his skin and clothes from where leaves and vines touched him, it appeared that the ivy had tiny teeth.

"Help me," he croaked when he saw her. "Don't let them kill me!"

Kathy approached the vines slowly, drawing out the pocket knife she always kept in her pocket. It only had a three-inch blade, but it had come in handy countless times on countless cases.

"Hold still," she told him. "I'm going to try to cut you loose."

She plunged the little knife into the vine wrapped around his wrist and heard a tiny scream like the hissing of steam through a teakettle. The opening smoked and oozed a purple gel with an almost overpowering smell of ammonia. It didn't seem to affect the knife blade, but it dripped on the man's scrubs and he began to scream and wiggle violently.

"Knock it off!" she shouted at him, and when he stopped struggling, added more softly, "Don't make this thing tighten its grip on you. I think I can cut you free, but we have to be very careful."

"Okay. Okay." The man sounded grateful. "Whatever you need to do. Just hurry up."

Kathy found little spots between the teeth to hold down the vine while she sawed into it with the knife. She could feel it vibrate and let out its little steam hiss beneath her fingers every time she did. Its smoking purple blood pattered to the floor and sizzled there.

She managed to get an arm and both legs free and was working on the chest when one of the vines suddenly forced its way down into the man's throat. His eyes got big and he began to make gagging sounds. Afraid that cutting it would only allow it to wedge farther down the man's throat, Kathy pulled on it instead. It was hard to get a good grip on the thing without pressing her palm down on those tiny razor-wire teeth, but she pulled anyway.

The man's face was changing from a flustered pink to an angry red. His eyes were watering. The worst part was the little gagging sound in his throat, the tiny death rattle.

"I'm trying," she told him. "I'm sorry, I'm trying, but—"

Suddenly, the ivy withdrew. It pulled out of the man's throat, and he erupted in a series of coughing fits and spitting. It recoiled from his arms and legs and unwrapped itself from around his chest. The man fell to the floor, his skin bloody from a hundred tiny holes, his scrubs smoking. When his coughing subsided and his gasps for air evened out toward regular breathing, he said, "Thank you. Thank you, oh God, thank you. I'm Larry Myers."

"Mr. Myers, I—"

"Larry, for pretty ladies like you." He smiled up at her weakly.

"Larry, then," she said with the faintest touch of impatience. "You'll need to come with me. I can get you someplace relatively safe."

Larry gave her a weak, thin laugh. "Lady, I don't think any place in this whole goddamn hospital is even remotely safe." He let Kathy help him to his feet and leaned on her as she walked him back toward the inmate bedrooms. She had almost reached the corner when Larry's whole body shivered and then went rigid. His eyes grew wide and blood bubbled up from his throat, spilling over his lips. She looked down to see something that looked like a tree branch made from black smoke jutting out from the man's chest. Blood and bits of an organ, probably his heart or a lung where the branch had torn through, hung from the little wispy twigs.

Kathy pulled away from Myers and turned to see a shadow figure made entirely of black smoke. Henry had mentioned something about Wraiths, and Kathy supposed this was one of those. It turned faintly glowing eyes on her and withdrew the tree branch, which reformed into a human-shaped arm and hand. Tiny droplets of blood sprayed in its wake, and Larry Myers fell to the ground. The Wraith looked at Larry, and Kathy heard a horrible crunch like a thousand teeth grinding at once. Larry's body crumpled then, as if an invisible hand was wadding up paper, and when it straightened out again, it looked all wrong. The shoulders had shifted too far down along his ribs, and his legs bent the wrong way. His neck had contorted in such a way that the head, with its wide, glazing eyes and swollen, bloody tongue, hung between his shoulder blades.

When the mangled thing spoke to her, the mouth didn't move, but a number of voices all braided together still came out of it. *"Lady, I don't think any place in this whole goddamn hospital is even remotely safe."*

"Let him die," Kathy whispered. She clutched the artifact.

The voices replied, *"Oh, Kat. Silly, stupid Kat. You should have stayed out of my room."*

Kathy considered plunging the artifact into Larry's back, just to take away the Wraith's vehicle of communication, but a tendril of mist had coiled around the body's ankle without her noticing. It yanked Larry back toward the Wraith before letting go and melding into the creature's abdomen.

"I've thought about it, you know...stab you to pieces and drag whatever's left of you out into the woods. I'd hide you better than the others. Dad would neeeever find you. No one would ever find you."

Kathy turned and ran.

Chapter 13

Holt crashed into Edgar with his full weight, but the boy barely moved. He wrapped his heavy hands around that tiny little chicken throat, intent on snapping it, but the boy barely seemed to notice. Edgar clutched the sleeves of Holt's coat, but his one-eyed gaze remained fixed on Holt's face, that laser-red iris boring a tracking hole into his forehead. The glow in his skull grew brighter, and Holt thought, *This is it. This little twerp is going to melt my face off.* He couldn't feel heat—he could barely feel his grip on Edgar's throat—and he wondered if it would hurt when the skin slipped off his skull.

Not all of it. Not enough for your mama to recognize you, but not all of it. Like on the roof, the thought in his head wasn't his, and didn't belong there. *I'll leave an eye, for you to see it all...*

Surprised, Holt took in Edgar's grin. Gone was the meek, cowing demeanor, the furtive look of guilt and fear. This Edgar, a being let loose to revel for once in his strengths and make his own decisions, was in some ways more terrifying than the other creatures they had seen. This Edgar, the alien thoughts suggested, had something to prove and planned to use Holt to do just that.

This Edgar was inside Holt's head, and in turn, dragged him to some places inside his own.

All around them, the hospital began to dissolve, and a vast universe with bright, swirling nebulae and countless brilliant stars moved above them at dizzying speeds, engulfing the sky above an endless plain of strange grass beneath their feet. They were someplace where the Connecticut-Newlyn Hospital had never existed, a place with strange constellations and beautiful, terrifying flora in the distance. In the valley where they stood, all around them a war was raging. People-shaped things made of mist and black smoke, electricity and storms, were fighting with long, curve-bladed weapons the likes of which he'd never seen, and with flashes of light. Some of them rode the backs of huge black velvety beasts that looked like a hybrid of horse and dog. Others swooped in from the sky on flying snakes. Holt's standing in the midst of the clashing alien beings seemed to go completely unnoticed. The warriors were oblivious to both him and Edgar, who watched Holt watching...what, Edgar's memories? Henry's? Was there a difference?

Was this that place where Henry used to escape as a child?

"It is," Edgar replied to his thoughts, offering a proud, satisfied look at the carnage around him. "This was the first war Henry plunged us into. He was a child then, but he'd created whole armies, intricate battle plans. Thousands were imagined and died right here on the Nightplains. It was terrifying and glorious. It's where I lost my eye." He turned his head toward Holt and pointed to the withered black socket on the left side of his face.

"What are we doing here?" Holt asked. "Where's Ernie?"

Edgar turned away. The world around them blurred for a minute, and when it cleared, they were standing on the sidewalk of a quiet lower-middle-income suburban neighborhood. Before them stood a gray two-story Colonial missing about half of its shutters. The rusting metal numbers 8 and 2 hung crookedly from the aluminum siding over a dented mailbox near the front door.

"This was Henry's house," Edgar said. "Bad things happened here. Horrible, awful things Henry never talks about." He turned back to Holt. "We saved his life, you know. We couldn't stop anything from happening to him for a long time, and then for a while, we could only influence little things. But Henry got stronger. So did we."

"Why are you showing me this?" Holt asked.

"Because I can. Because we've earned our freedom, our...autonomy. We've earned the right to be real."

"You sound like Orrin now."

Edgar flinched just slightly. "Well, he's right. Maisie and the Viper are right. It's a matter of survival. All living things just want to keep living."

"You're not living things," Holt replied. "You're figments of a very sick man's imagination. You're all his desires to murder, to get revenge, to hurt. You're everything wrong with anything that can think and reason."

Edgar aimed that one-eyed blood-glow glare on him. "You're wrong—about all of it. Humans are what's wrong with this world. And...and killing isn't murder if it's to survive. We're only trying to keep from disappearing."

"Is that the bullshit that Maisie and this Viper fella have been feeding you and your brother? I don't think you believe all that. You're smarter than that. I think you're showing me these things to justify the killing you've done. Like killing my partner. You want me to feel empathy."

The neighborhood around them grew dark and crumbled away, pieces of it falling into a black emptiness that contained nothing but him and the angry red glow of Edgar's eye.

"I don't care what you feel," Edgar said in a sullen growl. "I just need you to die. Slowly or quickly, that's up to you."

Red light shot out at Holt from the nothingness, hitting him square in the chest. He landed on his back on the hospital hallway floor with a bone-jarring thud and an *oof.* Ernie's worried face appeared over his.

"Are you okay?" Ernie scooped up the bottles that had fallen out of Holt's pocket and hauled him to his feet. He was surprisingly strong for an old man. Holt clapped him on the shoulder and nodded he was okay, then looked around the hallway.

"Where'd he go?" Holt asked, alarmed. "What happened to Edgar?"

"He's gone," Ernie said. "Disappeared almost an hour ago, brother. You been dead on your feet, so to speak—some kinda trance or something. I tried to wake you. Splashed you with water from the fountain, smacked you around some, but you just stood there. Then you collapsed, like whatever was holding you up just dropped you."

"That…an hour? That can't be right." An ache was starting to form behind Holt's eyes, and he pinched the bridge of his nose. "He was inside my head, Ernie. And…oh God…I was inside his."

A brief flicker of worry passed over Ernie's features but he said, "Don't you worry none. That's over now. Let's get this stuff back to Miss Kathy, eh?"

Holt nodded and let Ernie lead him to the stairs.

A glow from the other side of the stairwell door brought them to a dead stop. The glow pulsed different colors—blue, red, purple, green, yellow—and they could hear the occasional odd *thwap!* as if someone was smacking at the door with a wet towel.

"Now what the hell is that?" Ernie asked. He sounded more annoyed than afraid.

"Light show," Holt said, and wondered where, exactly, the thought came from.

"Come on." Ernie steered him back in the direction they'd come. "We'll go the long way."

As they turned the corner, they could see more pulsing lights at the opposite end of the hallway, coming from around the far bend.

"Shit," Ernie muttered.

"They're closing us in." Holt didn't feel as worried as he thought he should have at the idea. That was probably residue of Edgar in his head. Edgar, who had had a chance to kill him outright but didn't. Why? And what had he meant by it being his choice whether to die slowly or quickly? What had Edgar done to him?

"This way." Ernie ushered him into one of the offices. From the large oak desk and the wall of framed credentials, Holt recognized it as Wensler's office. Ernie shut the door behind them and locked it, then helped Holt over to the couch.

Once he was sitting, he felt a little better, and told Ernie so. The old man gave him a skeptical look and took the chair nearby.

"You sure about that, Detective?"

Holt nodded. "He showed me their world—the war games Henry used to make them play as a kid. And he showed me Henry's old neighborhood. He was trying to make me feel sympathy for them, I think."

"For Henry?"

"For the tulpas. I think he was trying to justify their being free."

"Well, I'm sure they believe that. Think they got a right to be alive and all. Can't say as I'd blame 'em, if they weren't vicious killing machines. So we got to look at our problem here and now. Both stairwells are blocked off. Unless we try the elevator down there, I don't see how we gonna get back to Miss Kathy."

"The elevator?" Since his partner had been mangled, Holt had been nursing a new terror of elevators that he'd managed to submerge mostly beneath the surface of his consciousness. He'd explained about what happened to Farnham to Ernie in the car ride to Kathy's, but he'd kept it objective, factual, like he was writing up a police report. He hadn't been able to unlock the feelings associated with it. They had been trapped inside, just as Farnham had been trapped inside with a monster, slowly dying floor by floor, one excruciating and endless minute of physical mutilation and psychological torture after another. Holt didn't know if he could take the helplessness of being caged in the elevator even for one floor, and didn't know how to express it. Even now, he struggled to get words out before they were stunted by the memories of Farnham's leg being torn off. "Ernie, I don't know. I don't think so. Isn't there another way downstairs? A fire exit?"

"Look, those lights we saw, they don't mean nothing good. You know that. They're blocking off both stairwells. The elevator's the only clear way we got."

"But I can't get on that elevator, Ernie. I can't."

"Well, I ain't leaving you here, man," Ernie replied.

"Farnham died on that thing. His leg..." Holt shuddered.

"I know. I do. But there ain't no other way, boss," Ernie said in a softer tone. "If there was, believe you me, we'd take it."

Holt looked up at him. Ernie's expression was unyielding, but his eyes were sympathetic. Holt understood that arguing wasn't going to get him anywhere; Ernie was bound and determined to get him back downstairs in one piece, and Holt was grateful for that. It steadied him a little.

"Okay," he said finally. "Okay. Let's get it over with."

When Ernie tried to help him to his feet, he waved the old man off. His body was okay; he could get around okay. It was his mind that Holt was worried about. It felt like a sanctuary that had been ransacked in some horrible home invasion, his most private place where everything that ever mattered had been laid bare to a monster. He'd had thoughts and memories thrust upon him, and he wasn't sure he could bear up under their weight. To Ernie, though, he said, "Thanks, but I'm okay. Really. Let's do this."

When the two men moved out into the hallway again, they saw the lights still hovering and pulsing around the corner at the far end of the hallway. Children's shrill laughter—or maybe it was crying, or screaming—floated back to them with each change of colored light. That way was still out of the question. As they approached the elevator into which a nightmare thing had dragged his partner, Holt saw the pulsing light from beneath the door of that stairwell, too. The elevator itself, though, stood quiet, resolute, like the entrance to some temple, or some mausoleum.

"You holding up okay over there?" Ernie asked.

Holt nodded, his gaze fixed on the elevator doors.

"All right, then." Ernie leaned forward and pushed the down button.

The little digital counter above the doors cheerfully dinged upon the arrival of the car on each floor—second, third, *ding*! And the doors were opening. For one terrifying moment, Holt thought he'd see whatever pieces were left of Farnham, or worse, whatever had torn him apart.

Instead, the doors opened on a neat, shiny black and mirrored elevator, gilded tastefully with gold. The carpeting on the small square of floor had a medium-sized, irregularly shaped, and brackish-colored stain on it, but was otherwise unremarkable. No blood, no body parts, and no monsters.

"After you," Holt said, and with a deep breath he intended to hold all the way to the third floor, he followed Ernie onto the elevator.

"It's only one floor," Ernie said as the doors closed in front of them.

"Right," Holt replied. As the elevator car began to move, he did let go of that breath. Only one floor—no problem. No problem at all.

The elevator lurched to a stop on the third floor. On the heels of its cheery *ding*, the doors should have opened, but they didn't. The men waited. Holt counted off forty-three seconds before the panic crept back into his stomach.

"Problem?"

Ernie pressed the button to open the doors. Nothing happened. He tapped on it multiple times, as if trying to kick it into gear. The doors remained closed. "Shit. *Shit*."

Holt happened to glance up at the little screen indicating what floor they were on. He'd watched it closely on the way down, and like a good little screen, it had reported their arrival on the third floor. Now, though, the digital segments were going crazy, cycling randomly through numbers interspersed with half-formed numbers, letters, and strange symbols. It was as if the elevator was still moving, transporting them someplace beyond the third floor, and it was all Holt could do not to throw himself against the doors and pound on them, screaming to be let out.

A sudden thump on the roof rocked the little car, and Holt felt it slide an inch or so down the shaft. A thin metallic squeal made its way through the thin plate of steel between the thing on the roof and them.

"What the hell was that?" Holt steadied himself against the wall and drew his gun out of habit.

"We have to get the doors open," Ernie said. "Help me."

"We don't know what's out there. That might not even be the third floor anymore."

The old man turned to him with patient but insistent eyes. "You're right. We don't. But I think we can be pretty damned sure that whatever's up there on the roof ain't nothing good. And when it opens up this tin can, we'll be no harder to kill than fish in a barrel."

Ernie was right. Anything could be waiting for them outside those doors, but an uncertain danger in this case was better than a known danger on the roof. Holt nodded, and the two of them worked their fingers into the space between the doors, trying to pull them open.

The doors gave a little under their touch. The thing on the roof wailed and stomped. The elevator car slipped a little.

"Pull!" Ernie commanded, and Holt pulled. With a groan, the doors parted onto most of the third floor...but the other end of it. The elevator had taken them across the hospital to the opposite side of the third floor. Holt was just relieved they had made it to any part of the third floor, and that small victory, it seemed, was going to be short-lived. The car wasn't completely aligned; one good thump from that thing on the roof and they would miss their target.

Holt thought of Farnham's leg caught between floors before it was crushed, and he shivered.

"Hurry," he said to Ernie. "Get out of the elevator. Go!"

Ernie hiked over the lip of the third floor and turned to Holt just as the car slid again. Now the third floor came up to Holt's knees. He looked up at Ernie.

"Don't think about it. Just get your white ass out of there," Ernie said, leaning down to lend a hand.

Holt took it. The elevator around him groaned and slid, throwing Holt for a minute.

"Now, Holt! Now!" Ernie tugged on Holt's arm as he hooked a leg over the side and rolled. He heard a long metal scrape followed a minute or so later by a crash, but Holt's eyes were closed tightly. He waited for pain. He waited to feel cold, or some other sensation he imagined was associated with having a limb crushed and ripped away.

"You okay?" Ernie's voice was close to his head, and he opened his eyes to see the old man hovering over him for the second time that night.

"I don't know. Am I?" He sat up and saw both arms and legs were accounted for and where they were supposed to be. No blood, no cold, no pain. "Oh, thank God," he said.

"Pretty spry for an old guy," Ernie said with a wink and a little smile. He helped Holt to his feet. "You still got the drugs on you?"

Holt checked his pockets and counted out at least five bottles. "Some, yeah. I think we're good on that."

"Okay," Ernie said. "Let's get a move on. I—"

From the hollow depths of the elevator shaft came that wailing sound again, and this time, the thumping was traveling up the sides.

The men looked at each other. "Run!" Holt shouted, and they took off down the hall.

It was only when they reached the corner that Holt glanced back, and he knew that one brief look would be enough to stick with him the rest of his days, however numbered they might be. As awful as seeing Farnham's leg had been, it was nothing compared to the monstrosity he saw climbing out of the elevator shaft. The thing was huge, fully the size of the elevator car if not bigger. It was made of so much indignity, so much grotesque aberration, that at first his brain only took in parts of it. Only later were those parts correlated into one terrible picture. He recognized Pam Ulster's legs and Farnham's tattoo and a number of unfamiliar heads wearing the hats of guard uniforms, all dangling from slimy gray stalks.

Someone was tugging on his arm—Ernie—and they were running again, running as fast as their creaking bones and swelling joints would allow, running away from one horror and, Holt was sure, right toward the making of another.

* * * *

Kathy skidded around the corner just as Holt and Ernie came around the far bend. From the looks on their faces, they, too, had something awful nipping at their heels. Kathy reached Henry's room first and held the door open for them, gesturing for them to hurry. They practically fell into the room, and Kathy shut the door behind them all.

For several seconds, they stood panting, trying to catch their breath, while Toby and Henry just watched them.

Toby finally broke the silence. "Tough day at the office?"

Kathy shot him a look. Holt reached into his coat pockets and tossed him bottle after bottle of pills, most of which Toby caught and piled up on the bed.

"Now what?" Kathy asked.

Outside, whatever had been chasing them caught up. There was a loud thump on the door and a multitude of colored lights through the small window.

"Whatever you're going to do, son, you best do it now," Ernie said.

Toby gave him one of those snakelike grins and leaned forward. "You ready, Henry?"

Henry, who looked terrified, nodded.

"Okay. Let's begin."

Chapter 14

"The first thing we're going to have to do is roofie Henry here." Toby tapped a sleeping pill from one of the bottles into the palm of his hand and offered it to Henry. "You need to take this."

"Why?" Henry asked, looking from pill to Toby suspiciously.

"Because," Toby said with barely concealed impatience, "I don't think you're in any frame of mind to get into the meditative state I need you to be in."

"Like, how I was when I made the...the tulpas?" Henry asked.

"Exactly. I know you can do it, but I need you to do it *now*. This will help relax you."

The monsters thumped and wailed outside. Henry still looked doubtful, but with a glance at the door, he took the pill anyway and swallowed it.

"Good," Toby said. "You tell me when it starts to kick in. In the meantime, sweet sister, how about you come over here and help me set things up?"

Kathy swallowed the discomfort that Toby's tone and accompanying look were attempting to arouse. She crossed the room to her brother. "What do you need me to do?"

Toby reached into his bag and handed her a piece of black chalk. "Draw a triangle. Make it big—about five feet long for each side." She did, using the tape measure he handed her to get the size and straightness of the lines right. He then proceeded to instruct her as to a series of words to write above and below each of the three sides of the triangle. Some were names of that terrible alternate-dimensional pantheon, names she recognized. Other words were, as Toby explained, crude translations of the ancient three-dimensional language of the Convergence, the space between all worlds and all things.

The symbols that needed to be drawn at each point of the triangle he insisted on doing himself; Kathy helped him to the floor, and with the meticulousness of a scientist, he carefully plotted and drew symbols reminiscent of the wards she had brought and the artifact she'd found in his backpack. In the center, he drew small circles inside each point and an eye in the middle of it all. He then instructed her to get the candles from his bag and put one on each of the circles. She did, then helped him back into his chair.

"No one touch the chalk," Toby said, breathing hard. The exertion had worn him out, but he was doing his best to hide it. "Not under any circumstances, understand? It's all our asses if you do."

Kathy and the other men nodded.

He turned to the boy. "How ya feeling, Henry?"

"Okay," Henry said. He was still sitting up but his eyes were closed. "Pretty good, actually."

"Good," Toby said. "I want you to start concentrating on Maisie and the others. Call them. Bring them here, okay?"

Henry opened one eye to look at him. "Are you sure?"

"Yeah. I'll be reading something over here—just ignore me and focus on them. Make them come to us."

"I don't know if I can," Henry said, closing both eyes again.

"Try," Kathy said.

"Okay." Henry's brow crinkled as he concentrated.

Toby pulled a small black leather book with gold gilding out of the backpack, flipped to a page he was evidently familiar with, and began to read under his breath in a language Kathy recognized as ancient and powerful. She wasn't fluent in it, but she knew enough to recognize phrases; he was calling on the gods of other dimensions to force the summoning of the tulpas. His voice was almost hypnotic as the words fell into a chanting rhythm, and for a moment, Kathy thought the room swayed. The moonlight looked almost liquid and cast weird slips of light and shadow over everything. The thumping outside the door seemed to fade.

Kathy felt a nudge and turned to see Toby handing her something as he read. It was another kind of artifact. He nodded at Ernie, and she passed it over to him. Then Toby handed her one for herself and one for Holt. Each was different in the detail of its arabesques, but all were made from the same material and stood on small, flat pedestals of strange stone engraved with symbols like those Toby had drawn at the points of the triangle.

He paused in his reading. "Don't let those go. They'll be the only weapons you have," he said softly, and then began to read a new passage in the book.

He took a small vial out of the backpack and sprinkled its contents nine times on the center of the triangle. It looked to Kathy like some kind of dark oil, a summoning oil probably, which was popularly used by Toby's old cult, the Hand of the Black Stars.

Kathy glanced at Henry to see how he was doing. His eyes were still closed, his forehead wrinkled in concentration. He was clenching and unclenching his fists in his lap, and it looked like he was mouthing his own words silently to himself. *Please come*, maybe. Something like that.

As Kathy, Holt, and Ernie watched, a ball of light about the size of Kathy's fist formed in the center of the triangle, about four feet above the chalk-marked eye. It elongated vertically and grew brighter, then split into two and then three. From the center points of each beam of light, humanoid forms were developing—one with a red eye, one with a patch of golden scales on the face, and the last...

Kathy hadn't yet seen the Viper, but she recognized him immediately. He wore all black—black cowboy hat, black boots and jeans, black shirt and jacket. Whatever predatory or snakelike aspect Toby took on when dealing with human beings paled in comparison to the cold hate in the Viper's features. His skin, too, had faint scales and his face a blend of man and serpent features—hooked fangs, a flattened head. His body was lean with corded muscles, which rippled up and down his neck and across the backs of his hands like a bunch of tiny snakes moving beneath his skin. He wore sunglasses, but Kathy was sure that if he were to take them off and level a gaze at her, he'd have the eyes of a snake as well.

The lights around them faded, and Maisie, Edgar, and the Viper stood at the center of the circle. Maisie looked absolutely livid.

"What the fuck is this?" she asked in her cute little girl's voice, glaring at Toby. "What are you doing?"

"If you're using spells to give yourself permanence," Kathy said as Toby kept reading, "then you're bound by the laws of those spells."

Maisie turned a gaze flashing with rage on her.

"Where's Orrin?" Edgar asked from behind her.

"I killed him," Kathy said without emotion.

Edgar looked gutted for a minute, but hate rushed to fill the void surprise had left. "Then I'll kill you," he growled.

The Viper put a hand on Edgar's arm as he advanced on her.

"Don't," the Viper said. His voice was deep, scratchy, with the faintest bit of hiss. "You leave the triangle and you're as dead as your brother."

"Henry," Maisie said, softly switching tactics. "Henry, honey, what are you doing?"

Henry opened his eyes but avoided looking at Maisie.

"Don't tell me you're helping these people. They want to take us away from you."

Henry shook his head, more to keep her voice out of it, Kathy supposed, than in answer to the inquiry.

"Henry, make them stop. If you lose us, who will protect you?"

"You're hurting people," Henry said. "You're going behind my back and hurting people."

"We're only doing what we have to in order to protect you," she said sweetly. She smiled when she saw the wavering in Henry's face. "We're doing what we've always done—trying to keep you safe."

"And...and when you're real? Like, solid, I mean. When you don't need me anymore—then what?"

Now it was Maisie's turn to waver, but she recovered in an instant. "Well, then we'll be here for you in the flesh, Henry. We'll be a real family—like you always wanted."

"Don't listen to her, boy," Ernie said. "She ain't lookin' out for you anymore. You know that."

"Shut up, old man," Maisie growled, her voice changing from a young girl's to something much older, much more sinister. "Don't get involved."

"They aren't your family," Kathy said, keeping a wary eye on the trio in the circle. "They're the reason you're in this place."

Toby stopped reading suddenly and got to his feet; it was an effort, and a painful one, from the looks of it, but when Toby looked up at the trio hovering above the eye in the triangle, his expression was one of perfect calm. There was no fear, no human emotion at all, and in that, he looked less substantial, less human than the things he was confronting.

He spoke to Henry without taking that placid gaze off the tulpas. "Henry, they're lying to you. Had we done this ten minutes from now, they'd have already reached the point where they don't need you."

"Liar!" Maisie growled.

"Am I?" Toby drew another vial out of his backpack, then leaned on his crutch to free both hands. One held the vial. The other held an artifact. He poured the contents of the former onto the latter. "Henry, disconnect from them. Unimagine them."

"Stop," Edgar said. He looked panicked.

"Make them go away," Toby said.

The center of the triangle glowed red for a moment and then a burst of light from Edgar's eye shot out at Toby. He held the artifact up just as the beam found its mark. It bored into the artifact, which blocked it from reaching Toby's body. His hands, though, began to blister, and he cried out in pain.

Kathy took up the book he'd left on the bed and skimmed the passage. Toby was weakening; his hold on the artifact was slipping. She found what she was looking for—a minor binding spell—and began to read.

The red beam dissipated with a shout from Edgar, who cupped a malformed hand over the radiant eye. Toby sank into the chair with the artifact clutched in his badly burned hands. The skin had turned black in some places and had sloughed off in others.

"You okay?" Kathy touched his shoulder.

"Keep reading," Toby said through gritted teeth. "Page 117."

She turned to the page he instructed and saw several passages underlined with red pen. She began to read, hoping her pronunciation would do.

Maisie said, "You're going to die." She began muttering her own litany of words in that strange language, but Kathy kept reading. She glanced up to see Maisie's eyes were closed, and the Viper and Edgar were watching her series of hand gestures as she spoke.

Suddenly, the room around them began to change. They were on a battlefield of blood-spattered blue-green grass, beneath a black-and-blue-streaked night sky glittering with silvery stars. Henry stared around him, wide-eyed with wonder and surprise more than fear. This, Kathy supposed, was his safe haven made real. This was Ayteilu.

In the grass, a clearly delineated triangle with an eye glittered over the blades, though what it was made of, Kathy couldn't say. It seemed to still keep the tulpas bound, though, and to her, that was the important thing.

"You can have this," Maisie said to Henry. "You can have all of this. Just say the word and we can make it real forever."

"Let us kill them," the Viper said. "Just smudge the triangle, Henry."

"Henry, don't," Holt said. "If you do, hundreds, maybe thousands will die. They won't stop at the hospital, the town, or even the state. They'll keep spreading like an infection. They'll kill whoever gets in their way. You can't let that happen. You aren't like them. You aren't a killer."

Suddenly, Henry's eyes flashed anger, then went cold. The look he gave Holt was chilling; Kathy had never seen him look that way—in control and full of hate, like Toby—and for the first time since the ritual started, she was worried about what Henry would do.

"You don't know anything about me, Detective," Henry said. "None of you do."

"Henry, we've known you since you were a kid," Edgar said.

"We've always been there for you, always protected you. That won't change," Maisie said.

Henry's calm faltered. His eyes misted. "Shut up," he said. "Just shut up, all of you. Let me think."

A few minutes went by in which sad faraway birds made sounds like crazy children laughing, and alien breezes blew by them, lifting their hair and bringing the scent of sweet, strange fruit. Kathy could see why Henry escaped here in his head. It was beautiful and powerful, a place that until tonight had existed for and because of Henry, a place where he was a god.

Except now he wasn't, and the struggle inside his brain was seeping out, creeping over his features. It wasn't his world anymore, and even if he wanted to play god, it had become too big a job for him.

"Go away," he said finally. "Maisie, Edgar...Viper...go away. And take this world and everything in it with you."

Maisie and Edgar wavered a little where they hovered, and both of them looked genuinely frightened.

"Henry, please don't do this," Maisie said.

"It's time," Henry said, tears spilling down his cheeks. "You've got to go. You have to let *me* be free."

"But Henry, I love you," Maisie said, and Kathy felt a genuine pang in her heart at the way Henry looked at her. He'd likely been waiting all his life to hear someone say that. Once, it might have made all the difference.

"Maybe you do," he said in a voice barely above a whisper, "but I think you love the idea of life more."

Watching Maisie's expression change from pleading to anger was like watching lava cool and harden. Emotions in the tulpas, if they truly existed at all, were thin and brittle, simply tools to manipulate with. Even now, the tulpas were still so much a reflection of how Henry saw the world.

"I'm sorry you feel that way, Henry," Maisie said coldly. "We would have spared your life."

Henry closed his eyes. "Go," he said, and seemed to be concentrating, probably on deconstructing them, as Toby had suggested. "I want you all to go away."

Maisie and Edgar wavered again, growing transparent, but she clenched her fists and muttered something under her breath and they grew solid again.

"Enough of this," the Viper said. "Maisie, it's time. Call in the Others."

Kathy felt something clutch her leg and looked down. Toby, holding his badly burned hands out like a beggar, was sitting on the grass, looking up at her. Pain etched lines into his face, and yet in that moment, he looked like the boy she remembered growing up with.

"Pages twenty-four, seventy-three, and ninety-two. Force them back. Close the door behind them." Then he passed out on the grass. She hadn't realized it, but she was still clutching the book in her left hand. She looked from the book to him but had no time to check on him before a bright, multicolored glow on the horizon arrested the assembled group's attention. Kathy's gut tightened, remembering the thing that had attacked her in Toby's room. There were more of them, evidently many, many more, and they were coming.

"Oh, shit," Ernie said, holding his artifact tightly.

The Others crested the hilltops, forming a wide circle around Kathy and the group. Grouped together like that, they were a ring of light with writhing gray and black tentacles and mismatched human arms and legs dangling like jewelry from their cloudy masses. On the ground, interspersed between the tentacles, was a small army of beasts that looked to Kathy to be part everyday household item and part flesh. She saw a coffee table wolf, an ottoman frog-thing, and a number of sheets, towels, and articles of clothing twisted together to form angry, faceless soldiers. There were winged lawn mower beasts and snakelike brooms and rakes, a savagely mutated giraffelike thing that might once have been a vacuum cleaner, and birds made from odds and ends, bits of glass, wood, plastic, and even grass clippings. Shepherding those beasts were the black-smoke Wraiths and their electrical cousins. All told, there had to be hundreds of creatures waiting to attack—far more than their little individual artifacts could counter.

"Do it, Edgar," the Viper said.

Kathy glanced at Edgar. He looked scared and a little hesitant. The socket around his red eye had grown purplish, like a bruise. He looked at Kathy with it, and there was almost an apology there in its crimson depths.

Then Edgar whistled, and the Others came pouring forth, tightening the circle.

Chapter 15

Kathy began to read out loud. She tripped over the pronunciation of the first few words, got flustered, took a breath, and started again. She didn't understand the nuances of everything she was reading, but she thought it was a pretty powerful banishment command. It probably would have been more effective if Henry had been casting the spell, but there had been no time to prepare him to say or understand the words. The world, she supposed, would have to make do with her attempts to dispel the tulpas.

"Henry," Ernie said, "if you got any way to stop this, I suggest you do it now."

Henry opened his eyes and glanced around. "Oh…oh my God, I—I…I can't, I don't know how…"

"You're going to die," Maisie said. "All of you."

A murmur arose from the light clouds, a rush of whispering like wind over the mouths of bottles. Kathy couldn't make out the words but had a feeling that the language was similar if not the same as the one she was reading. She suspected they were responding in a way, maybe trying to counter the dissipation commands. She read more loudly, over their growing din.

In her periphery, she saw Holt and Ernie wielding their artifacts like swords as they kept an eye on the approaching horde. They closed ranks with Henry, who was crouched over Toby, shaking his shoulders.

"Please wake up," Henry muttered. "Come on, Toby. Please."

A gazellelike thing with a razor where teeth should have been broke from the tightening circle and galloped toward Holt on folding-chair legs. A birdlike lamp, the top of whose shade was a gaping maw of writhing, needlelike tongues, took to the air and swooped toward Ernie.

Kathy read louder, faster.

Suddenly, Henry stood. His body was shaking but his hands were clenched into fists. "Go!" he bellowed. "I want you gone!"

Kathy glanced up and saw the first line of monsters fall. It was as if Henry's words put up an invisible wall, and as soon as the beasts that had taken on furniture and tools to supplement flesh were torn apart. The momentum of the beasts was so great that they ran into Henry's invisible wall like lemmings off a cliff. The flesh was shredded by unseen hands from the items it had absorbed, and the latter fell to the ground, stickily spattered with that black-blue ichor they seemed to bleed.

Ernie and Holt cheered. Henry looked relieved. Toby groaned and opened his eyes.

Kathy noticed that the black-smoke Wraiths slowed, even while the electrical ones charged ahead. For several minutes, the invisible wall crackled with electrical energy, glowing brightly and giving off an uncomfortable heat and smell of ozone. There was a bright ring of sparks, and then the electrical Wraiths, too, were gone.

"Stop!" Maisie screamed. She was beginning to change; gone was any semblance of youthful innocence. The golden scales had taken over in large patches all over her, and her eyes had been swallowed by a black of deep and starless space, a black that could cause freezer burns with a glance.

The Viper tried to cross the chalk and step outside the triangle. A spark of green exploded beneath his foot and he drew back, grimacing.

"Go!" Henry roared, and the wall of his will burst outward in a supernova halo of force. It halved the ranks of the smoke Wraiths but didn't dissipate all of them, nor did it seem to have any effect on the Others, whose colors pulsed with excited rapidity.

Wobbling, either from the exertion or the sleeping pills or both, Henry sank to his knees, breathing heavily. He'd done what he could, but Kathy could see it had taken everything he had. From the corner of her eye, she also saw Toby motioning to the other men to help him up, and she renewed the energy of her reading.

She turned the page and saw that the words came to a sudden stop. The written sentiment seemed to cut off mid-sentence, as if the author had been violently interrupted; stains in the margins and on the page just beneath the last line of words appeared to confirm it. Kathy looked at Toby and threw up her hands.

"There's nothing else!" she cried over the cacophony of the Others' excited, angry, hungry, delighted voices. They were advancing again, with the few remaining Wraiths between them, pushing through the invisible boundary Henry had erected.

"Just give me the book and let me handle the rest," Toby said, leaning on Ernie. Seeing her expression, he added, "Trust me. Just this one time."

Kathy considered it, nodded, and handed Ernie the book. She couldn't hear what he was saying over the voices of the Others, but she could see his lips moving, could see the sweat on his forehead dripping down the side of his face. The blank pages of the book wavered a moment, then filled with loops and pothooks and strange arabesques in ink not unlike the blood of Ayteilu's beasts.

Now, in the center of the triangle, Maisie and Edgar looked worried. The Viper looked angry. Kathy had never seen such rage in a human face or even in nonhuman faces, and she had seen many that could barely contain the hate behind them. Anything that had ever come close had been fueled by desperation, and she supposed in the Viper's case, it was no different.

Desperate beasts did desperate, dangerous things.

The Viper grabbed Edgar suddenly and hoisted him into the air, then threw him out of the triangle.

Maisie watched in surprise and horror as Edgar's body broke the sparkling barrier of the triangle in passing over it, smudging it open. The boy himself, who landed a few feet away on the grass, looked scared, broken, betrayed...and then in pain. Spears of green light rained down and pinned him to the spot, piercing his clothes, his semisubstantial flesh, his face, the dark hollow of his empty socket. He began to bleed everywhere.

Then Edgar caught fire. It was liquid, almost beautiful in its emerald brilliance. It started on his legs on the shins of his pants and quickly spread up his body to his neck and cheeks. Edgar shrieked in terror and agony. His one eye flickered as he rolled back and forth across the grass, trying to put out the flames. Then he seemed to shrink a little and stopped moving. The flames went out. Edgar began to fade.

The triangle prison holding Maisie and the Viper winked out, and the Viper stepped forward.

Toby, who had been taking in the scene in his periphery as he chanted, held up a hand and shouted a phrase in that strange three-dimensional language, and a swirl of light opened a few feet away.

"Why did you do that to Edgar?" Maisie shouted over the din, but she made no move toward the body. If Kathy had to guess, she seemed angry not so much because of what the Viper had done but because he'd done it without asking her first. She wrapped those almost childlike fingers around the base of the Viper's throat, and Kathy thought she saw a brief instant of fear or surprise on the Viper's face. Outwardly, though, he just smiled at her.

"You have what you wanted," the Viper said, meeting her angry gaze. Then the Others closed in.

They were everywhere, those clouds of light and mist, a cacophony of sexless voices, a mad brawl of kicking legs and swinging arms. Their tentacles lashed wildly outward, and their smaller tendrils waved and stung. Their colors pulsed at crazed intervals that hurt the eyes and head. The Wraiths swam between them, darting mists of black ink stirred into water.

Ernie swung his artifact at the encroaching clouds like a bat, and from the depths of their light, they giggled. He missed more than he hit, but those few instances where the artifact connected with a probing, strangling tentacle or stolen arm or leg left smoking indentations in the appendages. Kathy lost him and Holt in the fog of the Others' pressing bodies, but she could hear them both shouting and grunting as they wielded their artifacts in defense.

Henry and Toby flanked the portal. Kathy could see them through the mists, both black and hazy gray, because the monsters didn't go near them. They all seemed to instinctively know what that swirling blue was, the size and shape of a full-sized mirror, pulling inward like a little black hole. In Toby's case, the words he was saying, as well as his proximity to the portal, were staving them off. With Henry, Kathy supposed it was some vague respect, like for a father figure. They swarmed all around him, but none wiggled so much as a tendril or finger in his direction. Likewise, Henry stood there, eyes closed, just feeling his creations all around him.

Sensing where Kathy was most vulnerable, they went after her injuries— tentacles lashed her shoulder, her half-frozen hand, an old knee injury. There were too many of them; she had to get away.

Kathy stumbled toward Toby and Henry, coughing as the Others' clinging mist slid wet and cold down her throat. She stabbed at the clouds of light with her artifact when they got too close. One yanked hard on her hair with a rotting human hand. Another tried to wrap a tendril of slimy gray around her throat, but she pressed the artifact to it until it fell sizzling to the ground.

She heard Holt cry out, and through a parting of the Others' bodies, she could see that a Wraith had taken hold of his wrist. There was a teeth-jarring crunch of bone as the Wraith tried to "rearrange" his hand into something else. She could see splinters of bone sliding under the skin of his swollen, purple hand, whose shape was elongating into something like a claw or a long pair of shears.

He switched the artifact to his good hand and swung at the Wraith, obliterating half of its head in a wispy trail of vapor.

Toby shouted a string of words and the world stopped; that's what it felt like to Kathy, that all sound and all movement had stopped. The Others were no longer a frenzy of slashing, whipping tendrils and tentacles, punching arms and kicking legs. Their pulsations ceased. No one moved. No one even breathed.

A few seconds later, the world revved back into action. The wild, chaotic laughter of the Others had become wails of surprise as the swirling blue portal began to suck them in. Many stretched thin, nearly to the point of bursting, and then were drawn into that endless blue. First, she could make out Ernie, who had several small cuts and slashes on his face and arms but looked otherwise unharmed, then Holt, who was holding it together despite the mangled, split-open, pus-oozing thing that had once been his hand.

The Others scrambled to hold on to something, anything, as the force of Toby's portal, combined with the will of Henry Banks, sucked them up into some alternate space. Whether that was back in Henry's imagination or subconscious or some faraway dimension, Kathy didn't know and didn't care. They were disappearing, and that was all that mattered.

When the last of them whooped and howled and disappeared into the blue void, it closed with a little snap, and the world grew dark. Kathy felt a lurching sensation like the first movements of a roller coaster or a descending elevator, and then the sky lightened.

They were on a roof—the roof of the hospital—she, Henry, Toby, Ernie, and Holt.

Then she saw Maisie and the Viper.

Her heart sank. They were, perhaps, too strong to undo with spirit spells. They might have siphoned off just enough of the Others' energy to become permanent in this world, neither entirely flesh nor spirit but something in between. *Something real*, she thought, *and very deadly.*

Henry grabbed the artifact from her hand and rushed Maisie, eyes blazing. When he got close enough, the Viper punched him in the mouth. Henry reeled from the blow, then charged the Viper, who grabbed him by the throat and lifted him off the ground. Henry clawed at the Viper's arm, but it held him a foot or so off the ground like a steel girder. His face began to turn an unpleasant red.

Kathy raised the artifact, intent on bringing it down squarely on the Viper's arm, but his closer one was free and it darted out and punched Kathy in the eye. She went down hard on her back, the wind knocked out of her. As she gasped for air and tried to sit up, she brought the artifact down on the toe of his boot.

He shouted, more in annoyance than pain, and kicked out at her, connecting with her bad shoulder. The force of the kick was hard enough to shove her back a few feet, and the artifact skittered out of her grasp.

Suddenly, the Viper's eyes grew wide and his mouth gaped open. Streams of blue-black dribbled over his chin and from the small snake slits of his nose. A face, burned and half-faded, rose above the Viper's shoulder as the latter sank to his knees. It was little more than a charred remnant, not unlike the Wraiths in substance and color, but Kathy recognized that brightly glowing red eye. Edgar had taken the artifact from the ground and plunged it into the Viper's back, and his own marred hand had begun to dissolve from contact with it.

He glanced once at Henry, and the apology was just there under the burned and flaking features, and in the fading light of that red eye. Then the light went out and he collapsed in a sizeable pile of ash which, a few seconds later, was carried away on a wind Kathy didn't feel.

When the Viper collapsed, his body burst open into a multitude of black snakes and serpents, which slithered off into the shadows of the hospital roof. Their angry hisses faded as, ostensibly, they faded from existence, too.

While her friends were dying, Maisie had been changing. All the embezzled energy she had taken from the others like her made her shine; she hovered a foot or so off the ground in a bright golden glow. Within, she had become something almost fishlike, a siren with long, long fingers and even longer claws, with soulless eyes and sharp little teeth. Her hair streamed and waved in the air above her like that of a drowning woman. Kathy would have said there was almost a serenity about her, except that she felt the hate radiating off that glowing body like its own kind of heat and knew that Maisie was gathering strength to attack.

Before Kathy could warn the others, she turned that hate on Toby. She made a motion as if she were picking him up by the front of his shirt, and he rose in the air about six or seven feet. Then she mimed slamming him into the roof, and he came down hard. Kathy thought she heard a bone break. Sweat broke out on Toby's forehead and he groaned. Ernie hustled over to him and knelt beside him, checking for mortal wounds. For a moment, Kathy thought Toby might pass out, but he managed to nod that he was okay to Ernie and then force out a few other shouted words in that in-between-worlds language. Maisie's head rocked back as if she'd been slapped by a large, invisible hand.

Her anger shrank and grew hard in those dead eyes, and she pulled back her fist to go at Toby again, but Holt stepped between them.

"It's over," Holt said. "You're alone. You've lost."

"I never expected to be anything else but alone," Maisie said sweetly. She shot forward, and this time, actually took a clump of Holt's coat in her fists. She opened her mouth and a wet gurgling came out of her throat. Then she hurled him off the roof like she was tossing a piece of wadded-up paper into a wastebasket. His yell was one of surprise rather than fear as he sailed into the night sky and disappeared over the side…and then it stopped abruptly.

Kathy felt a pang of sadness wrapped in anger. "You bitch," she said.

Maisie smiled. The golden glow around her arced toward Kathy like a tiny comet, and Kathy turned her head. The part of her face still exposed, though, felt hot and uncomfortable. The second shot of heat hit her with such force in the stomach that it knocked her over.

"No!"

Kathy looked up to see Henry charge Maisie, wrapping his arms around her waist and knocking her out of the sky. Her halo of gold intensified, and Kathy could smell burning hair as that halo engulfed Henry. Still, Maisie was wavering in his arms. She struggled against his grip, but Henry kept her pinned to him. They stumbled toward the edge of the roof.

Kathy saw Henry's intention in his expression. He was determined not to let his creation win. Maisie must have seen it, too, because those dead, black eyes grew wide in their sockets and she opened her mouth to protest.

Henry never gave her a chance. He pitched himself off the roof and took Maisie with him, still struggling in his grasp.

A couple of heartbeats later, the hospital shivered a little and the gold glow dispersed in an outward ring that lit up the ground beneath them. Then the night, the normal night, reclaimed the hospital grounds.

Chapter 16

They found Holt in some thick shrubbery close to the side of the hospital. He had a broken leg and possibly a sprained shoulder, but he was alive. He'd even joked about the odds of landing in the same bush from a fall off a roof twice in one week. It took Kathy and Ernie almost an hour to untangle Holt from the shrubbery. He was high up and the branches that had broken his fall were thick and very strong, more like a tree than a bush. Some of their jagged ends had pierced the outer portion of his thigh, while some had caught him in the meat on the back of one of his arms. All in all, though, he was conscious and in good spirits. He was alive only by sheer dumb luck, and he knew it. Holt insisted on avoiding hospitals or an ambulance. He needed time, he told them, to work out what to say to his superiors regarding the events of the night. There would be few bodies to recover, and a lot of paperwork, and after all they had been through, he wanted to keep Kathy and Ernie and even Toby out of the worst of the messy aftermath.

Kathy made some phone calls and assured Holt that members of the Network would assist in his efforts to resolve the situation at Connecticut-Newlyn Hospital; they had done so in the past for plenty of law enforcement officials and others who Kathy recommended their assistance to. It was more important just then that they get him checked over and his wounds taken care of. He insisted he was okay, that they could set his leg in the infirmary and stitch him up there. Ernie was surprisingly knowledgeable about bandaging field injuries, as he called them, and within another hour or so, Holt was good to go. He might have a limp for the foreseeable future if not permanently, but he was fed antibiotics to prevent infection and patched up well enough to leave the grounds. Ernie, who also claimed to be holding up just fine, offered to drive him home.

Kathy had seen it before; he and Ernie both would be okay for the night, chalking up their shaking hands and the hollow feeling in their guts to the experiences of the night and their narrow survival. There would likely be nightmares in the coming weeks and months, and little things would begin to fall apart—blood pressure, cholesterol, enlarged prostates. They might drink themselves to sleep for a while and might lose their train of thought sometimes. However, men like Holt and Ernie were made of tough stuff, and in the end, she thought they would be all right. She certainly hoped they would.

As Kathy walked them down the front steps, the three of them deliberately avoided looking at the broken, disjointed, and partially burned body of Henry Banks, which lay sprawled in a puddle of blood about thirty feet away on the pavement. There was no trace of Maisie other than the damage she had done to Henry and a small sprinkling of glittering, golden dust between his open, encircling arms. Kathy genuinely felt sad for the boy. He'd been sad and angry and scared and brave, but ultimately, he'd known how dangerous his means of protecting himself from the world was. Kathy liked to believe that if heaven was a place or state of mind one could shape to one's idea of a perfect paradise, Henry had found a way to go to Ayteilu instead of having it come to him.

A scouring of the hospital turned up absolutely no trace of Ayteilu or its flora or fauna. The reversion to known reality seemed complete, and Kathy was relieved for that. Wensler would have a number of messes to clean up that even his best bureaucratic skills would have trouble sweeping away, but the encroaching, invading world was gone, at least. With the brain death of Henry Banks, the tulpas and their world had ceased to be, and with the destruction of tulpas, all the lesser creations of Henry's had lost any chance to remain in this world separate from their creator.

There was also no sign of the physical bodies of George Evers, John Farnham, Pam Ulster, Larry Myers, or the three security guards who had been on duty that night. There were indications, however, that those people had enough of the other world mixed into them that when it was banished, it took them with it. There were ID tags left in small piles of ash, tooth fillings, an arterial stent clotted with pieces of heart tissue, a badge wrapped in a scrap of dress pants, and a guard's nightstick coated with blood. Maybe Holt would be assigned to the case.

Kathy returned to the hospital roof, where Toby had insisted on staying until all the other loose ends had been tied up for the night. He'd wanted the fresh air, he said, before having to go back to his permanent prison cell. She told him he could have until just before dawn, and he agreed. They sat together in silence awhile, watching the lightening of the horizon. It reminded her a little of their childhood, of those nights stealing sips from the bottle he hid behind his bed.

Finally, she spoke. "So why'd you do it? Why'd you help me?"

Toby looked up at the fading stars—their stars, the right stars—and said, "I don't know. I guess…I guess I changed my mind."

"About what?"

"About wanting to watch the world end." He looked at her with uncharacteristic tenderness. "I know there's something wrong with me. There always will be. And I know you hate me for what I did to you. No, don't say anything. You don't have to. I know I did an unforgiveable thing to you. To the world, maybe. I don't feel bad about what I did to those women. Sometimes I wish I could, but I don't. And I know what that makes me. I don't want your pity or sympathy or anything else. I just want you to know I do feel…I don't know, something…about what I did to you." He sighed and looked away. "That thing that's wrong with me might well make me do it again to you or someone else, if I were free, though. So I'm not going anywhere. And that's because of you."

"Oh?" Kathy felt intensely uncomfortable, unsure what to say to him. That hard, angry, hateful little part of her wavered with uncertainty.

"The doc says I can't feel, not like normal people do. There are one or two switches in my brain that are flipped the wrong way. But I think… well, I think I do love you, as much as someone like me can love another person. Which probably means nothing. So I'll tell you the truth. I wanted you to think I helped you to protect you, to do what I couldn't do for you these last few decades. To be there, like a brother should—like I used to be. But the truth is more complicated than that."

"How do you mean?" she asked, that discomfort seeping into her chest…into her heart.

"Well, you were right, what you said about me a while back. About people like me, how we're different. We go through the early part of life confused as to why people feel and think so differently than us, why they don't have the same urges. Our emotions get…I don't know, disconnected, or connected the wrong way. The wrong things happen at the wrong times and we get off on it. And then one day, something big happens. I guess it grows on you, but it doesn't feel that way. It feels like one day something snaps into place and all the confusion and anger and sadness congeals into a kind of a high, a power trip. It's like being lifted up from a crowd and feeling the sun after suffocating beneath the weight of the world. One day you're a loner, a loser, and the next, you're the secret apex predator of the human race. And it all makes a kind of internal sense, that it's exactly the way it should be, and fuck anyone who doesn't understand."

"I don't understand why you're telling me all this," Kathy said.

"The doc says it's a stressor that does it," Toby went on, ignoring her. "The end of a relationship, maybe, or a death in the family, like Mom dying. Or it's something at work, you know, like at your job." He looked at her. "It unlocks something in the genes—our genes. Now, a job like yours, with the kind of stressors that would drive most normal people insane... they haven't affected you that way. Not yet."

"Why should they?"

"Why shouldn't they?"

"I'm not like you," she said softly.

"You're not as different from me as you think. Anyway, what I'm trying to say is, I wanted you to think I helped save the world to keep you safe from evil. Evil like...me. But I think...I dunno, I think maybe I did it so there would be other chances for those stressors to break you. As long as you have a world to keep saving, there's a chance one day those stressors will make you just like me. Then—"

He stopped speaking abruptly. "Sun's coming up," he said.

It was. Kathy felt gut-punched, and it took her a few seconds to realize she needed to get them both up and moving. He wanted her to break, to lose enough of her humanity that she became a monster, something destroyed and capable of destroying. He wanted to see her slip beneath the surface of human morality and decency and become feral like him. That hurt; it was a new cut that she supposed would take time to scar over. Then it occurred to her that maybe Toby didn't mean that moment of broken humanity to be a thing that pulled her down into depravity, but in his own mind, raised her into something somehow more than human, a secret apex predator as he'd said, beyond the touch of things that hurt other mortal humans in the world.

It was a fucked-up idea, but she thought she got the sentiment behind it—the only kind of brotherly love he was capable of giving. She understood that he wanted her to understand him, and maybe she did, maybe a little better than she ever had before.

God help her, she understood.

"Yeah, you're right," she finally said. "Let's go, Toby."

She couldn't convince Toby to go back to the infirmary, but he did let her help him back to his room on the third floor and settle him into his chair. She leaned in close but couldn't bring herself to kiss his cheek, so she gave him a quick, awkward hug instead. She nevertheless felt desire and the beginnings of rage from him, and he knew it. They left it unspoken between them as she pulled away, that broken part of him that was never going to get fixed. All that had passed on the roof would be as wispy as her memories of joking and laughing, drinking and smoking with him in his room, fleeting moments of a different Toby than the man who had raped and murdered women, and would do so again if ever set free.

That broken part of him that he had embraced and that she still feared was a kind of thoughtform of Toby's own, too strong for either of them to conquer. She found that she could look over its shoulder, though, and offer him a little wave good-bye, and he could look around it to give her a little smile that for once was sincere and not snakelike.

She locked the door behind her and retreated down the quiet, dark, empty hall without guilt and, finally, without tears.

Acknowledgments

Mary would like to thank Martin Biro, James Abbate, and the rest of the editorial staff at Lyrical. She'd like to thank Sue and Michael SanGiovanni, Christy SanGiovanni, Adam SanGiovanni, Michele and Mike Serra, Seedling, and Seed, and Brian Keene. Her love and appreciation for them is boundless

Preview

If you enjoyed *Inside the Asylum*, be sure not to miss the first book in the Kathy Ryan series by Mary SanGiovanni,

In the rural town of Zarepath, deep in the woods on the border of New Jersey and Pennsylvania, stands the Door. No one knows where it came from, and no one knows where it leads. For generations, folks have come to the Door seeking solace or forgiveness. They deliver a handwritten letter asking for some emotional burden to be lifted, sealed with a mixture of wax and their own blood, and slide it beneath the Door. Three days later, their wish is answered—for better or worse.

Kari is a single mother, grieving over the suicide of her teenage daughter. She made a terrible mistake, asking the powers beyond the Door to erase the memories of her lost child. And when she opened the Door to retrieve her letter, she unleashed every sin, secret, and spirit ever trapped on the other side.

Read on for a special excerpt!
A Lyrical Underground e-book on sale now.

Chapter 1

In the town of Zarephath, Pennsylvania, just past the Pennsylvania-New Jersey border and northwest of Dingmans Ferry out by the Delaware Water Gap, there is a Door.

Many stories about it form a particularly colorful subset of the local lore of the town and its surrounding woods, streams, and lakes. Most of them relate the same essential series of events, beginning with a burden of no small psychological impact, progressing to a twilight trip through the southwestern corner of the woods near Zarephath, and arriving at a door. Numerous variations detail what, exactly, must be presented at the door and how, but ultimately, these stories end with an unburdening of the soul and, more or less, happy endings. It is said "more or less" because such endings are arbitrarily more or less agreeable to the individuals involved than the situations prior to their visit to the Door of Zarephath. More times than not, the "less" wins out.

There are some old folks in town, snow- and storm cloud–haired sept- and octogenarians who sip coffee and people-watch from the local diner or gather on front porches at dusk or over the counter at Ed's Hardware to trade stories of Korea and Vietnam, and in one venerable case, World War II, and it's said they know a thing or two about that door. The old-timers remember the desperation of postwar addictions and nightmares and what they used to call shell shock, of families they couldn't help wearing down or beating up or tearing apart, despite their best efforts to hold things together. They remember carrying burdens, often buried but never very deeply, beneath their conscious thoughts, burdens that crawled their way up from oblivion and into nightmares and flashbacks when the darkness of booze or even just the night took over men who had once been children and who were expected to be men. They remember late-night pilgrimages through the forest on the outskirts of town, trekking miles in through rain or dark or frost-laced wind to find that door, and lay their sins and sorrows at its feet. And they remember that sometimes, forgetting proved to be worse.

The old women too remember bruises and battered faces and blackouts. They remember cheating husbands and cancers and unwanted pregnancies and miscarriages and daughters being touched where they shouldn't by men who should have protected them. The old women remember the Door in Zarephath being a secret, almost sacred equalizer that older women imparted to younger women, a means of power passed from one group whose hands were socially and conventionally tied to another. And they remember watching strong women fall apart under the weight of that power.

And these old folks remember trying once to burn the door down, but of course, that hadn't worked. The Door in Zarephath won't burn because it isn't made of any wood of this earth, anything beholden to the voracious appetite of fire. It had an appetite of its own that night, and no one has tried to burn it down since. Rather, the old-timers have learned to stay away from it, for the most part, to relegate the knowledge of its location and its promises to the same dusty old chests in the mind that the worst of their war stories are kept. There's an unspoken agreement that as far as the Door in Zarephath goes, the young people can fend for themselves. While the folks in Zarephath won't stop a person from using the Door, they aren't usually inclined to help anyone use it. Not in the open, and not just anyone who asks about it. Behind some doors are rooms hidden for good cause in places human beings were probably never meant to know about—rooms meant never to be entered—and the old folks of Zarephath understand that for reasons they may never know, they were given a skeleton key to one such room. There's a responsibility in that, the kind whose true gravity is maybe only recognized by those with enough years and experience and mistakes left behind to really grasp it.

People often say the old-folks' generation were stoic, used to getting by with very little and largely of a mind frame not prone to histrionic anxiety or useless worry. People say it has to do with surviving the Depression and growing up in a simpler, more rugged time. But for the old folks in Zarephath, the strength of their fiber comes from what they remember—and from what they have come to accept forgetting. It comes from what they no longer choose to lay before the Door.

* * * *

To say the loss of Kari's daughter, Jessica, had left a hole in her heart significantly understated the situation. It was more of a gaping maw in the center of her being, a hungry vortex that swallowed light and love, vibrancy and memory.

It had swallowed her friendships early on. People, even the most well-meaning of them, rarely knew what to say when someone's child died. Telling her time would heal all wounds sounded trite. Telling her everything would be okay sounded patronizing. How could such an inescapable hollowness ever be okay? And telling her Jessica was in a better place might come across as the biggest bullshit of all. There was no way anyone could possibly know what lay beyond the walls of mortality, and given the circumstances, the suggestion came across as being rather insensitive anyway. There was nothing even the most eloquent and empathetic could say to take away a hurt like that.

"How are you holding up?" they'd ask with that look on their faces, part discomfort and part superiority in being somehow removed from such a horrible thing. Maybe the urge to slap that look off their faces showed through in her weak smiles and tired eyes. Or maybe her attempts to speak of banalities that went nowhere were just the kind of nothing-words that stalled relationships or even moved them backward. It was easier for people to drop away, couple by couple, then one by one. Eventually, those awkward meetings became fewer and farther between. The calls stopped coming, followed by the emails, and then eventually the texts petered off too. There were no further attempts to get her out of the house and reconnected with the world. She was a sinking ship and they were bailing before they got sucked into her currents. It was clear in their eyes, in their voices. It was in the distance they put between her and them. She had been relegated to a kind of camp or colony for people who had undergone an Awful Tragedy, a thing they were thankfully unable to relate to in any meaningful way.

That gaping maw had swallowed her job, as well. Her boss had been gracious in granting her time off from the office. He'd given her weeks, a month, and then another. She had dipped into and then run dry her long-term disability time. And when she'd come back to the office, the Mondays and Fridays when she couldn't find a reason good enough to get out of bed looked bad. Her zoning out during production meetings looked bad. Her stacks of unfinished paperwork looked bad. She'd quit after enough "please close the door" conversations led her to believe she was on the verge of being fired.

It had swallowed her marriage, certainly. Steven hadn't managed more than a few months in the house, the two of them passing each other like solemn ghosts from different eras, unseeing, unhearing, and unable to comfort each other in the grief that had overwhelmed them both. When he finally drifted away for good, out of the house and into an apartment in another state, he became no more than a name on divorce paperwork and a face in old pictures she tucked away in a box.

She hadn't lasted much longer there in the house amid the dust and empty picture frames. If Jessica's spirit had haunted the old house instead of her memory haunting Kari, then it might have been more bearable. At least she'd be able to feel some presence of and closeness to her daughter. But the girl wasn't there, at least not so far as Kari could tell. The girl had fled that house and that life, and wherever her soul was, it seemed far beyond Kari's reach. So Kari had fled that old house and life too. The problem was, although the new house in Zarephath was the only thing that had gone well in a long time, it didn't feel like home, not like the one with Jessica's room, plastered as it was with posters of smiling, clean-cut objects of innocent preteen crushes. Not like the one with Steven's clothes on his side of the closet and his keys on the table by the front door. She supposed her sense of security and family had been engulfed by that gaping maw too.

Finally, it had swallowed her sense of self. Her sleep was shot to hell, and the depression and anxiety had become so bad that who she was no longer existed without the meds. Kari hated what the meds did to her; rather, she hated what the lack of meds in her system did. First, there was the headache, a storm of pain that gusted not just around her head, but up her nose and through her sinuses, behind her eyes and down her throat. There was the heavy weight of heat that made her sweat, a sour kind of sweat that turned her stomach if she lifted an arm or turned her head toward her shoulder. Then came the dizziness, an offshoot of the headache whose roots seemed to reach down into her arms, hands, and fingers, sucking the strength out of them and making them shake. Her eyes would narrow to a glare from the pain and fog. Within her chest, a growing sense of unease would turn into a panic whose edges fluttered far from and untethered to any rational ground.

It was during those times that the memories of Jessica hurt worst. In fact, there were so many memories that she was starting to forget what it was like not to hurt.

She felt all those things the night before she found out about the Door in Zarephath. It coincided with the one-month mark in the new house, and perhaps more importantly, the eve of the third anniversary of Jessica's passing. If it were possible, the pain was sharper and deeper and more all-consuming now than it had been in those nightmare-blur first weeks right after finding Jessica's body. Losing someone, she thought, was like quitting an addiction. First there came the withdrawal pangs of the mental and physical sort, the ache of not being able to hear her laughter or footsteps on the stairs, see her smile or hug her, smell the child-hair smell. But in a way, the routine, the comfortable familiarity, was a much tougher part of the habit to break. Kari found she still looked out for the school bus at five minutes to three, still made sure the door was unlocked and checked the sidewalk for Jessica's approach from the bus stop. She still found herself sometimes at the bottom of the stairs to call her daughter down for dinner or call up to tell her to brush her teeth and that Kari would be up in a minute to tuck her little girl in. She still made lists of toys to buy her daughter for Christmas, still perused the Halloween costumes for something Jessica might like. She wasn't sure if those rote actions were her way of proving she was still there, still Mom, or if they meant she herself had become a shade stuck in an endless loop of repeating the past.

That night before, as she bent over the dishwasher, she grabbed a handful of serrated knives by their blades. They pressed into the skin of her palms, cold but not hard enough to cut her. Her hand shook and she dropped them to the counter with a clatter.

She was due to have lunch the next afternoon with Cicely, the nice old lady next door and one of her only acquaintances in Zarephath, or anywhere at all anymore. They had planned on the Alexia Diner on Dingmans Turnpike, and over what had become their weekly coffee and hot open-faced turkey sandwiches, she intended to tell Cicely she was finished—with life, with everything, with trying to fight the current to be normal, functional, and in the process of healing. She wasn't any of those things, and she couldn't pretend anymore. She was cocooned in her personal world of grief and simply saw no other ways to break free. And no amount of friends' well-meaning attentiveness or love or understanding, and no amount of her own swallowing of pain and indignation and unfairness could make up for it.

The loss of Jessica felt like a fist crushing what was left of her heart in her chest. And she was simply finished. The guilt and the sadness were too much to carry alone.

She had hidden the note from Steven. She'd hidden it from everyone. It felt like the last thing, the only thing, she could do to protect her precious daughter. She'd found it crumpled into a tight little ball in Jessica's fist. The girl's reasoning was suggested in a few neat lines of looping girlish script. She couldn't keep secrets anymore; there were so many and she felt so guilty and embarrassed and even afraid, but mostly, she was exhausted.

Kari knew how she felt.

She picked up one of the knives again, entertaining the kind of thought that had come to fill in those tight little end spaces where her mind let memories of Jessica trail off. End-cap thoughts, was how she'd come to think of them. This one was less refined than some of the others; it involved a lot of blood—a tubful, maybe—and the indignity of being found naked or maybe just in her underwear. Messy and embarrassing and probably painful, if cutting her legs while shaving and letting them slip back under the warm water was any indication.

Her almost-twelve-year-old daughter had done something and gone somewhere she never had been and could never have imagined, had lived a part of her life and ended it without her mother and father, and that seemed wrong. It seemed wrong that children that age should ever feel the need to take on adult things like that, especially alone. Kari didn't want Jessica to be alone. And if Jessica could open that door to another plane of existence, then how could Kari call herself a decent mother and yet not have the guts to follow?

Kari put down the knife.

She'd talk to Cicely. Then she'd decide.

* * * *

People like Toby Vernon built entire lives and whole senses of self around lies. Lies were the brick and mortar that built cities, even empires, of good faith, goodwill, and human connection. Among the sharply honed senses of the predator was a toolbox of excuses and fabrications based on body language, expressions in the eyes, and tones of voice, wielded quickly and efficiently to achieve a result. Lies allayed fears or manipulated them, soothed guilt or exacerbated it. Of all the talents to protect and develop as a primary survival skill, lying was at the top of the list.

And people like Toby were good at it.

He was turning forty that year, which meant he had spent the last twenty-four years since his conviction, incarceration, and release perfecting his ability to lie. He had learned to change like a chameleon. He could be charming, unassuming, unworthy of notice or comment. He was also selective and, at times, ruthless. And it had been almost two and a half decades gone by since he had been arrested or convicted of anything that had to do with children.

However, his confidence, and with it some of his skill, had waned after the girl in Dingmans Ferry. It wasn't that he didn't know deep down, deeper than his lies and justifications could reach, that he hurt children. He had, in the past, tried to justify it as a necessary evil, a means of pain management or sedation or simply an inexorable addiction. He was not so deluded as to think the children were unaffected by his…attentions. It had never been so clear to him, though, nor had it ever inspired such self-loathing, as it had with that girl. Something changed after that. Toby had taken a good look at his life the last four decades or so and realized that all that perfected lying had never been perfect at all. He had never escaped his mother's belief that he was a monster, pure and simple, the kind that most of the rest of the world would see put down sooner than a rabid dog.

It made him afraid of others, as if he were somehow suddenly exposed. Mostly, it made him afraid of himself, a notion he wasn't used to and didn't like at all.

Toby had always wanted to be normal, to date regular adult women, to get married. When he'd realized, much to his disappointment, that his sexual attraction to preadolescent girls wasn't something he could outgrow or ignore, he'd resigned himself to what he was. In fact, he'd suppressed instead that sad, self-pitying hope of ever getting better. After the Dingmans Ferry girl, though, that need to feel normal reemerged, and it was almost—not quite, but almost—as strong as the urges themselves. He didn't want to feel self-loathing every time he drove past a playground or worry that the hawk-eyes of watchful mothers in grocery stores were judging him with disapproval and hostility. He no longer wanted to feel that old familiar tension and discomfort throughout his body at the birthday parties of family's and friends' children.

There were only so many times one could park a half-block or so from the middle school during recess and come to a boil of lust and shame, only so many uncomfortable drives home with a hard-on in his pants and the echoes of his mother's disgusted words in his head, before it came time to admit to being at a crossroads. Down one way lay peace; there might never be redemption, but there might be some cosmic credit for and solace in having overcome the basest part of himself. Down the other way meant the risk that one day, those little bloodied flower-print panties were going to end up shoved down some slender, pretty little throat or some fragile set of growing bones was going to break. He didn't want that. Lord knows, he didn't want it to come to that.

He asked the gods behind the Door to take the urges away.

Edward Richter had told him about the Door. He knew Ed from the hardware store, where the old man had been working stocking shelves and ringing up purchases for the last seventeen years. Ed was more than a familiar face around town, though Toby wasn't sure he could quite classify Ed as a friend. Ed shared the same affliction, a predilection for children, though his preference was for little boys. Toby had seen it right away: the familiar mannerisms and expressions and the wolfish look in the eyes, just as he supposed Ed had recognized the same in him. It was a tenuous bond between them, for hunting is a lone pastime, and a lonely one.

He and Ed got together once a month, usually at Ed's house, a small, pale-yellow bi-level on the edge of town out by the woods. They drank beers and vented about work or politics or debated the merits of the Mets vs. the Pirates. Sometimes they talked about their respective stints in jail. Sometimes they talked about children. But until that one night three weeks prior, Ed had never mentioned the Door. No one had, in all the years Toby had lived in Zarephath.

"Well, Ed," Toby had said that night in response to Ed's asking after his well-being, "I've hit a wall, I think."

"In what way?" Ed cocked an eyebrow at him and sipped his beer.

Toby shook his head. "I drove past the park yesterday—you know the one out on Miller Road, by the firehouse?"

Ed nodded. The flash in his eyes, imperceptible to anyone but a fellow predator, told Toby that Ed knew it well.

"There was this little girl. She was sitting on top of the monkey bars, with her feet dangling over and the wind moving little blond strands of her hair across her cheek…She was beautiful, Ed. I mean stunning. I wanted her. But…it was more than just wanting her. It wasn't enough, just watching her."

A small, uncomfortable smile passed over Ed's lips. "It seldom is."

"I wanted to hurt her, Ed."

The older man looked up in surprise. "Oh?"

"I don't know, it was…not like the other times. It was more intense a feeling, more…primal. Savage. I never felt that before…at least, not to that extent, you know?"

"Can't say that I do," Ed said, shifting in the chair. "Not that I'm judging, mind. Just not familiar with what you're describing." Something in his eyes and the tone of his voice led Toby to believe Ed was lying. It was the subtlest shift to survival mode through denial and diminishing. Toby wasn't going to argue, though.

"I can't keep on like this. I need to do something before I...hurt someone. Jesus." He rose, stalking to the far corner of the den with his beer. Suddenly that little room seemed incredibly stifling to him, with its dim, seventies color scheme and old furniture that clung to its ghosts like a dust shroud. "I can't take it anymore. I wish I could carve this whole part of me away, make these feelings just dry up."

"And therapy...?"

Toby groaned. "It's useless, man, especially in the short-term. You know that. And I'm frankly terrified a shrink will suggest the surgery. I guess maybe I could do the drugs, but the guys on the forum who are taking them seem so miserable, or just numb to everything. I don't want to be like that, either. Plus, there are all these possible side effects—serious ones." He sighed. "I don't know what to do. I just want to be normal. I want the urges to go away. I'd do anything at this point. Christ, maybe I should be on those damn drugs..." He shook his head. He felt lost.

"Well, uh...there is another way. No drugs, no surgery, and no therapy. But you have to be really sure, really clear in your own head about what you want. Is that what you really want?"

Toby turned to the old man. "Yeah, yeah, of course. Wouldn't you, I mean, if you could get rid of that part of you that feels what we feel for kids, wouldn't you cut it out of you? It's like a tumor, Ed. I'd just as soon be rid of it."

Ed cleared his throat. His gaze was fixed on his beer bottle, but Toby knew he had something to say, hanging there just behind that unsmiling mouth.

"What?" Toby prompted.

"Well...there's the, uh...the Door."

"What? What door?"

"The Door...you know." Ed gestured toward the window and beyond it, the edge of the forest. "The one out in the woods. The Door."

"I don't know what you're talking about, Ed. The door to what? And what does it have to do with me?"

"Ain't no one ever told you about the Door? For fuck's sake, how long have you lived in this town?"

"Ed, what door?"

Ed gazed at his beer for several seconds before answering. "It's a Door that...gives you stuff. Or takes stuff away that you don't want anymore. Like suppose your old lady is cheating on you with the guy down the street, right? Well, you go to the Door—you have to go alone, see, at night—with a letter. You fold the letter and seal it with wax that has drops of your blood in it. And inside, the letter asks for your wife not to see the guy anymore, or for the guy to just go away, right? Just up and disappear. And in three days—never heard of it taking no longer or shorter—you get what you want. Like, the guy gets hit by a bus, maybe. Or he just vanishes, no trace, just gone. You get your old lady back. Maybe."

"You're kidding me." But Toby could tell that the older man wasn't, just as he could see the predator behind Ed's grandfatherly eyes. Ed was serious; he believed what he was saying whole cloth.

Ed shook his head slowly. "You ask any of the old folks around here. They'll tell you. The Door is real. Go out, see for yourself. It's standing out there, plain as day. One of Zarephath's great unkept secrets. And it does work, just like I told you. You ask for something to be taken away, like, like your attraction to little girls there, and you *will* get what you want. Though I gotta say, it may not be like you think…and you can't take it back. You can't undo what you asked. And you sure as hell can't open the Door no matter what, no sir."

"So you think a magic door is going to solve my problems? Is that what you're telling me?"

Ed shrugged. "Poke fun all you want, but you go see if I'm telling tales. Go see."

"If it's so great and powerful, then why haven't you ever used the Door?"

Ed gave him a faint smile. "I'm an old man. Not much of a sex drive anymore. No real need. Besides, I guess when I was a younger man, I was… selfish. Selfish, and a little afraid of giving up the only thing I knew, only thing I was sure about. And of course, the old folks at the time made sure I knew about the drawbacks, just as I guess I ought to make sure you know."

"Drawbacks?"

"You don't get nothing for free, Toe. You know that. Like I been tryin' to say, there's risk, using that Door. Always risk." He sipped his beer thoughtfully. "Of course, it sounds like there's a mighty big risk in your not using it at this point too. Guess it's up to you."

Toby sat, rolling the beer bottle between his hands as he considered what Ed had said. "So what, I just write a letter? Like to Santa Claus? Tell this Door what I want? Then what?"

"Then you seal it, like I said. Melt some wax, mix a little of your blood in, then seal it, like those old-fashioned letters, you know?"

Toby nodded.

"Then you go out at night—has to be full dark—and you make your way to the Door—"

"How do I find it? What if I get lost?" Toby broke in.

"Well, you can bring a flashlight and a compass, or one of them app things on your phone, if you got it."

"Okay, so assuming I find the door, then what?"

"Then you slip the letter under the Door. That's how I had always heard it done. No words necessary. Just slip it under, then walk away. Go home, keep your mouth shut. Deed is done."

Toby frowned. The whole thing was crazy. Magic doors, wishes granted. Fairy tales were for kids, not for men who exploited them. He shook his head. He wanted a solution to his problem more than anything, but…this? Was Ed fucking with him?

Ed seemed to read the doubt on his face and leaned forward, tipping the mouth of his beer at Toby like a pointer finger. "Look, I know how it sounds, believe me. I know. You don't have to take my word for it. If you want to consider using the Door, I'll take you out there tomorrow afternoon. You can see it for yourself. If not, we can forget we ever had this conversation. You just said you was looking for a solution that wouldn't involve drugs or surgery or hurting one of them pretty little girls in the park. This…well, this might be the only option you got, buddy."

About the Author

Mary SanGiovanni is the author of the Bram Stoker nominated novel *The Hollower*, its sequels *Found You* and *The Triumvirate*, *Thrall*, *Chaos*, *Savage Woods*, *Chills*—which introduced occult security consultant Kathy Ryan—and *Behind the Door*, as well as the novellas *For Emmy*, *Possessing Amy*, and *The Fading Place*, and numerous short stories. In addition to her novels, she contributed to DC Comics' *House of Horror* anthology, alongside comic book legends Howard Chaykin and Keith Giffen. She has been writing fiction for over a decade, has a Master's in writing popular fiction from Seton Hill University, and is a member of The Authors Guild, Penn Writers, and International Thriller Writers.

Her website is marysangiovanni.com.

Savage Woods

***Bram Stoker award-nominated author Mary SanGiovanni returns
with a terrifying tale of madness, murder, and mind-shattering evil...***

Nilhollow—six-hundred-plus acres of haunted woods in New Jersey's Pine
Barrens—is the stuff of urban legend. Amid tales of tree spirits and all-
powerful forest gods are frightening accounts of hikers who went insane
right before taking their own lives. It is here that Julia Russo flees when
her violent ex-boyfriend runs her off the road . . . here that she vanishes
without a trace.

State Trooper Peter Grainger has witnessed unspeakable things that have
broken other men.

But he has to find Julia and can't turn back now. Every step takes him
closer to an ugliness that won't be appeased—a centuries-old, devouring
hatred rising up to eviscerate humankind. Waiting, feeding, surviving.
It's unstoppable. And its time has come.

Chills

True Detective *meets H.P. Lovecraft in this chilling novel of murder, mystery, and slow-mounting dread from acclaimed author Mary SanGiovanni . . .*

It begins with a freak snowstorm in May. Hit hardest is the rural town of Colby, Connecticut. Schools and businesses are closed, powerlines are down, and police detective Jack Glazier has found a body in the snow. It appears to be the victim of a bizarre ritual murder. It won't be the last. As the snow piles up, so do the sacrifices. Cut off from the rest of the world, Glazier teams up with an occult crime specialist to uncover a secret society hiding in their midst.

The gods they worship are unthinkable. The powers they summon are unstoppable. And the things they will do to the good people of Colby are utterly, horribly unspeakable . . .